P9-CRB-121

GONE IN A FLASH

A Selection of Recent Titles by Susan Rogers Cooper

* *available from Severn House*

GONE IN A FLASH

Susan Rogers Cooper

This first world edition published 2013
in Great Britain and the USA by
SEVERN HOUSE PUBLISHERS LTD of
19 Cedar Road, Sutton, Surrey, England, SM2 5DA.

Copyright © 2013 by Susan Rogers Cooper

All rights reserved.
The moral right of the author has been asserted.

British Library Cataloguing in Publication Data

Cooper, Susan Rogers
  Gone in a flash. – (An E.J. Pugh mystery; 11)
  1. Pugh, E. J. (Fictitious character)–Fiction.
  2. Women novelists–Fiction.
  3. Women private investigators– United States–Fiction.
  4. Detective and mystery stories.
  I. Title II. Series
  813.6-dc23

ISBN-13: 978-0-7278-8292-9 (cased)

Except where actual historical events and characters are being
described for the storyline of this novel, all situations in this
publication are fictitious and any resemblance to living persons
is purely coincidental.

All Severn House titles are printed on acid-free paper.

Severn House Publishers support The Forest Stewardship Council [FSC],
the leading international forest certification organisation. All our titles that
are printed on Greenpeace-approved FSC-certified paper carry the FSC logo.

MIX
Paper from
responsible sources
FSC
www.fsc.org   FSC® C013056

Typeset by Palimpsest Book Production Ltd.,
Falkirk, Stirlingshire, Scotland.
Printed and bound in Great Britain by
TJ International, Padstow, Cornwall.

ONE

SATURDAY

We were the lead car in a caravan heading for Austin. I should say lead truck. Willis and I were in his huge, four-ton pickup with the ridiculously fat tires that even I, at five feet and eleven inches, had to use the sissy bar and the running board to get into. Before he bought the new love of his life, back when he was a thinking man, we used to laugh at trucks like this, what a friend had dubbed 'Texas Clown Trucks.' And to add insult to injury, this one was painted mustard yellow (or, alternately, depending on to whom I was speaking, baby-poop yellow). We were in this monstrosity because we needed the cargo space for all of our son's stuff. In the next car in the caravan, a 1993 Toyota Celica, was our son Graham with his more personal stuff and, in the last car of the caravan, a Volkswagen so old even my VW snob husband approved, was Leon, Graham's best friend since the second grade, and his personal stuff. Our cargo area also carried some of Leon's bigger items.

Where were we going with all this stuff? To Dobie Hall on Guadalupe Street in Austin, right on the edge of the University of Texas campus. U.T. has no dormitories on campus – they're all off. Dobie was very close, within walking distance to most of the buildings where undergraduate classes would be, and was the dorm I lived in when I went to U.T. The bottom floor, street level, was filled with fast-food places and the basement held a theater. Fortunately they played mostly art films, so my 'if the lead doesn't have superpowers then it really isn't a movie' son probably wouldn't spend a lot of time there. I tried not to dwell on the fact that he was going to be in the same dorm where I drank my first whiskey, smoked my first weed, and lost my virginity – at least the latter part was down to my son's father, who deflowered me shortly after we met. These are not the kinds of things a mother wants to think about.

It took an hour and a half to drive there, and then we had to eat at Threadgills, the original, on North Lamar, where Janis Joplin was known to show up unannounced and do a duet or two or three with Mr Kenneth Threadgill himself. Their second location, in the southern part of the city, was practically a museum for the old Armadillo World Headquarters, the first of the premier music venues in a city self-proclaimed as the 'live music capital of the world.' Unfortunately the Armadillo had been torn down in 1980, several years before I made it there for my freshman year. And Janis's days at Threadgills had been even longer ago than that.

If I actually *lived* in Austin, Threadgills could be my downfall. Even though I'd been able to keep off the thirty-five pounds I'd lost last winter, I couldn't help but order the chicken fried steak and cream gravy (the best in Texas and Texas has the best in the world), the San Antonio squash, and the broccoli rice casserole. And all this with plenty of melt-in-your-mouth yeast rolls and cornbread.

Even though we knew the boys were eager to get started on their new lives, Willis and I lingered over coffee and a shared dessert – buttermilk pie. We hadn't discussed it, but both of us needed to slow this whole thing down, keep our baby boy with us a little bit longer. An extra minute or two. Because this would be it. He'd come home for a weekend here or there, and holidays, but after four years and his degree, he'd probably stay in Austin – so many graduates of U.T. did. There would be more work for him there and, let's face it, Austin was an exciting city, a hell of a lot more fun for a young adult than Black Cat Ridge. We'd had the pleasure of his company for eighteen years, and now it was time for the world to get to know Graham Pugh, and for Graham Pugh to get to know the world.

I was able to keep the tears contained as we unloaded the two new roommates, found their room – a carbon copy of the one I'd had back in the eighties – and got them semi-unpacked. And then Willis and I just stood around for a while.

And the boys stood there and watched us standing there.

And we watched them watching us standing there.

And so on.

'Well,' Willis said.

'Yeah,' Graham said.

'See ya!' Leon said.

'I guess we should be going,' I said.

'Ya think?' Leon said, and I wanted to take him over my knee and beat the crap out of him. Of course, I've wanted to do that for eleven years and have yet to succumb to the internal pressure.

'Leon, shut up!' Graham said. To us he said, 'Come on, I'll walk y'all down.'

And so he did. Except we took the elevator. The stairs would have taken longer. We should have taken the stairs.

And we stood by the shotgun side of the truck, all three of us, until a very pretty girl walked by and both Graham and his father turned their heads to watch her pass.

'OK,' I said, hitting Willis on the arm. 'Go meet her,' I said to my son. 'We're out of here.'

I hugged Graham to me, still surprised at how I had to reach up to get my arms around his shoulders. And I kissed him on the cheek. OK, maybe more than once.

'Call!' I said, my voice breaking and the tears starting to flow.

I jumped in the passenger seat and tore my eyes away from my husband and my son embracing. Then Willis was in the driver's seat and I looked out of the window to see my son's retreating back.

I looked at Willis. Tears were brimming in his eyes. 'Shit,' he said. 'I wish I had a cigarette.' This from a man who had quit smoking right about the time he graduated from this same university.

SUNDAY

The next morning, we packed our overnight bags and headed downstairs to breakfast. We'd made plans and reservations to stay overnight at the Driscoll Hotel, a beautiful old hotel downtown with lots of history. The night before we got to our room, we went downstairs to the dining room and discovered we were both too bummed to eat. Turned out later we were too bummed for sex, too.

Willis sat on the edge of the bed, elbows on knees, and said, 'We should have just driven straight home and saved the money.'

'Yeah,' I said, too bummed to even argue the point.

By morning, his appetite had improved considerably, as revealed by his purchase and consumption of half the menu items, but my stomach was still processing the pain of losing my son – and maybe the over-indulgence of the whole Threadgills experience. I had coffee and fruit; he had enough food to feed a high-school football team.

He ran away from them as fast as he could, but he'd had that knee operation last year and he wasn't as fast as he used to be. Rounding the corner in the parking garage, he saw one of those great big trucks with the even bigger tires, this one painted mustard yellow. It had one of those silver boxes attached to the bed, right at the back by the cab. He knew from having seen his brother-in-law's truck that there was a space underneath that. He threw the satchel in the bed of the truck, shoving it under the big silver box.

Two men, one big and beefy, the other smaller and more agile, but both light in the intelligence department and heavy in the following orders department, rounded the corner just as the first man shoved the satchel under the box. Seeing them, he turned and headed away, up, up, and up the winding ramp of the parking garage.

The two men communicated silently, the smaller one following the first man up the ramp, the other heading for the pickup, just as a couple came out of the elevator two cars away from the pickup.

'You can't be hungry, we just ate,' the man said.

'You ate! I just had coffee,' the woman said.

'And fruit,' the man said.

'Well, it wasn't filling,' she said.

'I'm not stopping between here and home, and that's final.'

'Says you.'

'Yeah, says me,' he said, throwing the bags he was carrying into the cargo area of the pickup. He clicked the remote and the two got into the cab of the mustard-yellow truck, still arguing.

The man who had been heading for the pickup hid between two cars. Taking a felt-tip pen out of his shirt pocket, he wrote the license plate of the truck on the palm of his hand.

Then, when the pickup had gone around the corner, he came out of hiding and ran up the ramp after his partner and their quarry.

We'd just left the parking garage adjacent to the hotel, hauling our bags ourselves since my cheap-ass husband hadn't wanted to pay valet parking the night before. We headed east, back home to Black Cat Ridge, where our three daughters were being watched over from next door by our neighbor Elena Luna, the cop. All three were a little in awe of her, which I hoped meant they'd behaved themselves.

What had been an hour-and-a-half trip yesterday took about an hour today. Speed limits? Willis Pugh didn't need no stinking speed limits! Not now that his son was gone. We reached the house and I got out, letting my husband deal with the bags. Sometimes I play the southern belle card. Not often, but when it's needed, like not hauling crap, I know it's available to me. And as I walked in the back door into the family room, thoughts of my son zoomed out of my mind.

'I didn't say you could wear it!' Megan yelled at Alicia.

'You didn't say I couldn't!' Alicia yelled back. I smiled. Alicia's our foster daughter and I was happy she was finally getting enough spunk to yell at Megan, who usually needed to be yelled at.

'You're supposed to ask!' Megan yelled.

'And you're supposed to pick it up off the living-room floor! Anything I find in a communal room I shall deem wearable!'

Good one! I thought. 'Hey, girls!' I said.

'Hey, Mom,' came a new voice from the sofa. Bess, our adopted daughter, was lying there reading a book.

'How can you read through all this?' I asked.

She pulled earphones from her ears and said, 'Huh?'

'Mother! Alicia's wearing my sweater and she didn't even ask to borrow it!' Megan wailed.

'She's just jealous because I can wear her clothes and she can't wear mine!' Alicia, three sizes smaller than Megan, shouted back.

'I can't help if it you don't have boobs! I do!' Megan said, sticking said boobs out. 'And wearing your clothes would just make me look cheap.'

Alicia: 'Well, wearing your own clothes so tight already makes you look cheap!'

Megan: 'Oh no! You didn't just say that!'

Alicia: 'Uh huh! I did! And I'll say it again!'

Megan: 'Do and I'll slap your face!'

Alicia: 'Yeah? You and what army?'

New voice: 'What the hell's going on here?'

Both girls in unison: 'Daddy!'

'Well, you see,' I said, turning to Willis. 'It seems that Megan has big breasts—'

Turning red in the ears, Willis, who still held our bags, said, 'I don't need to hear this!' and headed to our room beyond the kitchen.

'Mom!' Megan said, hands on hips.

The family room and my beautifully large kitchen are connected with an open bar area separating the two, and a larger open space. I glanced to my right. The cabinet under the sink was pushed open by trash accumulation spilling out of the can inside.

'What's this mess?' I said, or yelled, or whatever, pointing to the trash.

Alicia said, 'We divvied up chores and guess whose chore that was?' The look she sent Megan was – only one word for it – smug.

I sighed. 'Megan, deal with that now, please.'

'What about my sweater?' she yelled, pointing at the too-big cotton-knit blue-and-gray-striped sweater that fell to Alicia's knees. She appeared to be wearing nothing else. I prayed for panties.

'I think Alicia's idea is a good one. And it goes for all three of you. You leave something – anything, not just clothes – in the common rooms, whoever finds it can use it.'

'Mom!' Megan wailed.

'Trash! Now!' I said, pointing.

'I can't believe this shit—' Megan mumbled under her breath as she headed for the kitchen. I didn't get on at her about language. With Willis and me as role models, it's just a miracle they didn't start cussing while they were potty training.

We have satellite TV, and get most of our local stations from Austin, although we do get a couple from Houston. Black Cat Ridge on the north of the Colorado River and Codderville on the south are sort of in the middle, between the two cities, although slightly closer to Austin. I was in the kitchen fixing dinner and the girls and Willis were in the family room arguing over the remote.

'There's something on MTV I want to watch!' Megan said, grabbing for the remote in Willis's hand.

'I'm watching the news!' her father said, and I saw him swing the remote out of Megan's reach, this way and that, while trying to watch the news around her body.

'Daddy!' she wailed.

'Go watch it upstairs!' he said.

'This TV gets better reception!'

'Bullshit! It's just bigger!'

'Well, yeah, duh!'

'Stop!' Willis shouted. 'Get out of the way! E.J.! Come here!'

By the sound of his voice, I didn't think it had anything to do with my daughter's hijinks. I went into the family room, my hands dripping water.

Willis turned up the sound as a reporter appeared on screen. 'The man appears to have jumped, or possibly fallen from the top of the parking garage. His identity is being withheld pending the notification of his family. Again, the body of an unidentified man was found just moments ago outside the kitchen entrance of the Driscoll Hotel in downtown Austin. The APD and hotel security are looking into the matter, but at this time they will not say whether or not the man was a guest of the prestigious and historical Driscoll Hotel.'

'Oh my God!' Alicia said. 'Isn't that the hotel y'all stayed in last night?'

'Yeah,' Willis said.

'God, how awful,' I said, setting a hip down on the arm of the sofa next to my husband.

'Mom, you think it was murder?' Bess asked.

'They didn't say a word about murder, missy!' Willis said. 'They said fell or jumped. Nobody said a word about him being pushed.'

'Well, if they found him just now, then no one really knows, do they?' Bess said.

Willis shot her a look. This was all we needed – one of the girls trying to start sleuthing. Willis and I had separated briefly during the summer over my involvement in too many murders. I can't help it. I feel like I need to help people in these situations, and that I can, so I do. And, yeah, sure, I like the puzzle. I admitted that to Willis. And he admitted that he was scared I was going to get myself or the kids killed. We got back together because we love each other, and we're trying for a ceasefire, which has been fine since the summer's puzzle was solved. And now here was Bess trying to build a puzzle out of nothing.

I stood up and headed back into the kitchen. Over my shoulder I said, 'Bess, honey, the guy fell, or he jumped. Don't try to make a mountain out of a molehill. The only point of interest here, other than for his wife and family, of course, is that your father and I were in that very parking garage only this morning.'

Bess jumped up. 'Then you might have seen something!'

'They only found him a little while ago, honey,' Willis said. 'We left the parking garage at around eleven this morning.'

'So how often do the kitchen people go out that door? Hum? How long could he have lain there?' Bess all but shouted.

'I'm sure the police will look into that,' Willis said.

I decided to ignore them and went back into the kitchen. Since losing thirty-five pounds, I've been learning to cook in a more healthy fashion. Tonight we were having broiled salmon with corn on the cob and a green salad. I knew my husband would go to the pantry and pile his plate with a couple of pieces of bread – wheat not white, there's no white bread in the house! – but it was still better than having mashed potatoes or pasta. I know, I know, corn is a carb, but it's still better than the alternatives.

'It wasn't on him,' the smaller of the two men, Mr Smith, said into the phone.

'Then where is it?' the man on the other end of the phone, Mr Brown, demanded.

'Mr Jones saw him throw a satchel into the back of a pickup truck. He got the license plate number.'

'Give it to me!' Mr Brown demanded.

Mr Smith grabbed Mr Jones' arm and read the numbers off the palm of his hand to Mr Brown.

'Stay put,' Mr Brown said. 'I'll call you back with a location.'

'Yes, sir,' Mr Smith said and hung up.

'What's this?' I asked Willis that night as we got ready for bed. He had finally brought our bags up from where he'd deposited them right next to the back door when we first came home. I was pointing at a black satchel that wasn't mine and wasn't his.

'Isn't that yours?' he asked.

'No, I only had the one bag,' I said.

I sat down on the edge of the bed, bringing the satchel to my lap. 'There's no ID tag on the bag. Should we look inside?'

'Cool!' Willis said, always waiting for that pot of gold to show up. He sat down beside me. 'Open it!'

I did. No form of ID inside either. Nothing but men's clothes – a couple of T-shirts, a pair of jeans, and some underwear. And a Dopp kit. Opening the kit still didn't give us an ID, or a pot of gold, just some Aqua Velva aftershave, an old electric razor, a can of Right Guard, some nail clippers, and all the stuff the Driscoll puts out in the bathroom for their patrons to use – little bars of soap, little bottles of shampoo, conditioner, body lotion, and hand lotion, all shoved in the corner.

'OK, so this guy's a thief, but that's all I see,' Willis said.

I could feel my face heating up as I defended him. 'They put that stuff out there for you to use! So what if you use it at home or at the hotel? They *want* you to use it, for God's sake!'

'How much of that shit did you steal?' my husband asked me with a grin.

'That's not the point,' I said, and deflected further questioning with a question of my own. 'You think any of this stuff will fit you? Anything in the Dopp kit you want?'

He pulled out one of the T-shirts. 'If I weighed a hundred and fifty pounds maybe,' he said, looking at the clothes. 'Which I haven't since I was in eighth grade.'

'What about the Dopp kit?'

'That razor's older than I am, and you won't let me wear Aqua Velva.' He took out the can of Right Guard and shook it. He frowned. 'I'm not so sure about using another man's deodorant.'

'Jeez, Willis, it's not a roll-on.'

'Naw.' He stood up and took both the Aqua Velva and the Right Guard and put them in the bathroom trash can.

'This Dopp kit is older than mine, but it's real leather. It's in pretty good shape,' he said.

'Are you going to keep it?' I asked.

'Should I?' he asked.

'Why not?'

'Is it stealing?'

I shrugged. 'I don't think so,' I said. 'Somehow this got in our truck and possession is nine-tenths of the law, right?'

'Actually, that's wrong,' he said. 'But we have no idea who to give it back to, so I guess we're in the clear. And I like this leather. Really soft and aged. Classy.'

'Did you just say "classy"?' I said, raising my eyebrows.

'No,' he said, going back in the bathroom.

I put the clothes back in the satchel, zipped it up, and set it by the bed.

Willis came out of the bathroom. 'What are going to do with that?' he asked.

'Take it to Goodwill in the morning,' I said, turning off my bedside light.

'Yeah, that's best,' he said. 'I'm going to read for a while. That OK with you?'

'No problem,' I said, turning over and shutting my eyes. I may have been asleep before my eyes were actually shut, I was that tired.

*   *   *

The phone rang in Mr Smith's hand. 'Hello?' he said.

'There's a place called Black Cat Ridge, right outside a town called Codderville, either side of the Colorado River, on the way to Houston. The truck is registered to a guy named Willis Pugh, lives at 4210 Sagebrush Trail in Black Cat Ridge. Get that satchel, find what I want and do it now.'

Before Mr Smith could say, 'Yes, sir,' Mr Brown had hung up. Mr Smith turned to Mr Jones. 'Road trip,' he said.

VERA'S STORY
MONDAY

It was six-thirty on Monday morning and I was standing around the parking lot of my church, waiting for the bus and my friend Gladys Cook to show up. She was to be my roommate. At least it wasn't cold, I said to the woman standing next to me, who nodded her agreement.

Now, I've been a God-fearing, twice-on-Sunday Southern Baptist for most of my life, and I believe a preacher, especially a Baptist preacher, should be spouting fire and brimstone if his mouth is open. Scare those sinners half to death, I always say. Only way to get their attention.

But then our long-time preacher, Brother George, ups and retires and we wind up with Brother Joe Logan. I'm not sure if we're being punished for something or not. Not only does he not preach fire and brimstone, he's pretty damn close to being a liberal, if you ask me. And I'm sorta an authority on liberals in my church, seeing as how my son, Willis, married the queen of liberals, my daughter-in-law, E.J. That about says it all right there – won't even go by her Christian name. She'd rather go by initials. I've tried calling her Eloise, her Christian name, but by the looks she gives me when I do that, I've always been afraid she'd keep my grandchildren away from me. Now that they're all teenagers, I guess I don't have to worry about that. Not that I see 'em much anymore.

But back to this new preacher. The most damning thing about him, of course, is that he's a bachelor, which just isn't right. I don't think he's one of them homosexuals you hear about all the time, but I do believe he's got an evil eye for the ladies, and some of 'em aren't quite old enough for him to be having even a good eye on, if you know what I mean.

Little Beth Simpson just about drools every time she looks at him, and she's still in high school. And that Rachael Donley, that young, *separated* woman in choir, she's all up in his business. And he don't seem to mind it a bit. Did I mention she's just *separated*? She's not divorced. I think a Baptist preacher should be a married man, preferably with children – at least two. If we're all for family values, then the preacher should be leading an example, right? Now, that's just my opinion, but a bachelor Baptist preacher? Uh uh. That's just wrong. And there's a commandment against what him and Rachael Donley are thinking of doing – or have already done, but I'm not one to talk out of school.

At least that Donley woman is an alto, so I don't have to stand near her in the choir loft because I'm a soprano. But myself and everybody else in the loft get to see the googly eyes the two share almost the entire service. I can hardly keep my mind on the sermon, thinking about the way the two of them were looking at each other. It's downright disgusting.

Our former preacher, Brother George, was a good man, married with four children, and his wife was a perfect preacher's wife. Not too pretty, not too thin, not too ugly either, and certainly not fat. Sister Edith was just a medium woman's woman, who cooked and sewed, and did her own housework. And she started a quilting club while she was our church's first lady. I belonged to that quilting club for nigh on twenty years, and then her and Brother George up and retired, and Brother Joe comes in and doesn't even *have* a first lady. Well, it sure didn't take long for the quilting club to disband. Heck, there were only three of us left, anyway. These younger women can't get off their cell phones long enough to sit and have a chat without Tweeting or IM'ing, or texting, or whatever it is they're doing!

We got a notice back in the summer, before Brother George and Sister Edith left for their retirement home in the Hill Country, that our choir had been chosen to perform at the Southern Baptist National Meeting in the fall in, of all places, Washington, D.C. I say of all places because, really, who could use a little Southern Baptist influence more than those politicians up there?

So here we were in the parking lot of the church, ready to board the bus for the trip to D.C., when we get word that my would-be roommate, Gladys, and Sister Sharon, our choir director, both got the flu, and that Brother Joe, our bachelor preacher, was gonna go in Sister Sharon's stead, having directed the choir in his old church. Well, I can tell you one person who was happy about this chain of events, and that would be, of course, Rachael Donley. And a couple of the other younger women – all of them married. Let me just say that in thirty-three years of marriage, I never looked at another man. Ever. And that's the gospel truth! These younger women, I swear to God, are all depraved! Even my own daughter-in-law likes to say how she'd do this or that with this or that actor, just because he looks good without his shirt on! I only know this because I occasionally stumble across her Facebook page – purely by accident.

If all this fal-de-ral with the preacher wasn't bad enough, I was still reeling from saying goodbye to my grandson, Graham, who'd gone off to college over the weekend. Saying goodbye to the boy was hard – almost as hard as saying goodbye to his daddy twenty-something years ago when he went off to the same college.

If I wasn't such a strong woman, I might cry.

MONDAY

I was in the kitchen doling out breakfast. It was a typical Monday morning, with the exception that my son was missing. The new school year hadn't started yet in Black Cat Ridge, but the girls had junior orientation today. They needed to be at the school by nine o'clock, and it was now after eight.

Alicia was already downstairs, eating Fruit Loops and orange juice. A short while later, Bess was down.

'Whatja eating?' she asked Alicia, leaning over her shoulder to see. She made a face. 'Do I have to have cereal?' she asked me.

'Of course not. Would you like me to fix you a bagel? I have cream cheese.'

'Oh, yeah! That sounds good!' Bess said, crawling up into one of the high stools by the bar that separated the kitchen from the family room.

'Where's Megan?' I asked Bess.

'In the bathroom. Still,' Bess said. 'She's been in there forty-five minutes. I'm going to have to put my make-up on in the car. I barely got a chance to pee!'

'Not at the table,' I said.

Both girls giggled.

I sighed. 'I didn't mean don't pee at the table, I meant—'

But then they were laughing out loud so I just gave up.

The girls finished, grabbed their backpacks full of back-to-school goodness (they'd be getting their assigned lockers today), and headed for the front door. 'Call up to Megan, please,' I asked.

Both girls started shouting up the stairs. 'Meggggggan!' Bess yelled. 'We're leeeeeeaving you!'

'Megan! Come on! It's time to go!' yelled the more mature Alicia. It was hard to believe they were all sixteen.

I packed up the perishables and headed for the back door. Bess and Alicia were already out, heading to the minivan in the garage. I'd campaigned vigorously for a new vehicle last summer, thinking we wouldn't need the minivan since Graham had a car and would take the girls anywhere they wanted to go. But then Willis reminded me that Graham would be going off to college in the fall and taking his car with him. I was in total denial at that stage. So we compromised. I'd received a very nice book check (I write romance novels and it's getting pretty lucrative after twenty years), and we decided I could get my Audi R8 Spyder (a silver two-seater to die for) and keep the old but reliable minivan for the girls.

All three had taken driver's ed during the spring so all three were eligible to drive. We'd have to draw straws every morning to see who drove, or make a schedule or something. But today I was taking them because I was on the refreshment committee for the orientation program. Two more years and no more of this high-school crap, I thought as I started up the car. Megan ran out the door and tried to jump in the shotgun seat but Alicia was already sitting there.

'Hey! I called shotgun last night!' Megan yelled.

'You snooze, you lose!' Alicia said and stuck her tongue out at Megan.

I was able to suppress my giggle as I handed a granola bar to Megan. I may be cruel, but I'm not mean.

Mr Smith and Mr Jones had been watching from across the street as Willis Pugh left his home in the pickup truck. They followed him back across the Colorado River, which Mr Smith assured Mr Jones was not the same Colorado River as the one in say, Colorado, and to an office building in the town of Codderville.

Pugh parked his truck, got out and walked into the building. He wasn't carrying the satchel. As soon as he was inside the building, Mr Smith told Mr Jones to go get the satchel from the truck.

Mr Jones got out of the rental car, went up to the pickup truck and looked in the cargo space. There was nothing there. He tried the lid of the silver box that stretched the width of the truck. It was unlocked. Inside were jumper cables, a tool box, a plastic bottle of coolant, a plastic bottle of windshield-wiper juice, and several red rags they sell at auto parts stores. Mr Jones looked up and made eye contact with Mr Smith, then shook his head. Mr Smith waved him back to the rental car.

They said nothing as Mr Smith turned the car around and headed back to Black Cat Ridge.

'Hey, Mom, what's that?' Alicia asked, pointing to the satchel sitting on the console between us.

I glanced down. 'Oh, that. We found it in the back of the truck.' I shrugged. 'Somebody must have gotten confused and put it in the wrong truck. Unfortunately there's no ID in it, so we can't return it. I'm taking it to Goodwill later.'

'Can I have it?' Alicia said, eyeing the satchel. 'It looks like one of those old-fashioned house-call doctor bags, ya know? That would be a really cool schoolbag, rather than a backpack like everybody else!'

'I want it!' Megan shouted from the next row of seats.

'Why?' I asked her, glancing at her face in the rearview mirror.

'Because she does!' Megan said, and stuck her tongue out at her sister.

'You are so childish,' Alicia said, arms across her chest and looking straight out of the window.

'Yes, you may have the satchel,' I told Alicia. 'Just take the clothes out and put them on the floor, and I'll take those to Goodwill later.'

'Thanks!' she said with a grin, and proceeded to transfer everything from her backpack into the satchel.

'I think it looks stupid!' Megan said.

'Oh, Megan, give it up,' Bess said.

'Bite me,' Megan said.

'Really?' Bess said. 'May I?'

'Cut it out!' I said as I pulled into the high-school parking lot. We got out of the minivan and headed into the school, Bess and Megan with their backpacks, Alicia with her satchel, and me with one hundred mini-muffins that I'd bought at the grocery store but put in a basket with every intention of saying they were homemade.

TWO

MONDAY

Mr Smith and Mr Jones watched from across the street as the woman, presumably Mrs Willis Pugh, and her three daughters got out of the minivan and went into the school. 'That's it!' Mr Jones shouted.

'Not so loud, stupid!' Mr Smith said. 'Where?'

'The second girl!' Mr Jones thrust his finger toward Alicia. 'The one with the long brown hair. She's got the satchel!'

'OK, so we know they have it. Let's just wait it out. School hasn't started yet, right?'

Mr Jones shrugged. 'I don't know.'

Mr Smith got out his phone, looked up the school by the name carved into the white rock cornice of the building, and called the number listed. It took four rings, but a frustrated-sounding voice finally said, 'BlackCatHighhowmayIhelpyouPleasehold.'

Mr Jones looked at Mr Smith. 'Well?'

Mr Smith gave Mr Jones a disgusted look. 'I'm on hold.'

'Yes?' came the frustrated voice.

'Are you in session today?' Mr Smith asked.

'School starts Wednesday, sir.'

'What time do they get out today?' Mr Smith asked.

'Orientation lasts approximately two and a half hours,' she said.

'Thank you,' Mr Smith said and hung up.

'My, aren't we polite?' Mr Jones said with a smirk.

'Shut the fuck up,' Mr Smith said.

I was one of six eleventh-grade mothers at today's orientation. Tomorrow would be orientation for the seniors, and Wednesday school would start. Basically, one more day without killing my daughters and I'd be home free. I can do it, I can do it, I repeated under my breath, my new mantra. What I might not be able to do was put up with Collette Newberry, this year's head of the refreshment committee. I'd been an idiot, it seems, when I turned down the 'honor' at the end of year last spring. If I'd taken the proffered position of head of the refreshment committee, I would have been able to tell Collette to go . . . well, do something organic with herself. As it was, I had to shut up and take her crap. And crap it was.

'We decided at our meeting in July, E.J., to only bring homemade goodies for our children. And healthy ones at that. These,' she said, handling my basket of mini-muffins, 'are neither healthy nor homemade.'

I had so many excuses, the first of which was my emotional wreckage at having given away my son to semi-adulthood, but Collette Newberry was not someone who was want to take excuses, nor was I want to give her one. I shrugged and did not reply. She just looked at me hard, then sighed, equally hard.

'Well,' she said, 'I'm so glad to see that everyone else complied with my orders from the summer. Now, if y'all . . .'

She went on, and I suppose on, but I stopped listening when a voice in my ear said, 'Orders? She's giving *orders*?'

I turned to find Lacy Kent, one of my neighbors, sitting behind me. 'Can we kill her?' Lacy whispered.

'You go ahead and I'll back you up,' I said.

'Ha! With your reputation, you'll hunt me down and turn me in!' Lacy whispered.

'Not for killing that bitch!' I whispered back.

Lacy giggled and sat back, forcing me to once again pay attention to Collette Newberry. 'So I've added a few more occasions when we should bring treats,' Collette said, 'other than the usual six – first of year orientation, of course,' she said with a slight twitter escaping her lips, which I could assume was supposed to be a laugh, 'Halloween, Thanksgiving, Christmas, Easter, and end of school. I thought it would be nice to add the Fridays before Monday holidays, and of course teacher work days.'

There was some mumbling but no one said anything loud enough for Collette to assume they were talking to her. That didn't sit well with me. So I stood up.

'Excuse me, Collette, but two of those teacher work days, I believe, are for seminars and work sessions at U.T. Are we to follow them to Austin with our baskets of goodies?'

That got more giggles than just Lacy's.

Collette turned pink around the ears. I was quite proud of myself.

'No, E.J., of course not. But they'll gather at the school to carpool, according to my extensive sessions with Vice Principal Mallon, and we thought it would be nice if some of the mothers were there to meet them with coffee and doughnuts. One mother from each class. Can I put you down as the junior class representative?'

I stared at her a full half a minute. She just stared back. Her ears were no longer pink, but I would have bet a donut mine were. 'Sure,' I finally said and sat down.

'Great!' Collette said, smiling her big, toothy smile. 'I'll jot your name down! Oh, and E.J., they need to be at U.T. by eight a.m., so you'll need to be at the school by six.'

I vowed then and there to try to keep my big mouth shut, already knowing that vow would be shattered before the day was over. What can I say? I have a big mouth.

The kids took a break after an hour and we spread out our refreshments in the cafeteria. I was happy to see that my basket of mini-muffins was empty by the end of break, whereas Collette's plate of homemade yogurt treats had been pawed, but was basically still pretty much intact.

An hour later the girls found me sitting in the cafeteria talking to Lacy Kent. We'd been able to trash Collette Newberry like the old pros we were, and had gone on to other people we jointly disliked. Say what you will about gossiping, but there's no better way to bond with another woman than through that time-honored tradition.

My girls and Lacy's son, Dex, showed up, and Lacy and I hugged.

'Coffee, my house, Thursday morning?' I said.

'I'd be there even if you didn't invite me,' Lacy said.

I laughed and turned to my daughters. 'Where are your backpacks?' I asked.

'We got our locker assignments and left them in there, with all our school supplies. Why lug it all back home?' Bess said.

I shrugged. 'I hope nobody needs anything before Wednesday,' I said, leading them out to the car.

The dark blue rental Ford pulled back to the spot across the street from the high school. There were two large Slurpee cups in the cup holders. They could see both the school and the minivan from this vantage point. Finally, after half the junior class had taken their leave, the woman, Mrs Pugh, and her daughters came out of the school.

'Where's the bag?' Mr Smith said. 'Where's the fucking bag?' he screamed.

'She doesn't have it,' Mr Jones said. 'Look, none of them have the stuff they came in with, 'cept the mom has that basket. I bet they left their backpacks and the satchel inside.'

'Ya think, dumbshit?' Mr Smith snarled. Then he sighed. 'OK, we wait an hour, for everyone to leave, then we break in and find the bag.'

'I dunno,' Mr Jones said. 'That's an awful big school.'

'Shut the fuck up,' Mr Smith said.

We dropped by the Goodwill on our way home, then went straight to the house. We'd barely been back half an hour before all three girls were back downstairs dressed in swimsuits and cover-ups.

'Can we take the minivan to the pool?' Bess asked. 'There's going to be an impromptu party there in half an hour.'

'How can that be impromptu?' I asked.

'Huh?' Bess said.

'Never mind. Sure. Who's driving?' I asked.

The three girls all said, 'Me!' in unison.

'Rock, paper, scissors,' I said.

They did. Megan won.

'Be careful!' I cautioned as they piled out the door. 'Dinner's at seven! Be back by then.'

No one answered. 'Do you have your phones?' Again no one answered. They were already in the minivan.

After they left I looked around my domain. I could clean up the breakfast dishes, wash a couple of loads of laundry, vacuum the living room, or read a book. I settled onto the sofa, my feet on the coffee table, a can of almonds in my lap, ice tea at my side, reading glasses on my nose, and the newest Maggody mystery in my hands.

No one had left the school for thirty minutes, which meant all of the people were probably gone. Mr Smith and Mr Jones left the rental car at the curb across the street from the school, and walked up to the front doors. They were shut, but unlocked. Mr Smith opened the door and walked in, followed by Mr Jones. Then Mr Smith stopped short.

'Shit!' he said. In front of him was a sea of lockers.

'What?' Mr Jones asked.

'If you were in high school, assuming you ever went to one, and I'm assuming a lot here, where would you put your shit?'

'I dunno,' Mr Jones said. 'One of these lockers?'

'Yeah, dumbass, one of these lockers. But which one?'

Mr Jones shrugged.

'Shit,' Mr Smith repeated. 'Come on,' he said in resignation, and led the way back to the rental.

I almost choked on an almond I was laughing so hard at the antics of the Buchanans, when the phone rang.

'Hello?' I managed.

'Hey, babe, what's wrong?' my husband asked.

'Nothing. Just busy,' I lied.

'Doing what?'

Well, there's only so much I'll lie about. Evasions, half-truths, a yes when a no is in order, or vice versa, but a total invention? Not so much. I sighed. 'I'm reading. So sue me.'

Willis laughed. 'It's OK. You're allowed. Now that you're the one bringing in the big bucks.'

'And don't you forget it, buster!' I said.

'Where are the girls?'

'At an impromptu swimming party at the pool.'

'Are they closing the pool tomorrow?'

'I have no idea.'

'You want to meet me in town for a sexy one-on-one dinner tonight?'

'Ooo, baby,' I said. 'Meat and everything?'

'I can even make it red.'

'Let me check and see if the girls have their phones. I'll call you back.'

They did. At least the first one I called, Bess, had hers.

'Your dad and I are meeting in town tonight for dinner. You three are on your own. I'll leave pizza money on the kitchen table.'

'OK, Mom. Y'all have fun!'

I planned to.

'That's new,' Mr Smith said, as they sat in the Taurus across the street from the Pugh home.

'Huh? What's new?' Mr Jones asked.

'Wake the hell up, asshole. We have a new vehicle in the mix,' Mr Smith said.

'Huh?'

Mr Smith sighed. 'The woman. Mrs Pugh. She's driving one of those new Audis. The two-seater.'

'Cool,' Mr Jones said, watching it turn out of the driveway.

'The truck's gone, the minivan's gone, now this. That means nobody's home, dumbshit. We can go in,' Mr Smith said.

'Why?' asked Mr Jones.

Mr Smith rotated his neck, hearing and feeling the satisfying clicks. It came from gritting his teeth every time he had to communicate with Mr Jones. 'Because maybe we can find out what locker number the bag is in,' he said, enunciating each word, and saying it slowly. Hoping for a response other than Mr Brown's usual 'huh.'

'Yeah, OK,' Mr Jones said. 'Both of us or just one?'

'There are three girls,' Mr Smith said. 'We might have to split up.'

'Right.'

Mr Smith got out of the car and walked casually across the street. He knew exactly how to play this. If they acted like normal visitors, no one would bat an eyelid. Deliberately making a bit of a production, he rang the doorbell, looked at his watch, rang the doorbell again, and said, out loud, 'I guess we'll try the back door.'

They were walking up the driveway toward the back of the house, when the door to the house with the neighboring driveway opened and a woman came out.

'Hey,' she said.

She was a big woman, Latina, with a scowl on her face.

Mr Smith turned to her and smiled. 'Hey, yourself!' he said cheerfully.

'The Pughs aren't home right now,' the Latina said.

'That's OK, they said we could leave something for them in the backyard,' Mr Smith said.

'Really? What would that be?'

The smile on Mr Smith's face was getting tight. 'That's between the Pugh family and us, ma'am,' he said.

'I've seen your car parked across the street several times today, and last night,' the woman said. 'I find that suspicious.'

'I'm afraid you're being paranoid, ma'am,' Mr Smith said.

'No,' she said, pulling a badge out of her pocket. 'I'm just being a cop. Now who should I say stopped by?'

Mr Jones sprinted off and, cussing himself – and Mr Jones – Mr Smith saw no alternative but to follow him.

I was halfway to Codderville when I got a call from Luna. 'Two guys just tried to break into your house,' she said.

'Excuse me?'

'I really think you heard me the first time.'

'Did you call the cops?'

'I *am* the cops, Pugh. Remember?'

'I mean the on-duty cops.'

'No, but I got the license number. It's a rental out of Austin. Rented to a Mr Brown on a Visa card.'

'What's Mr Brown's first name?' I asked her.

'As far as I can tell it's "mister." The kid at the car place – first day solo, of course – actually wrote that down. "Mister." Go figure.'

'Did they break anything? Any windows or anything?'

'No, I nailed them in the driveway. I'd noticed that car parked across the street last night and on and off today.'

'Well, gee, thanks for telling me!'

'You know, Pugh, here's the thing: why in the hell did I call and even tell you about these assholes if all you're going to do is give me grief?'

'You know, Luna, I'm not that sure myself—' I started, but I was talking to dead air. She'd hung up on me. She is *so* sensitive sometimes.

I called Willis. 'Hey, babe,' I said after he said hello. 'Luna just called. Two guys tried to break into the house—'

'What the—'

'So I'm turning around. We'll have to do date night another time. I don't want the girls coming home alone with these guys on the prowl. Luna said the car has been hanging out across the street last night and on and off today.'

'Why didn't she—'

'I know! I said the same thing!'

'I'm coming—'

'Home? Good. I'd feel better if we were all there. Should I call Graham?'

'E.J.—'

I sighed. 'I know, I know. 'Bye.'

*   *   *

'We're gonna have to change rental cars,' Mr Smith said into the phone.

'Why?' Mr Brown asked.

'Because we've been spotted in this one.'

'Who saw you?' Mr Brown asked.

Mr Brown was a bit of an unknown to Mr Smith. He'd never worked with him before. He was paying big bucks for the job, but Mr Smith hadn't seen a penny of it yet. The gig had been set up by an older partner of Mr Brown's, who had also set up the annoying Mr Jones. Mr Smith had still not actually met Mr Brown, only doing business over the phone. But he was aggressive and paying a whole lot more for this gig than it seemed worth – which made Mr Smith think maybe Mr Brown was connected – like with the Mexican cartels, or the Mafia, or even worse, the Russians. Mr Smith had heard some hairy things about those Russians. So he planned on being just as nice to Mr Brown as he could possibly be, and to hedge his bets whenever possible.

Should Mr Smith tell him the 'who' was a cop? Probably not a good idea. 'The wife,' he said. 'I saw her writing down the license plate number.'

'Maybe you were too fucking close?' Mr Brown said.

'Yes, sir, you're right. We were too close. We'll use the binoculars from now on,' Mr Smith said, thinking it wise to agree.

'Jesus!' Mr Brown said and hung up.

He couldn't really tell how pissed off Mr Brown was, as he didn't know the man, but if heads were going to roll Mr Smith had big plans that that head would belong to Mr Jones and not to himself.

I was pacing the family room when I heard Willis's monstrosity of a pickup pull into the driveway. I ran to the back door and opened it, meeting him as he got out of the driver's side.

'They're not home yet!' I yelled.

'Did you call them?' he asked, propelling me back into the house.

'Are you an idiot? Of course I called them! I called all three of them and nobody, not one of them picked up!'

'They're OK. It's a party, they probably didn't hear—'

'I told them to come home by seven, and now it's seven-thirty!'

'E.J., how many times have they, individually and as a group, been more than half an hour late? I'll tell you. Hundreds!'

'But there's somebody out there trying to break into the house! What if they're after the girls? I can't lose another child!' I said, burst into tears and fell to the sofa.

I could hear my ever-supportive husband sigh. 'Ya think maybe you're overreacting? Just a smidge?'

'Shut up!' I mumbled into the sofa.

'We didn't lose Graham. We know exactly where he is. And we know where the girls are. Do you want me to go pick them up?'

'They have the minivan,' I said into the sofa cushion.

'I know that. But I can round them up and make them come home,' he offered.

I was just about to demand that he do just that when I heard the not-so-subtle sound of the minivan's muffler.

I jumped up and started to run for the door.

'You really want the girls to see you like that?' Willis said.

I looked at my reflection in the shiny aluminum toaster on the counter near where I stood. I was a mess. Mascara smeared, eyes blotchy, snot – the whole nine yards.

'Shit,' I said and headed for our bedroom right off the kitchen.

When I came out, all three girls were on the sofa watching TV, wearing flannel pajamas and their hair in towels. Except Megan – her hair was not in a towel. She'd taken some babysitting money last week, gone to a hairdresser and had all her beautiful, strawberry-blonde curls that almost reached to her waist cut off. She now sported a short, curly bob. As much as I hated to see the hair I'd so lovingly tended all these years gone, I had to admit the new do looked great on her. The other two, still sporting long hair, had towels twisted around their heads.

Willis was sitting in his recliner watching TV with them. I leaned in and whispered, 'Did you tell them?'

'Tell them what?' he whispered back.

'Yeah, tell us what?' Megan said. My God, that girl has ears.

I took the remote out of Willis's hand – I've found if you don't telegraph the move, just make a smooth grab for it and surprise them, it is possible to take a remote away from a man. It's not easy, but it can be done. I muted the TV.

'Hey!' four voices said in an echoing pattern.

'Mrs Luna saw two men trying to break into our house today. She said their car has been sitting outside our house off and on since last night. Did any of you notice anything out of the ordinary?'

Alicia: 'No.'

Bess: 'Uh uh.'

Megan: 'What does "ordinary" mean?'

I rolled my eyes. Leave it to Megan. 'Ordinary: as in the usual, the same, what has been deemed expected.'

'Hum,' Megan said. 'I guess not.'

I put my hands in my pockets. I couldn't strangle her if my hands were in my pockets.

'Megan, don't be a douche,' Bess said.

'Who are you calling a douche?' Megan demanded.

'No one. I didn't *call* you a douche, I *suggested* you not be one,' Bess said, which elicited a giggle from Alicia.

'OK, girls,' Willis said. 'What your mom is trying to say is that these guys are hanging around for some reason and you need to be careful. Stay together. Nobody goes off on their own, got it? E.J., did Luna describe the car?'

'No,' I said and pulled my new iPhone out of my pocket. The five. It's fabulous. I selected Luna's home number and waited until she said, 'Hello?'

'It's me,' I said. 'Describe the car please. I'm going to put you on speaker.'

'No, don't— I'm on speaker, right?'

'Loud and clear,' Willis said.

'I hate being on speaker. Who else is listening?'

'The girls. I think they need to know what to look out for,' I said.

'Well, I'll tell you what they were driving, but I'm sure they've changed it by now. It was a rental, a dark blue Ford Taurus. So basically be careful of everything *except* a dark blue Ford Taurus.'

'What do they look like?' Bess asked.

'One was short and stocky, with black hair. Swarthy-looking, but not Mexican. Not middle eastern. Not Indian – native or the other. Maybe Italian. The other one was taller, well over six foot, *very* well built, serious blue eyes, also dark hair.'

'Jeez. He sounds cute,' Megan said. 'Maybe he was my blind date!'

I glared at my big-mouthed daughter. Yep, a chip off the old block. Me being the block, of course. 'OK, Luna, thanks—' I started.

'So what have you done now, Pugh?'

'Nothing!' I turned to my husband. 'Tell her!'

He gave me a look, then said into the phone, 'To my knowledge she has not gotten herself into anything. Yet.'

'Jeez, Willis!' I said, while the girls punched each other and giggled. 'I have done nothing. Absolutely nothing. I've thought about doing terrible things to Collette Newberry—'

'Jason's mom?' Alicia said, and all three girls burst into another fit of giggles.

'But I have as yet done nothing more than piss her off,' I finished.

'Well, make sure you keep it that way. If anything happens to Mrs Newberry, I'll know where to look,' Luna said and hung up.

To the room in general, I said, 'Try being on a committee with her. She'd turn Mother Teresa surly.'

Mr Smith and Mr Jones turned in the dark blue Ford Taurus, walked to a nearby convenience store and used a pay phone to call a taxi.

'Why are we doing this?' Mr Jones asked. 'Why didn't we just rent another car at Codderville, for pity's sake? My dogs are barking,' he said, sitting down on the curb and rubbing his feet.

Mr Smith tried not to lose his temper, but did anyway. He'd done some pretty bad things in his time, but couldn't think of anything so bad that he deserved to be stuck with this dumbass. 'The cop saw the car, right? She knows it's a rental. She probably called the rental agency, right? So we rent another car there, the guy'd just tell her what it was, idiot! So, we take a cab, we go here,' he said, looking at a map, 'place called La Grange, and rent a car there.' He paused for breath, hoping Mr Jones would sprout a brain cell while he did so.

'So what if she calls the cab company?' Mr Jones asked.

'Why the fuck would she call the cab company?' Mr Smith demanded.

'I dunno. 'Cause how else we gonna get around, huh? Answer me that!'

'Shut the fuck up!' Mr Smith said.

He took off, walking around the outside of the convenience store, circling the building before coming back to stand over Mr Jones where he still sat on the curb, rubbing his feet.

'What's wrong with your feet?' Mr Smith asked.

'Ah, they're all fucked up. Corns, bunions, you name it,' Mr Jones said.

Mr Smith picked the map up yet again. 'OK, so we take a taxi to here,' he said, pointing at a speck on the map. 'Merleville. They may have a cab company, but even if they don't, I'm sure we can get a ride to La Grange where we can rent another car. That way, if the cop does call the cab company here, all she'll know is we were headed for Merleville, which is on the way to Houston, so she might think we went there.'

Mr Jones looked up at Mr Smith and smiled. 'That's a good one!'

Mr Smith tried not to beam at the compliment, but he *was* pleased.

VERA'S STORY
MONDAY

Since we were two hours late leaving the church, we only made it as far as Little Rock, Arkansas, before we had to stop for the night. Following the itinerary set up by Sister Edith before she left, we should have been as far as Memphis, but that surely didn't happen. We had reservations at the Motel 6 in Memphis, so our driver, an excellent baritone, figured we'd try a Motel 6 in Little Rock. No such luck. Seems there was a jazz festival going on in Little Rock, and there wasn't a motel room to be had in the entire city. So we kept driving, until Brother Joe, who proved to be about as worthless as tits on a boar hog, said to pull over in the parking lot of an all-night Wal-Mart.

'Y'all go on in and use the facilities,' he said, standing up at the head of the bus like he was in charge or something. Well, I suppose he was, but still and all. 'Take your toothbrushes and sleepwear with you, and if anyone tries to stop you, tell them to see me. I'll be in the front of the store.'

Personally, I'm not one for walking around a store in my nightgown and robe. I mean, I'm totally decent and all, but it just seems inappropriate. Knowing I'd have to walk back in in the morning, wearing the same thing and changing clothes, made me decide to sleep in what I had on and change my blouse in the morning. I went in the Wal-Mart, but with just my toothbrush and night cream in my purse.

So imagine everyone's chagrin when we woke up the next morning to find out we'd been traveling most of the night. Brother Joe had taken a turn driving – he said he had a license to drive a bus, whatever. And we were back on Sister Edith's itinerary. We should arrive in D.C. late tonight.

TUESDAY

I got up the next morning, threw a robe on over my sleep T-shirt (one of Willis's from a Grateful Dead concert years ago – the holes aren't in any awkward places), and headed into the kitchen.

Willis was right behind me, jeans and a button-down shirt, running shoes and crew-socks, and his briefcase. Being your own boss does have its privileges – like every day is casual Friday.

I handed him an orange juice and his vitamins, all of which he consumed in one swallow, then his cup of coffee and he was out the door by seven-ten. I went back into our bedroom, threw the robe on the floor, and crawled back into bed.

I woke up again around nine-thirty when I heard a commotion in the kitchen. One of my not-so-favorite things about building our new bedroom onto the new addition of kitchen and family room is that it was too damn close to the kitchen.

I stretched, picked the robe up off the floor, and opened the door. Alicia and Bess were in the kitchen, Bess making coffee and Alicia fixing bagels.

'Don't drink that,' I said to Bess. 'It'll stunt your growth.' I crawled up on a stool. 'But make enough for me.'

'It's cigarettes that stunt your growth, mother,' she said. 'And I gave those up weeks ago.'

I started to react, then realized she was joking. Probably. I'd been joking, too, of course. Bess had just turned sixteen in the summer, and was still five foot nothing, so her growth had already been stunted by something. Her birth mother had been short, too, but more like five foot two inches. As Bess was already sixteen, I didn't see a big growth spurt in her future. And yes, there were a lot of short jokes in the family, but she seemed to handle it well. I think knowing that Megan, at five feet ten inches, felt like an awkward behemoth around her perfectly proportioned and quite beautiful younger sister eased the pain of a few playful short jokes. With Alicia now in the works, when she stood in the middle between the other two, I had stair steps. Alicia was five-five and ninety-eight pounds, so if she leaned just a little, it almost looked like Bess/Megan. That's a joke.

'Is Megan up?' I asked the girls.

'Not that I noticed,' Bess said.

'She'll probably sleep 'til noon,' Alicia said.

'What do y'all have planned for the day?' I asked.

'Why?' Bess asked. 'So you can get us out the door quickly and go back to bed?'

'Coffee,' I said, having heard the noise from the coffee machine stop. 'Actually,' Bess handed me a cup, into which I emptied two packets of Equal, 'I hadn't thought of that, but it seems like a plan,' I said, thinking going back to bed was an excellent idea.

Alicia turned to Bess and said, 'You're right. I do see where she gets it.'

'You're comparing me to Megan, aren't you?' I said. 'That's an awful thing to do.'

'That's an awful thing for a mother to say!' said a voice from behind me.

I glanced. It was, of course, Megan. 'It was a joke,' I said.

'At my expense!' she said.

'A joke is usually at someone's expense. This time it was you,' I said.

Megan went to the counter and poured herself a cup of coffee. She got the cream out of the refrigerator, poured in half a cup, then added three Equals.

'Like a little coffee with your sweet cream?' I asked.

'Gosh, Mom, you are just a barrel of laughs this morning, aren't you?' she said and, me being queen of sarcasm, I could tell she was trying out for the role of princess.

Looking at my other two daughters, it was like they were watching a tennis match: heads going this way and that, following the play by play from the mother and daughter match in front of them.

I took my coffee and wandered into the family room, turning on the TV and honing in on *The Today Show*. Five minutes of that, and there was a break for local news. It basically all went over my head until I heard the name 'Driscoll.' As in the hotel. As in the hotel Willis and I stayed at in Austin, where a dead body had been found.

'. . . Driscoll Hotel. The identity of the man who fell or jumped from there Sunday morning has been verified as James Unger, thirty-nine, of Houston, Texas. He was a chemist at a laboratory in Houston that he owned with his wife, Elizabeth Unger. Mrs Unger was unavailable for comment.'

'Huh,' I said. I picked up the landline as I had no idea where my iPhone was, and called Willis. When he picked up, I said, 'They identified that guy who fell off the garage roof at the Driscoll.'

'Yeah? Who?' he asked.

'James Unger. He was a chemist from Houston. He and his wife owned a lab there.'

'Well, what a shit,' Willis said. 'I mean, if he jumped. That's a shitty thing to do to his wife. If he fell, then hell, what an awful thing to happen.'

'Very well put, dear,' I said, albeit a little sarcastically. 'I think you've covered all the bases.'

'Unless, of course, as Bess mentioned, he was murdered.'

'Then what would the correct response be?' I asked.

'Quite like the "if he fell" response, with an added, "the assholes!" You know, for emphasis.'

I sighed. 'Are we terrible people?' I asked.

'Probably,' he said. 'Another call, babe, gotta go,' and he hung up.

THREE

We arrived in our nation's capital as it was turning midnight. The hotel had been notified that we were getting there pretty late, so they were ready for us. I know my place in this world, and I know God wouldn't give me anything more than I can handle, but I figured He and I were gonna have to have a little talk about my hotel roommate. Yes, you guessed it: Rachael Donley, the separated alto who made googly eyes at Brother Joe. Since my friend and supposed roommate Gladys was down with the flu, and since Rachael didn't have a roommate assigned, I got her.

The room was real nice, with two queen-sized beds, a kitchenette, a table and four chairs, and a large, flat-screen TV. Willis and E.J. bought me one of them last year for Christmas, and I gotta say, going back to one of them regular TVs woulda been a burden. Not that I was gonna sit around our nation's capital and watch TV. No way. I had a few things to say to the president, and I was gonna get in to see him if it hare-lipped Texas.

So me and Rachael Donley got in our room and looked around. I wasn't sure I could look at her because, well, I didn't want to judge.

'This is nice,' she said.

'Uh huh,' I said.

'Which bed do you want?' she asked.

'You choose,' I said.

'Do you want to be near the window? Or do you think it would be too cold?' she asked.

'What part of "you choose" do you not understand?' I said, finally looking at her. She seemed a little taken aback by the question, and I felt a little bad. 'You take the window,' I said. 'I *do* get cold at night.'

'OK,' she said, and threw her suitcase on the bed closest to the window. Then she turned to me, smiled, and said, 'Let me help you with that,' and picked up *my* suitcase and put it on *my* bed.

Hum, I thought. This could work out to my advantage. She thinks
I'm some ditsy old bat, too weak to lift a suitcase. Maybe she'll
bring me my coffee in bed in the morning. And the newspaper.
There are some things about getting ready to turn eighty that might
not be all that bad.

Things had not gone well the night before for Mr Smith and Mr Jones.
The cab *did* take them to Merleville and let them out at the service
station there, but took off before Mr Smith realized that the
service station, a rundown Texaco, was the *only* establishment in
Merleville. There were a few buildings, but after a second glance they
all appeared to be abandoned. The Texaco seemed to be still func-
tioning, but not at nine o'clock at night. It was closed for business.
After an hour of standing around, the taxi cab remained the only
vehicle they'd seen in Merleville. Mr Smith assumed there were houses
somewhere, probably hidden in the trees, but he didn't feel up to a
walk that could end up being miles long. And besides, he wasn't sure
what he would say to anyone who opened a door. The thought did
occur to him that he could use his gun and insist on a bed, but he
thought he'd get very little sleep in that case. These country people
usually had a lot of weapons. He thought seriously about calling Mr
Brown, but decided to keep him out of the loop; he needed to prove
he could handle these things himself, in case Mr Brown had any
better-paid jobs in the future. Besides, when he tried calling earlier,
Merleville appeared to be a dead zone. No cell phone service.

So he and Mr Jones sat on the cement drive of the gas station,
their backs to one of the bay doors, and tried to sleep. Mr Jones
appeared to have no problem, and fell asleep quite readily, his head
lolling onto Mr Smith's shoulder. Mr Smith removed it at once
and scooted further away.

Mr Smith finally fell asleep around midnight, but was haunted
by unfriendly dreams. He awoke around two a.m. to a voice singing
the Beatles' 'Yesterday' very nicely.

There was a man walking down the road singing that song, with
gestures and a bottle of something Mr Smith could only assume
was alcohol in his right hand. Mr Smith stood up and yelled, 'Hey!'
to the man.

The man turned, saw him and stopped, losing his balance for a
second, then stood fairly steady, although weaving just a bit. 'Well,
hey, yourself, fella! You know this song?'

'Of course—'

'Well, then, let's sing it together!' And the man began again, his voice a beautiful, lilting tenor one could imagine doing a wonderful job on 'Danny Boy.'

'Can you help us?' Mr Smith called out.

'Probably not,' the man said and smiled. He waved at Mr Smith. Mr Smith waved back.

'We need to get to La Grange,' Mr Smith said.

The singer shook his head sadly. 'We all need to get somewhere, don't we? La Grange would be a nice place to need to get to.' His face brightened with a big smile. 'Hey! Ya know they used to have a big ol' whorehouse there? The Chicken Ranch! Made a Broadway show out of it! "Best Little Whorehouse in Texas" was the name of it. Made a movie, too, with Burt Reynolds and Dolly Parton!' The smile faded and his sad face was again present. 'She has really beautiful breasts, donja think?'

'Can you take us to La Grange?' Mr Smith begged.

'Don't have a car,' the singer said. 'If I had a car, I couldn't drive it. Don't have a driver's license. See ya!' he said, and started his sloppy march up the road, breaking into 'Do a Little Side Step' from *The Best Little Whorehouse in Texas*.

Mr Smith sat back down and eventually awoke again at four a.m. when it began to rain. This also awakened Mr Jones and the two hustled to the tiny alcove of the front door of the office of the station, with an overhang of less than three feet, and bundled up as best they could to keep out of the rain.

When Mr Smith awoke next around five a.m., he noticed two things: one, it had stopped raining, and two, a dog was peeing on him. But he didn't bat an eye. He just closed them both and went back to sleep.

VERA'S STORY
TUESDAY

Well, she did bring me a cup of coffee the next morning, made with a Mr Coffee machine in the kitchenette, but I'm thinking she just passed the coffee over the filter without actually putting any in, it was that weak. Just as well I'm not one to complain.

She was walking around OK, so I had to ask, 'You get them contacts in OK?'

Rachael laughed, and it was a nice laugh, I'll give her that. 'Yes, thank you! All's well in that department.'

She'd told me the night before about her contacts. I'd remarked upon the fact that she'd put a bunch of stuff in the bedside table drawer.

'You're gonna go off and forget that stuff,' I'd said. 'Sure as shooting.'

'No, not this stuff! I'm blind as a bat, and these are my glasses,' she said, holding up a pair of glasses that really didn't need to be introduced, for goodness' sake, 'and this is my contact stuff. My eyes are weird and I can't wear the soft contacts. Mine are glass and I can only wear them like eight hours without taking them out.'

'That must have been hard on the bus!' I said, more sympathetic than I should have been, under the circumstances.

'It was difficult,' she said, 'but with the stop at the Wal-Mart it worked out OK.'

I patted her on the back as we headed down to breakfast.

According to Sister Edith's itinerary, Monday was travel day, Tuesday was sightseeing day, and the meeting started on Wednesday. Very important business took place during the Southern Baptist National Meeting every year. Like voting on whether or not women could be preachers, and whether or not to baptize homosexuals, or allow them in church at all. Real important stuff like that. But also there was a lot of fun, I'd heard. I'd never been to one and I was pretty much excited, I can tell you.

But today was sightseeing, and I knew we'd be heading to the White House and I had to work on getting me an invite to see the president. I'd contacted my congressman, Avery Mapleton, and told him I'd be visiting, but he didn't reply, which p.o.'d me some since I called people to vote for him during his last campaign. I figured he owed me. I was gonna handle him first. Then the president. I had some words for him about social security and Medicare. A lot of my friends shunned me for a while because I'd voted for a black man, but personally, I don't care what color he is as long as he doesn't mess with my social security and Medicare, know what I mean? So now we had to talk. I needed to keep him on the straight and narrow.

But it was gonna take a while to get there. The itinerary showed us going to Monticello in the morning, and the Smithsonian in the afternoon. She hadn't even put in a time for the White House. But I figured, the Smithsonian's a museum, right? How long could we hang around a museum?

'So what do you want to do today?' Alicia asked Bess.

Bess shrugged. 'I dunno,' she said. 'Maybe we should wake up Megan.'

They were sitting on the sofa in the family room, watching MTV. E.J. was in her under-the-staircase office, writing about somebody ripping somebody else's clothes off.

Alicia leaned her head back and screamed toward the stairs, 'Megan!'

Bess laughed. 'Oh, that's gonna work!'

Alicia's feet were in Bess's lap. 'I didn't want to disturb you by getting up.'

'Excuse me? Taking your feet off me would not disturb me! Putting your feet *on* me disturbed me!'

Alicia swung her long legs off Bess's lap and the sofa, and made it to the bottom of the stairs. 'Megan!' she screamed. 'Get up!'

'Gawd! You people!' Megan said, coming to the head of the stairs, a pillow in one hand while the other dragged her comforter. She plodded down the stairs barefoot, came into the family room and, upon seeing Bess on the sofa, said, 'Get up!'

'No-oo!' Bess said, stretching the tiny negative into a two-syllable word.

Alicia had wisely chosen the comfy chair, leaving the loveseat open.

'Take the loveseat!' Megan told Bess. 'My legs are too long for that. I need the sofa!'

'So cut off your legs,' Bess said, staring intently at the TV. 'Ha! Did you see that?' she squealed, turning her head toward Alicia.

Megan took that opportunity to continue Bess's momentum to the left and pushed her off the sofa. Megan got on the sofa, bed pillow under her head, comforter covering her body.

'You bitch!' Bess shouted from the floor.

'Bite me,' Megan said calmly from the comfort of the sofa.

Getting to her feet, Bess said, 'Mom said I couldn't bite you anymore, even when you ask for it, but she said nothing about pulling your hair out!' Which she proceeded to do from the head of the sofa.

'Get your hands off me!' Megan yelled. 'Mom! Help!'

'Jeez, Megan, leave Mom alone, she's trying to work!' Alicia said.

'Then you help me!' Megan pleaded, now her back was balanced like a seesaw on the arm of the sofa, her hands on Bess's hands as they pulled her hair. 'She's trying to kill me!'

'That would be fine, too,' Bess said through gritted teeth.

'What the hell is going on in here?' E.J. asked, coming in. 'Bess, let go of Megan's hair!'

Grinning like the Cheshire cat, Bess let go, and Megan's tentative balance on the seesaw sofa arm was skewed a little to the upper body, and she fell on her head on the hardwood floor of the family room.

When she landed, Bess laughed out loud. Megan jumped up and Bess ran, Megan not that far behind.

'Girls! Stop it right this minute!' E.J. shouted.

They didn't stop.

'I'm gonna kill you!' Megan shouted.

'You're so fat you'll never be able to catch me!' Bess shouted back.

'Mom! She called me fat!'

E.J. sighed. 'Bess, don't call your sister fat.'

'Fatty, fatty two by four, couldn't get through the kitchen door! So she starved to death!' Bess called out, laughing as she made yet another circle around the family room.

'I've got five dollars,' Alicia said lazily. 'Y'all got any money? We could go to the movies.'

The other two stopped, mid-run. Bess fell onto the loveseat and stuck her hand in her pocket. 'Ooo, a ten!'

'Let me go check my purse,' Megan said, and headed out to the foyer where all the purses hung on the coat rack. She came back in, her purse under her arm, her wallet in her hands. 'Three, four, ooo, a five, nine, ten, eleven, twelve. I have twelve dollars.'

'Bring in my purse, wouldja?' Bess asked.

'Mine, too,' Alicia said.

'Get 'em yourselves,' Megan said, 'I have to go change.'

The girls dug through their purses and came up with a total of thirty-eight dollars. Bess had her original ten, Megan twelve, and Alicia, who'd had a five in her pocket, found six more in her purse. All together it was enough to get the three of them into the seven-dollar matinee and buy a large popcorn to share. Megan came down dressed for the movies in skin-tight jeans, a tank top and sweaters over her arm. She handed one to each of her sisters and kept one for herself.

'It gets cold in the theater,' she explained to her mom.

'I understand,' her mom said.

They then proceeded to pull sodas out of the refrigerator and stick them in the bottom of their purses.

'OK, Mom, we're off,' Bess said.

'Do you know what's showing and what time it's showing?' E.J. asked.

'No,' all three girls said in unison. Megan said, 'It doesn't really matter, Mom. We'll find something once we get there.'

'Well, don't get caught with those sodas. And remember to cough when you open them.'

'Yes, ma'am, we've only been doing this since we were like five!' Bess said.

And they were out the door.

The next morning had gone better for Mr Smith and Mr Jones. A trucker pulled into the Texaco station fairly early and agreed to take them as far as La Grange. From there it was a piece of cake finding a rental car agency (a different company than the last one, of course), and heading back to Black Cat Ridge.

They'd parked three doors down on the same side of the street as the Pugh home, hopeful that the cop on the other side of the Pughs wouldn't see them. They'd been there almost half an hour when Mr Smith sat up in the new rental. 'It's them!' he said excitedly. 'They're getting in the minivan!'

'The one in the middle,' Mr Jones said, 'she's the one that's got the satchel thing.'

'Yes, that's right, Mr Jones,' Mr Smith said.

Mr Jones looked excitedly at Mr Smith. 'Now we can get the satchel!'

Mr Smith shook his head and gritted his teeth. 'The satchel is in the school, remember? We can't get it from them today. Maybe tomorrow.'

'But what if they go to the school? What if that's where they're headed right now?'

Mr Smith thought about it for a moment, then pulled out after the minivan as it left the driveway. 'OK, so we'll follow them for a little while.'

It was Bess's turn to drive the minivan. She pulled the seat up as far as it would go and started the engine. As they pulled into the Metroplex's parking lot, she asked her sisters, 'What color was that car Mrs Luna said was parked across the street from the house?'

'Blue?' Alicia said.

'Yeah, I think so,' Megan agreed.

'Hum,' Bess said, pulling into a parking spot only four city blocks from the theater.

'What "hum"?' Megan said, turning around in her shotgun seat to look behind them. 'I don't see a blue car!'

'Me neither,' Bess said, 'but that white one has been following us since our street.'

She turned off the ignition and all three girls watched the white car slowly drive by.

'Two dark-haired men,' Alicia said. 'One is taller – at least, he sits taller than the other.'

'Is that what Mrs Luna described?' Megan asked.

'You really just don't listen, do you?' Bess said in disgust.

'Get off my back!' Megan shouted.

'Hey, guys! Give it a rest! Is that them or not?' Alicia said.

'I dunno,' Bess said. She sighed. 'Let's just go see what's playing, OK?'

After the girls left, I fixed myself some lunch – a small salad and some fruit – and sat down in the family room to watch the noon news. After finding out we were in for at least seven more days of sunny weather, with highs of one hundred degrees for the third day in a row, and that one of the U.T. coaches had passed out during practice the day before from the heat (and he was just sitting on the sidelines), the real news came on.

'A couple of days ago we reported that a man fell or jumped from the parking garage at the Driscoll Hotel in downtown Austin. The police released a statement today, saying that from information gleaned from the medical examiner and the crime scene investigators, they are declaring the death of James Unger from Houston a homicide.'

'Shit!' I said.

'The report states that it appears Mr Unger was pushed. His wife, Elizabeth Unger, vice president of Pharmacopia, the pharmaceutical company owned by the Ungers, is still unavailable for comment. In other news . . .'

I muted the TV, picked up my iPhone and dialed Willis's number at work. 'Guess what?' I said when he answered.

'The kids have all run away and we are allowed to use their college money to retire and move to the South Pacific,' he said.

I sighed. 'Ah, if only. No. That guy – James Unger?'

'What guy?'

'The guy at the parking garage at the Driscoll!' I said. How could he not know what guy?

'Oh, yeah, the guy who jumped or fell—'

'Neither!' I said with an 'ah ha' to my voice. 'He was pushed!'

There was a silence on the other end of the line. 'Oh, come on, Willis! I'm not going to go rushing back to Austin to solve the case! Give me a break!'

'Every time I give you a break, you take a mile,' he said.

'That's an inch, idiot. And besides, who the hell are you to *give* me anything? I am woman!'

'Don't roar,' he said. 'Please don't roar.'

'Then don't start that sexist crap on me now!' I said. 'I called you because we were following the story, and this is a new development! That's all. Now I'm hanging up.'

'Please, don't hang up on my accou—'

I think he was going to say account, but I really didn't want to hear it. The issue of me getting involved in murder cases had not been resolved. We just didn't talk about it. Since the upheaval of the summer there hadn't been another murder so everything had been hunky-dory up until now. Now there was a murder. But we were very, very peripherally involved. So peripherally involved as to be totally uninvolved. So what was his problem? Did he really think I was going to jump in my Audi and rush off to Austin to SOLVE THE CASE? Jeez, was I Nancy Drew?

But jumping in my Audi and rushing off to anywhere wasn't out of the question. That would be fun. I sat a while, the TV on mute, contemplating places I could rush off to in my Audi. Some would include Willis rushing with me, some not. As was so often the case, I wished I had a close girlfriend I could rush off with, but since the

death of Terry Lester, Bess's birth mom, there hadn't really been
any to speak of. Elena Luna, the Codderville cop who lived next
door, was the closest thing I had, but we spent most of our time
sniping at each other, like an old married couple. Hell, Willis and
I have been married for close to twenty-five years, and we don't
snipe at each other as much as Luna and I do. Over the summer
I'd got sort of tight with the woman who lived across the street, but
the family had moved.

So basically I had no girlfriend to jump in the shotgun side of
my Audi and rush off to have an adventure with somewhere. I suppose
I could take one of my daughters, or even my mother-in-law . . . I
got up and took my lunch dishes back into the kitchen. For obvious
reasons, neither of those two ideas would work. I couldn't take just
one daughter, I'd have to take all three; and my mother-in-law?
Really? Where had that thought come from? I mean, yeah, we've
gotten along better over the past few years, but still and all. Why
would I even *think* that? Luckily she was either in D.C. or on her
way for some Baptist thing, so I couldn't even be tempted.
Getting up, I thought again about cultivating a friendship with Lacy
Kent, who I'd bonded with at the school yesterday. She seemed like
fun.

I headed back into my office under the stairs to have my heroine,
Naomi, the passionate and exotic Jewess, seduce young Daniel, the
heir to the throne of Maldovia.

It was a couple of hours later when all three girls came running
in the back door screaming, 'Mom!'

It was so loud and so forceful that the phrase I was typing, 'width
and breadth' came out 'width and brrrrrrrrrrrrrr.' I jumped up and
ran into the family room.

'What?' I yelled back.

But they were already through the family room and into the living
room at the front of the house. When I got there, they were standing
to the side of the front window, peaking out at the street one at a
time through a crack in the wooden Venetian blinds.

'What?' I said.

'Shhhhh!' Bess said, index finger to mouth. She hit the floor and
crawled below the windowsill to the other side of the window, where
she stood up and peeked through a crack in the blinds on that side.

Alicia, who was the odd girl out at the moment, ran up to me,
took my hands and forcibly lowered me to the sectional sofa.

'Mom, listen!' she said in an excitable stage whisper. 'Those men in the blue car?'

I started to stand up but she said, 'Listen! They changed cars! They followed us to the movies and when we got out they followed us home! And they're out there right now!'

I grabbed my hands back, went to the window, and yanked the cord that pulled the blinds all the way up. A white car was parked across the street, in front of the McClures' house with its 'for sale' sign, and the guys in it favored Luna's description. With my girls flanking me, we stared out at the white car, which started up immediately and drove off, as I wrote down the license plate number.

'Uh oh,' Mr Jones said.

'Shut up!' Mr Smith said.

'But now they know we're watching 'em,' Mr Jones said.

'Shut up!' Mr Smith repeated.

'Mr Brown's gonna be all kinds of mad,' Mr Jones said.

'Shut the fuck up!' Mr Smith screamed.

'Jeez, ya don't have to get pissy about it,' Mr Jones said.

Mr Smith gritted his teeth for the umpteenth time and drove out of the neighborhood.

I called Luna at her office at the police station in Codderville.

'Lieutenant Luna,' she said upon answering. She used to just say 'Luna,' but with the promotion, she's all about rank. I'm embarrassed for her.

'It's me,' I said. 'The blue car is now white. They were parked in front of the McClures' house.' I read off the license plate number. 'They followed the girls to the movies, waited for them, then followed them back! What are you going to do about this?' I demanded.

'Not my jurisdiction. Call the Black Cat Ridge police,' she said, and hung up.

I said some words I shouldn't say in front of my children, even though they're old enough now to teach me some new ones, hung up, and redialed the Black Cat Ridge police – the 311 number, not the 911.

I explained the situation, told the lady on the other end of the phone that Luna had witnessed these men sitting in their car outside my house and then attempting to break in. And that the same men had followed my girls to and from the movies today and had been sitting outside the house in another car just now. I gave her the license plate number of the white car they were driving.

'Did they actually break into your home?' she asked.

'Well, no—'

'Did they park their vehicle in your driveway?' she asked.

'Ah, no, but—'

'Did they speak to your daughters?' she asked.

'No, but listen—'

'Ma'am, I don't see that there's anything we can do about this at the moment. If they break a law, we'll be happy to—'

'But they trespassed!'

'Ma'am?'

'They walked up my driveway!' I said.

'Is your driveway posted?'

'Posted?'

'Is there a "no trespassing" sign posted at the front of your driveway?' she asked.

'No, of course not—'

'Then they did not trespass, ma'am. Please call us back if—'

'If what?' I shouted. 'They attack one of my children? Break into my home? Kill us all in our sleep?'

'Yes, ma'am,' she said. 'Any of the above.'

And the line went dead in my hands.

Boy, was I pissed!

'Go steal that license plate,' Mr Smith said to Mr Jones. 'Front and back.'

'Huh?' Mr Jones said.

'Go get those fucking license plates, moron! Are you deaf as well as stupid?' Mr Smith shouted.

Mr Jones squared his broad shoulders. He'd had just about enough of Mr Smith and his attitude. 'That was really uncalled for, Mr Smith,' he said. 'And if you want those "fucking" license plates stolen, I suggest you do it yourself!' Mr Jones crossed his arms over his chest and looked out the passenger-side window.

'You are fucking kidding me, right?' Mr Smith said between his gritted teeth. 'Tell me I didn't hurt your goddam feelings!'

Mr Jones said nothing, just continued to stare out his window, his body language speaking volumes.

'Oh, for Christ's sake!' Mr Smith said and got out of the white rental.

They were in the parking lot of the new Wal-Mart that had just opened in Codderville. The place was packed and they had their pick of vehicles. Mr Smith had picked a fairly late-model white Ford – a Focus, not a Taurus like their rental, but close enough. Using the screwdriver setting on his Swiss Army knife, he unscrewed the front plate, threw it in the back seat of the car, got in, and drove off down the row of parked cars. Mr Jones did not ask what he was doing. Mr Jones was still not looking at him.

Mr Smith circled the row and came back to the white Ford Focus. Stopping the white Taurus two cars down, he walked up to the Focus, then went round the back and unscrewed that license plate, thinking how much easier this kind of thing was in states that didn't require a front license plate. Mr Smith threw the back plate in the back seat of the Taurus with the front plate, and took off.

Several miles later, Mr Smith pulled into the parking lot of an office building, and proceeded to change the Taurus's plates to those of the Focus. Let it be noted that Mr Jones did not help.

'I'm coming home,' Willis said.

'Good,' I said. 'The girls are pretty nervous.' That was not exactly true. The girls were climbing the walls, but more from the excitement of it all than fear.

I'd called Willis to let him know what had happened, and informed him about the response from the Black Cat Ridge police.

'That's because I won that contract!' Willis had said.

'What contract?' I'd asked.

'The Chemco deal,' he said. 'Barry's son-in-law was also bidding, but Dave always bids way too high. Meanwhile, Barry and his wife are supporting their daughter and Dave and it's all my fault? I don't THINK so!'

Barry Donaldson was the chief-of-police for the small Black Cat Ridge police department.

'Well, just come home,' I'd said. 'We'll sort it out together.'

And he did. Come home, that is. And he'd stewed in it all the way home. By the time he walked in the door, if Barry Donaldson had been in the room, it's a possibility he wouldn't have made it out alive.

'I'm calling that son-of-a-bitch! He can't ignore you—'

'Honey, I didn't even talk to Barry! I talked to a dispatcher.'

He stopped, turned and looked at me. 'Why didn't you call Barry directly?' he asked.

'He's your friend, not mine,' I said.

'He's not my friend – we just shoot hoops once a week.'

'That's certainly more of a relationship than I have with him.'

'So why didn't you call me so I could call him?' Willis demanded.

I sighed. 'Because I didn't think about it! I called Luna first, and she said it wasn't her jurisdiction, that I should call Black Cat Ridge police, so I just dialed their three-one-one number.'

Willis pulled out his iPhone and looked at it, then put it back in his pocket and went into my office, coming out seconds later with the tiny Black Cat Ridge phone directory. He sat on the sofa, pulled out his phone yet again, and dialed the number.

'Chief Donaldson, please. Willis Pugh calling.'

I sat down in an easy chair opposite him. We waited.

Maybe I should take this waiting period to explain the existence of Black Cat Ridge, the town in which we lived on the north side of the Texas Colorado River. It is what they call a 'planned community.' Codderville, on the south side of the Colorado River, was more haphazard. It came about as a cattle-drive stop back in the 1800s, then got bypassed by the railroad and almost died out, only to have a highway come through in the 1930s, which perked it up again, only to be bypassed once more by the freeway system in the 1960s. But by the 1960s, people had dug themselves in: there were some businesses, lots of churches, retail, etc. Codderville, although sleepy, remained.

Then came a developer who saw an expanse of wooded acreage on the other side of the Colorado, and thought: trees! Must destroy now! But, of course, being a smart developer/tree killer, he opted to keep enough trees to make the homes costly. And not only homes: churches and grammar schools, and retail. Lots and lots of retail. From the beginning we had a fire substation, manned by two firemen from the Codderville station and one junior fire truck. The real fire truck would come over the river and through the former woods if needed. Which would only take like twenty minutes or so. Not enough time for the entire subdivision to burn down, but close. Luckily, the few fires the substation dealt with were small. They mostly tended boo-boos, rescued the occasional loose-riding lawnmower, and drove people to the emergency room at the Codder Memorial Hospital.

That was at the beginning. We now had a middle and a high school, a full fire station that employed four full-time firefighters and a list of eighteen volunteer firefighters (of which, I'm proud to say, Willis and I are two), and a full-time police department with a police chief and five police officers, backed up, when necessary, by the Codder County sheriff's department. And the fire station has an ambulance and two ENTs to drive people to the emergency room at Codder Memorial Hospital. We don't have our own hospital. Yet.

I perked up when Willis perked up. I told him to put his iPhone on speaker and he did. He said, 'Barry? Hey, got a problem here and I'm hoping you can help out.'

'Yeah, you backing out of tomorrow's scrimmage? I wouldn't be surprised the way we beat your asses last week.'

'Yeah, good game. But tomorrow's gonna be a totally different story, my friend.'

'Ah, you fire guys got no balls,' the police chief said.

'Hey, drive by sometime – you can hear our balls clanging all the way out in the street.'

'Sheee-it!' Barry said. 'You calling just to harass me, or you wanna gloat about taking the food out of my daughter's mouth?'

'Sorry, Barry. I'm just a better engineer, what can I say?' Willis said.

'No, son, you're a better negotiator. Dave's an asshole when it comes to bidding. Ah, hell, let's face it: Dave's an asshole all the time.'

'True,' Willis said, and I gave him the move it along signal. 'Reason I'm calling, Barry, is that we got a problem here.' And he went on to explain about Luna seeing the guys parked across the street two days straight and them coming up the driveway to our back door on the second day. And how, today, the same two guys were seen by our daughters in a different car following them to the movies and then following them home.

'What the fuck'd you do, Pugh?' Barry said.

'Me? I didn't do squat!' Willis said, his voice rising in tenor as well as volume.

'You get the license number on the new car? I know Luna got the one on the blue car.'

I handed Willis the slip of paper I'd written the plate number down on. He read it off to Barry.

'OK, great,' he said. 'I'm gonna call Luna, see what she says, just to confirm everything, then I'm gonna come out and talk to the girls. That OK?'

'Yeah, that's fine.'

And they rang off.

'He doesn't trust you?' I asked my husband.

'What?' he said.

'He has to call Luna to verify?'

'Let it go, babe,' he said.

'What? He thinks we'd lie about this?' Now my voice was rising in tenor as well as volume.

'Of course not,' Willis said in that condescending tone he gets when he thinks I'm being unreasonable. God, I hate that. Then he put his arm on my shoulder, which is condescending squared. 'I think he just wants to get it all first hand, that's all.'

'First hand this!' I said, removing his hand from my shoulder and showing him a well-known hand gesture most of us learn as kids.

FOUR

'Oh, shit!' Megan said, coming in to Bess's room. Bess and Alicia were sitting on the bed playing liar's poker.

'Ummmmm?' Bess inquired, not looking up from her game.

'Listen!' Megan demanded. When neither sister looked up, she plopped herself down between them, thus stopping any gamesmanship that might have been going on.

'Get your fat ass up!' Bess said, shoving Megan.

'Say what you want, but my ass ain't moving!'

'Why must you use improper grammar, Megan? You know it makes my ears bleed!' Alicia said.

'Do y'all want to hear what is going to happen to us in the very near future?'

'What?' Bess said, as she stopped shoving her sister.

'The police chief of Black Cat Ridge is coming to interview us,' Megan said in as dramatic a voice as she could conjure up.

'Why?' Bess demanded.

Alicia rolled her eyes. 'About the white car, dumbass,' she said.

'I'm not sure, Alicia, dear, but is "dumbass" actually proper English?' Megan said.

'Bite me,' Alicia said.

'Oh, you mean because of those guys. Well, good,' said Bess. 'We need the police on this and there's not much Mrs Luna can do since she works for the Codderville force.'

'You would think her living in BCR, she'd take a job here,' Megan said.

'I'd venture a guess that BCR doesn't pay nearly as much as she's making in Codderville, especially now she's been promoted to lieutenant,' Alicia said.

Megan shrugged. 'Yeah. That's probably right.'

'So when is this interview going to happen?' Bess asked.

Megan shrugged. 'All I heard was "he's coming by later." I have no idea what constitutes later.' She turned to Alicia and grinned. 'How'd you like that one? Constitutes. Good word usage, huh?'

'Piss off,' Alicia said. 'Even better word usage.' She hopped off the bed and headed for the door. 'I hope he doesn't come too late. We have school tomorrow, remember?'

'Oh, Lord,' Megan said. 'I've been trying to forget. What are you wearing?'

'That new black-and-white-striped tee with black leggings and that new red mini,' Alicia said.

'Oh, that'll look good,' Bess said. 'I'm thinking about that tie-dye maxi with the blue shrug.'

'I'm going old skool,' Megan said. 'Jeans and a tee. Probably the one from that Taylor Swift concert.'

'Can't,' said Alicia, heading out the door. 'New rule: no tees that advertise anything, even bands, etc.'

'Well, that sucks!' Megan said.

'Tell me about it,' Alicia said as she headed down the stairs, followed by her sisters.

The girls found their parents in the kitchen: Willis at the stove stirring a pot and E.J. at the bar, cutting veggies for a salad.

'What do you have there, Dad?' Alicia asked. She still felt a little uncomfortable calling him that, after the drama of the summer when Willis had left E.J. and Alicia had found out it was partially her fault, but now he seemed to preen every time she called him dad, so she figured it was all good.

'My two-alarm chili, without beans, of course, and a small batch of no alarm for the ladies,' Willis said.

'I guess I'm no lady,' Megan said. 'Bring on the two-alarm for me!'

'You know, Dad,' Bess said, taking the plates from Alicia, who had pulled them down from a cupboard that was too high for Bess to reach, 'it's now three against two, what with Graham off at college. The small batch should be the two-alarm, not the no alarm.'

'She's got a point, Willis,' E.J. said.

'Who eats seconds around here? AND takes leftovers to work for lunch? Me, that's who!' Willis said. 'The big batch will, as always, remain two-alarm. Thank you very much,' he finished with a bow.

Megan applauded.

'Megan, use your hands for something more useful – like setting the table,' her mother suggested.

'They've got it taken care of,' she said, head-pointing at her sisters.

'We need napkins, or really a whole roll of paper towels. This is going to get messy,' Alicia said. 'And pour drinks, please.'

'Jeez, you're needy! And bossy!' Megan said, but set about doing her chores.

By the end of the meal they all agreed that their respective chilies had been great, even though there might have been a bit more heat than advertised in the no-alarm chili. The salad and the plate of fruit dealt with that successfully.

The girls were cleaning the kitchen and arguing when the front doorbell rang. E.J. and Willis went to the front of the house and all three girls looked at each other.

'That's him, I bet!' Megan stage-whispered.

'Should we go in now?' Bess whispered back.

'Maybe we should wait until they call us in,' Alicia whispered.

So the three dried their hands and stood in the kitchen, waiting. They could hear talk from the living room – mostly two male voices, their dad's and another man's – with an occasional female laugh. Then they distinctly heard their mother say, 'I'll just go get them.' And in she came. 'The police chief is here to get your statements about that white car,' she said.

The girls nodded and walked single file into the living room, like stair steps going up – first Bess, then Alicia, with Megan at the end.

Willis and the man were both standing up. 'Girls, this is police chief Barry Donaldson. Barry, my daughters, Bess, Alicia and Megan.'

The chief was shorter than their father, maybe just six foot, with snow-white hair and skin darkened by years in the sun. He was just a little overweight, mostly in the stomach, but still wore his uniform well. He had bright blue eyes that sparkled.

'Ladies,' he said, and bowed slightly. 'Why don't y'all have a seat while I ask a couple of questions.'

They all sat down on the long part of the sectional sofa, with Willis and E.J. taking up one end and the chief the other.

Chief: 'Now when did y'all first notice this car following you?'

Bess: 'I was driving and I noticed the car pulling out of our street as we left, but didn't really pay any attention. I noticed it because there aren't any white cars on our street.'

Chief: 'And when was the next time you noticed it?'

Bess: 'We were talking, you know? So I wasn't really paying attention until we pulled into the shopping center. I saw the car behind us and it didn't really mean much at the time, but I'd pulled into the wrong driveway – the theater is the second driveway not the first, and I had to go all around Kohl's and Academy to get to the Metroplex and, when I found a parking place, I saw that car again. It was right behind us.'

Alicia: 'She called it to our attention, and Megan and I both looked and it looked like the two men Mrs Luna had described the day before.'

Chief: 'Dark hair, swarthy complexions. Is that right?'

Alicia: 'Yes, sir.'

Megan: 'Yes, sir.'

Bess: 'Yes, sir.'

Chief: 'Did any of you notice the make or model?'

Alicia: 'It was a white Ford Taurus. Fairly new.'

Everyone in the room turned to look at Alicia. She turned pink and said, 'I like cars. I notice these things!'

The front door opened and a young patrol man burst in. 'Chief! A white car just came up the street, saw us, and went speeding off!'

'Well, follow 'em, for God's sake!' the chief said.

'Morris went after 'em. He sent me in to tell you.'

The chief sighed. 'See that thing up there on your shoulder, boy?'

'Yes, sir?'

'What is that thing?'

'It's a radio,' the patrolman said, his face turning red.

'Now you and I are both stuck here without transportation and Morris's driving solo after two miscreants. Is that about the situation as you see it, boy?'

The patrolman hung his head. 'Yes, sir,' he said.

Willis stood up. 'Come on, Barry, we'll take my truck. You can deputize it.'

You!' the chief said, pointing a finger at the patrolman. 'Stay here. On the front porch. Anybody, I mean anybody, comes by this house, you radio me, you got that boy?'

'Yes, sir!'

The chief sighed. 'Let's do it, Pugh.'

VERA'S STORY
TUESDAY

OK, so the Smithsonian isn't just a museum. It's like a hundred and fifty museums. Well, maybe not that many, but a bunch. Monticello was very nice – that's the house Thomas Jefferson lived in – and took up the morning, then we had lunch at a cafeteria that was very good, but a tad expensive, then we headed to the Smithsonian. And that shot the entire afternoon! I'm not kidding! The whole baritone section didn't come with us when we left the Air and Space building, wanting to see *everything*, not just the interesting stuff, and we lost a few more in the Lifestyles or whatever building – the one with Archie Bunker's chair from *All in the Family*. I wasn't really interested in any of that fal-de-ral, but then I found this building that had this big walk-in display of the dresses worn by the first ladies over the years. Now that was something! Me and Rachael sorta got stuck in there, discussing the intricacies of some of the hand work. Who knew? Rachael sewed, just like me, and she didn't need a pattern either. There was a bench, and we just sat there for the longest and oo'ed and aw'ed over those dresses.

But by the time we were more or less through with the Smithsonian (and we hadn't even seen *all* the buildings), it was time for dinner back at the hotel. I decided to go up to the room and get room service because, and I hate to admit this, I was tired. A couple of the other people my age also left for their rooms. Three hours later, Rachael still wasn't back in the room. And all I could say to that was, 'Told you so.' I turned off the light and went to sleep, hoping, sorta, that she didn't stumble getting to her bed in the dark.

'I think we should call Mr Brown,' Mr Jones said, looking behind them as Mr Smith sped out of Black Cat Ridge. He could see the cop car trailing behind them, lights flashing. This was not a good sign.

'Shut up!' Mr Smith said, trying to lose their tail by weaving his way speedily through the streets of the subdivision.

'I think he'll be interested in hearing how you've botched this whole thing,' Mr Jones said.

'You know I'm going to kill you, don't you?' Mr Smith said.

'I'm calling Mr Brown right now!' Mr Jones said, pulling out his cell phone.

Mr Smith took one hand off the wheel, reached into his shoulder holster and brought out his Beretta. He shot Mr Jones in the foot before he dialed the first digit.

Willis and Chief Donaldson met up with Morris, the driver of the chief's car, about seven blocks from the Pugh home. He was standing outside the cruiser looking around.

Willis pulled up next to him and the chief got out of the car.

'Whatja doing, Morris?' he asked.

'Well, sir, I was chasing that white car, but then I lost it, but I think it was OK because it wasn't the same license number as the one reported.'

'Did you get the license number of *this* white car?' the chief asked.

'Yes, sir, I called it in.'

At that moment, the dash computer let out a ping. Morris looked at the chief and the chief said, 'Go on, see what it says.'

Morris crawled in the front seat of the squad car. 'Those tags belong to a white 2010 Ford Focus—'

'So it wasn't even a Taurus you were chasing?'

'Sir, it says those tags were reported stolen earlier today at the Wal-Mart on highway twelve.'

'So it *was* them?' Willis ventured from his vantage point, still in the cab of his truck, but with the window down.

'Yeah, coulda been,' the chief said. 'Shit.'

'You shot me in the goddam foot!' Mr Jones screamed.

'So don't threaten me, asshole!' Mr Smith screamed back. 'You're not calling Mr Brown, you got that?' He brandished his weapon at Mr Jones. 'You got that?'

'Yes!' Mr Jones screamed. 'I got that! I really, really got that!'

'OK, then,' Mr Smith said, settling back in his seat, a calm mist descending over him. He looked over at Mr Jones, who was trying to get his foot up in the seat, but was having trouble because of his long legs. 'Guess we should deal with your foot,' he said.

'Ya think?' Mr Jones asked, the sarcasm abundantly clear. 'Take me to a hospital!'

'Can't do it,' Mr Smith said. 'They have to report all gunshot wounds to the police.'

'Well, you should have thought about that before you shot me!' Mr Jones said.

Mr Smith found his way out of Black Cat Ridge without being

followed and pulled onto a side road that went down to the river. He pulled under the bridge that connected BCR to Codderville, shut off the engine and turned on the interior light.

'Get your foot up here,' he said to Mr Jones.

'I can't!' Mr Jones said. 'My leg doesn't bend that way!'

Mr Smith sighed. 'Get out of the car and lift your foot onto the seat.'

Grumbling, Mr Jones got out of the car, limping and, holding on to the door, stuck his injured foot onto the passenger seat.

Mr Smith studied the foot. The motorcycle boot Mr Jones was wearing had a hole in it in the baby toe vicinity. 'OK,' he said to Mr Jones, 'I'm gonna take off the boot. So hold on to the door.'

Mr Jones held on and screamed like a little girl when Mr Smith yanked off the boot.

'Big baby,' Mr Smith said. There was a lot of blood on Mr Jones' white sock. Mr Smith pulled that off, eliciting yet another child-like scream of pain. Taking the already ruined sock, Mr Smith cleared the area of blood. There was a small divot cut out of Mr Jones' foot, right below the smallest toe. It was less a wound and more a severe scrape. But in his position, Mr Smith noted a large hole in the floor of the car.

He threw the bloody sock at Mr Jones. 'Jesus, Jones,' he said, 'the car got it worse than you did. Get in.'

Mr Jones looked down at his foot. 'It's still bleeding,' he said.

'Then keep the sock on it. Jeez, get in the car and let's go.'

Mr Jones got in the car, leaning down to wrap the bloody sock around his wound before shutting the door. 'Where are we going now?' he asked Mr Smith.

'Now we gotta get another car.' Mr Smith sighed. 'This is getting old.'

WEDNESDAY

The next morning was hectic. Nobody got much sleep the night before, knowing those two men were still out there, but it was the first day of school, the first day of being juniors for all three girls. It wasn't as cool as being seniors, of course, but they were now upper-class women, and that was something. They got dressed, Bess and Alicia just as they'd described the night before, and, after much throwing of tops hither and yon, Megan managed to find a three-quarter sleeve, handkerchief-hemmed gauzy Indian print top, low-cut enough to show boobage, but not so low cut as to instigate a riot – either with the boys at school, the school authorities, or, she hoped, her mother.

Megan lucked out. Her mother was too busy making breakfasts and fixing lunches to care.

'I'd rather eat in the cafeteria,' Megan said, turning her nose up at the brown bag her mother had prepared.

'Eat it and shut up,' E.J. said. 'Email notice last night. The kitchen will be closed for at least one week pending the completion of the remodeling.'

'That's what you get when you go with the lowest bidder,' her father said from his stool at the counter.

'Where are we going to eat?' Megan demanded.

'The cafeteria will be open. The kitchen is cordoned off,' her mother said.

'Just great,' Megan mumbled.

'You'll live,' Alicia said from her stool where she was finishing up her cereal.

'I'm driving this morning!' Megan called.

'Nope.' E.J. pointed to a whiteboard on the refrigerator. 'It's Alicia's turn.'

Alicia stuck her tongue out at Megan. 'Very mature, Alicia!' Megan said, sticking her tongue out back at her.

'Gawd,' Bess said. 'Mother, may I please take the bus?'

Megan pushed Bess, who pushed back.

'Finish eating, please,' their mother called out. 'And don't anyone touch anyone else. At all. Do you hear me?'

They ignored her but bent down to their cereal bowls.

Ten minutes later they were out the door and piling into the minivan, both Bess and Megan shouting 'shotgun!' at the same time.

VERA'S STORY
WEDNESDAY

In a way, I hate to admit it, but I *was* right. I woke up Wednesday morning and the bed next to mine was empty – never slept in. I would have thought that Rachael and Brother Joe would be a little bit more discreet, but things aren't like they used to be. People living in sin and having babies out of wedlock like it's no big deal. Homosexuals having babies willy-nilly, and people talking out loud in mixed company about sex. But you'd think they would at least keep this stuff at home and not flaunt it in front of the entire choir like this.

I went down to breakfast and ran into my friend Ethel, another soprano. I said, 'Guess who never came back to the room last night.'

She made an 'O' with her mouth and her eyes got big. 'Not at all?'

I shook my head. 'Not seen hide nor hair of her since we got back to the hotel last night.'

Then she elbowed me in the ribs. 'Look! There's Brother Joe.'

I looked. Sure enough Brother Joe was in line at the breakfast buffet, loading his plate like he thought calories didn't matter. I couldn't help noticing he was alone, though.

'Do you think we should let them drive to school alone?' Willis asked me as they pulled out of the driveway.

'Ha! A little late to be asking that!' I said.

'Yeah. I didn't think about it until I saw them pulling away,' he said, the look on his face so tragic I wanted to take him in my arms and kiss his worried brow. I restrained myself.

'They'll be fine,' I said.

'Yeah,' he said, although I could tell he didn't mean it.

'Tell you what,' I said, picking up my new iPhone, 'I'll call them and have them call you as soon as they get to school, OK?'

He smiled. 'Yeah,' he said. 'That would be good.'

I got Megan on the first ring. 'Call your dad as soon as you get to school,' I told her. 'He's a little worried.'

'Yeah, whatever,' she said.

'Megan,' I said, putting my voice on stern, 'did you hear and understand my instructions?'

'Yes, ma'am,' she said, her voice on attitude.

'Just do it, OK?'

'OK, jeez!' she said and hung up.

I smiled at my husband. 'All taken care of.'

'So when I don't get a call, should I panic or just assume she forgot?'

'The latter,' I said, and kissed him goodbye at the door; a habit we'd gotten out of over the years, but one I'd brought back after the events of last summer. It felt good, somehow.

In a flash he was gone, the girls were gone, and I was left with dirty dishes and an entire day on my own. But my mind has a mind of its own, so to speak, and I couldn't help wondering about the entire situation we found ourselves in. Was it just a coincidence that these men showed up shortly after the incident of the man at the Driscoll garage, or was there a connection? I had no idea what the connection could be, but something felt off to me; I just didn't know what. I was still in my reverie twenty minutes later when the phone rang. 'Hey,' Willis said. 'Megan actually called me.'

'Yay!' I said. 'They're OK, I assume?'

'Safe and sound,' he said. 'You want to meet me for lunch today?'

I thought about my full day of leisure versus lunch with my husband. 'Sure,' I said. 'What time?'

'OMG,' D'Wanda said.

'Did you just die?' Azalea said.

'I tried to keep the other girls calm,' Megan said. 'They were getting hysterical.'

'And you actually saw a gun?' Azalea asked, wide-eyed.

'It sure looked like one,' Megan said. 'I thought it was best to err on the side of caution, of course,' she told her friends, 'so I took the girls home and had our father contact his friend, the chief of police.'

'Boy, you sure do get in a lot of adventures!' D'Wanda said, her voice, her eyes, and her smirk all showing a bit of skepticism.

'It's just something in our genes,' Megan said. 'My mom has it and she passed it down to me. I'm her only *real* child, you know.'

'What about Graham?' Azalea asked. Having had a crush on Graham since middle school, Azalea tended to bring up his name a lot.

'Why would I count him?' Megan asked seriously.

'Your mother gave birth to him too, for gawd's sake!' D'Wanda said.

'True.' Megan shrugged. 'I've just never considered him to be a real person.'

The twins looked at each other then back at Megan. 'Why the hell not?' asked D'Wanda, the more outspoken of the two.

'Well, for one, he's not a girl, and for two, he's like, you know, my brother.' Megan shuddered and made a face.

'You know, girl, you crazy,' D'Wanda said, and turned her head around to see if there was someone in the cafeteria more sane she could sit with. Not finding anyone that fit that criteria, she said, 'Well, if this all is really happening, whatja gonna do about it?'

'What do you mean "really" happening?' Megan demanded. 'You don't believe me?'

D'Wanda shrugged. 'You have a tendency toward hyperbole, girlfriend.'

'I believe you,' Azalea said.

'Thank you,' Megan said. 'And what am I going to do about it?' she said, looking fiercely at D'Wanda, 'I'm gonna cut them suckers!' she said, and all three broke into hand-over-the-mouth snickers.

VERA'S STORY
WEDNESDAY

We had a nine a.m. choir practice with two other choirs we were going to sing with – one from Atlanta, and one from a little town outside of Baton Rouge. With our numbers at twenty-two, the Atlanta choir at thirty-four, and the Hixton choir (the one near Baton Rouge) at fourteen, we had a bunch, but the risers we were to stand on could have accommodated more like a hundred, so we were OK. We'd known for a while what songs we were going to sing, so it was just a matter of getting the three choirs to work together. But with three choirs there had to be three directors, and therein lies the rub. You know, egos.

Once we were up on the risers, I leaned forward a bit to check out the alto section, but Rachael wasn't there.

Mr Smith's phone rang. He looked at the caller ID. 'It's Mr Brown,' he said to Mr Jones.

'Yeah? Well, tell him you shot me in the foot!' Mr Jones said.

'Shut up!' Mr Smith cleared his throat, rotated his shoulders, and clicked the button to speak. 'Hey, Mr Brown,' he said, putting a smile on his face in hopes it would put a smile in his voice.

'What the fuck is going on?' Mr Brown demanded.

'Sir?'

'Where the hell are you and where is that goddam satchel?' Mr Brown demanded.

'Things have gotten a little complicated, sir,' Mr Smith said.

'You know, I hired you two because of your reputation as go-getters, guys who really got the job done. It should have taken you no more than a day to get that goddamn satchel! I don't see no job getting done around here, Mr Smith. Do you see a job getting done around here?'

'We're working on it, sir, swear to God.'

'Swear to your fucking shoes for all I care, asshole, just get me that goddam satchel, or it won't just be your reputation in shreds, it's gonna be that plus your liver, your spleen, and your intestines. Get my drift?'

'Oh, yeah,' Mr Smith said, but the phone had gone dead in his ear.

They were sitting on either side of a king-sized bed they'd shared the night before. The only room left in the motel. It had been uncomfortable for Mr Smith, but more uncomfortable for Mr Jones because of his foot, or so he claimed.

Mr Smith stood up from the bed, still clad only in his Rule Britannia boxers, and looked out the window at the sad result of their car theft of the night before. It was a twenty-year-old white panel van, perfect for a child molester, but not so great for two guys trying to remain inconspicuous. It seemed to Mr Smith that everything that could go wrong had gone wrong on this job. And it was a big job, too: fifty thousand split two ways. But, Lord, was it a fucking mess or what?

Mr Smith knew in his heart that it was all Mr Jones's fault. Everything that had gone wrong could be laid squarely at his size thirteens. Mr Smith had plans for this money, big plans. He was gonna ask Sheila to marry him. After all these years together, she might even say yes. Then a nice honeymoon in Hawaii; the perfect way to start their lives together. She'd always wanted him to go legit, so maybe he could use some of the money to buy into her brother's western-wear shop. In Houston there was always a reason to dress up like a cowboy – the rodeo, the fat stock show, Thursdays. Texans loved to dress up.

But this job – this crazy job! From the get-go it was weird. Following that guy, the one with the satchel all the way from Houston, finally tracking him to an Internet café downtown, then he runs up the ramp at that parking garage. That crazy bastard, jumping off the roof like that. He, Mr Smith, had barely touched him. Really. The man just flew off the roof like he thought he was Superman or something. Then Mr Jones coming up onto the garage roof, asking him if he threw the man over the side. What kind of question was that? Why would he throw the man off the building? Was he bat-shit crazy? No, he mighta shoved him a little, but the guy just flew off the roof – again, like he was Superman or something. Mr Smith had nothing to do with it. That's what he told Mr Jones, and that's what he told Mr Brown. That man just flew off the roof. Like Superman. And to top it off, Mr Jones didn't have the satchel. The truck's owners had come before he could get it.

Now all Mr Smith had to do was get that satchel from the brown-haired girl and they were off, back to Houston. They'd get their fifty grand, and he and Sheila could get married. That's all he had to do.

VERA'S STORY
WEDNESDAY

We finished up with the practice by eleven-thirty, and everyone headed to their rooms to get ready for the opening luncheon that started at noon. I, however, waylaid Brother Joe instead.

Grabbing him by the arm, I twirled him around and said, 'OK, where is she?'

He looked at me, blank-eyed. 'I'm sorry, Miz Vera, where's who?'

'Rachael! I know she didn't come back to my room last night and she wasn't here this morning. So what did you do with her?'

Brother Joe looked around. 'You're right, she wasn't here this morning, was she?'

I didn't say 'duh' like my grandkids woulda said, but I sure thought it. 'No, she wasn't. And I don't see her now, do you?'

'Well, no, I don't,' he said, in such a way that it was like he was talking to a person without all their faculties. Well, he had the wrong old lady this time!

And then he patted me on the shoulder. Patted me! 'Miz Vera, are you sure she didn't come back to your room last night? Maybe she just got in late?'

The man was patronizing me. I don't truck with that, I just don't. 'Gee, maybe she didn't come on this trip at all,' I said. 'Maybe I was sitting on a bench at the Smithsonian with a ghost yesterday.'

This time he rubbed my arm! 'We don't believe in ghosts, do we, Miz Vera?'

Good God, the man didn't recognize sarcasm when it slapped him in the face!

'That was sarcasm, you fool!' I said, then immediately regretted calling him a fool. The Bible says not to call people fools. 'Sorry, Brother Joe. But no, she didn't come in late last night – she didn't come in at all. Her bed was never slept in.'

'Well, go on to your room and get ready for the luncheon, Miz Vera, and I'll ask around, see what I can find out.'

I nodded, still ashamed about calling him a fool, and headed to my room.

'So did you get all the classes you wanted?' Bess asked Alicia.

'Yeah. Except behavioral psychology. They gave me adolescent psychology instead.'

'Great,' Bess said. 'Maybe you can figure out Megan.'

'Not funny,' Megan said.

'Yeah, it is,' said Alicia.

'I don't like it when you two gang up on me,' Megan said, pouting.

'We're not ganging up on you,' Bess said, as she and Megan walked to the shotgun side of the minivan. 'We're just teasing. Come on,' she said, patting her sister on the back. 'Lighten up.'

'Really, Megs,' Alicia said. 'I didn't mean anything— Hey!' Alicia screamed.

The other two girls looked up to see that a white van had pulled up to the driver's side of the minivan and someone from inside the van was yanking on Alicia's satchel. Alicia was yanking back. Megan and Bess ran around the minivan, screaming 'Nine-one-one!' at the top of their voices, and grabbed hold of Alicia's satchel with her. Kids began swarming the white van; one boy grabbed hold of Alicia by the waist and began chopping at the arm of the man trying to take the satchel. The man fell back inside, screamed, 'Get the hell out of here!' and the white van tore off.

A bunch of kids were standing around. 'You OK?' asked the young man who still had his hands around Alicia's waist.

'I'm fine, thanks,' Alicia said, blushing.

'I'm calling the police,' the boy said, pulling out his cell phone.

'Already did it, dude!' called another boy from the crowd.

Alicia's hero took his hands off her waist. 'I'm Damon Scarpacci,' he said, holding out his hand.

Alicia didn't take it right away, so Megan shouldered her aside and took the outstretched hand. 'Thanks so much for saving my sister, Damon. I'm Megan Pugh, and this is Alicia and our other sister, Bess.'

Damon took back his hand and grinned. 'Oh,' he said, nodding his head. 'The Pugh girls. I should have known. Glad I could be of assistance.'

He turned and left the scene.

'What's that supposed to mean?' Megan demanded of her sisters. 'The Pugh girls? Do we have a reputation? I finally meet somebody really cute at this school and he's put off by our *reputation*?'

'Get in the minivan,' Alicia said, noticing that half the school was still in the area and listening to Megan mouth off.

They all crawled in and Alicia started the engine. 'Was that them?' she asked.

'Sure looked like 'em,' Bess said.

'Oh, yeah. That was them, all right! But were they trying to take you or the satchel?' Megan asked Alicia.

'The satchel, I think,' Alicia said. 'I think they would have left me alone if I'd have let go. But, dammit! That satchel is mine!'

'Maybe we should wait here for the police?' Bess suggested.

'I just want to go home,' Alicia said, tears in her voice. 'I'm sick of this shit!'

The girls came home just as the chief of police's car pulled up in front of the house. I was torn between unlocking the back door for the girls or rushing to the front door for the chief. I figured the girls had at least one key amongst them, and headed to the front door instead.

'Chief?' I said as he walked up the front walk.

'Hey, Miz Pugh,' he said.

'Please, call me E.J.,' I said.

'If you call me Barry,' he said. Having reached the front porch, he held out his hand and I shook it, ushering him inside.

I heard the back door open as we stepped in.

'Followed your girls here from the school,' Barry said.

'Oh?' I led him into the formal living room and called, 'Girls!' into the family room.

They shuffled in.

I looked from my daughters to the chief. He spoke first.

'Got a nine-one-one call from the school. Seems a white van was accosting your daughters, trying to pull one of them into the van,' he said.

'Oh my God! Who? What happened?'

'It's OK, Mom,' Alicia said. She pushed me toward the sectional sofa. 'Sit down, OK? Don't have a fit.'

'I'll have a fit if I damn well feel like having a fit!' I said, resistant to sitting down.

Alicia sat down next to her sisters, so I followed. The chief sat, too.

'It was my turn to drive and we were getting into the minivan when this white panel van came up alongside me and this guy leaned out of the open side door and grabbed my satchel. I wouldn't let go. But I saw the guy pretty clearly and I'm pretty sure it was one of the guys who've been stalking us. Do you have a sketch artist, Chief? I could definitely describe the one who tried to grab my satchel.'

'No, sorry, we don't, but they have one in Codderville. Let me call Lieutenant Luna and see what we can set up,' the chief said and got up and left the room, walking into the dining room to make his phone call.

'Are you OK, honey?' I asked Alicia, stroking her arm.

'Yes, Mom, I'm fine,' she said. 'I wasn't about to let that asshole take my satchel.' Then she blushed. 'Sorry, Mom.'

'About calling the guy an asshole?' I asked. She nodded. 'Fair game,' I said. 'He's definitely an asshole, and so is his running buddy.'

The chief came back into the room. 'OK', he said. 'Luna is gonna bring the sketch artist by on her way home. Then the artist will drop the sketch off at my office when he leaves. Meanwhile, can I have a look at this satchel?'

'Just a minute,' Alicia said, and went into the family room, coming back with the black satchel. She handed it to the police chief. 'It's just got my schoolwork in it.'

'Where'd you get it?' the chief asked, opening the case to look inside.

'We found it in the back of Willis's pickup when we got back from Austin on Sunday,' I told him. 'Our oldest started U.T. this semester and we drove him over there.'

'And it was just in the back of the pickup?' the chief asked.

'Yes. When we got home Willis brought it into the house thinking it was mine. I'd never seen it before. We opened it, looking for ID, but didn't find any. I was going to take the whole thing to Goodwill but Willis wanted the Dopp kit and Alicia wanted the satchel.'

'What was in it besides the Dopp kit?' the chief asked.

'Men's clothes. Couple of T-shirts, a pair of jeans and some underwear,' I told him.

'What did you do with that?' he asked.

'I took all that to Goodwill.'

'Young lady, could you take out your schoolbooks, please?' he asked Alicia.

She took out two books and a notebook, and handed the chief the satchel. He put his hand inside.

'What are you doing?' I asked him.

'Well, some of these old things used to have trap bottoms. Just wanna see if this one does.' His hand came out. 'Not so you'd notice,' he said. The chief stood up.

So,' he said, heading for the front door, then turned back to face them. 'Unless you got a tag number off that van?' All three girls shook their heads. 'Then I'm off. Y'all want me to post someone out here tonight? Gonna have to be a volunteer since we don't have that many people. And he – or she – (he said, nodding in my direction) – would be unarmed . . .'

I followed him to the door. 'Then what would be the point?' I said, and shrugged. 'We'll be OK.'

He left and I looked at the girls. 'Make a sweep of the house. Lock every window and door. Put the chains on.'

This was touching my family now, and I was beginning to think, even with the satchel being empty, that all this had to be connected. Somebody was after my family, and Willis couldn't fault me for fighting back – or could he?

I leaned my back against the front door, wondering how Willis and I were going to protect our precious cargo.

FIVE

I changed into my Sunday-go-to-meeting outfit and headed downstairs, finding some of our choir members milling about the lobby. I started asking about Rachael, and it seemed that the last person to see her the night before was John Blevins, a tenor, old enough to have gone to high school with me, if he was bright enough to have made it that far. Sorry, I have a tendency to get catty when I'm upset, and this whole thing with Rachael was surely upsetting me. I was beginning to think that maybe she hadn't been with Brother Joe the night before. I wouldn't call her a friend, but our shared experience at the First Ladies exhibit had gotten me to like her some.

'Yeah,' John said, 'I saw her. I was standing here waiting for the elevator, and saw Rachael head up the stairs,' he said, pointing to the grand staircase that went from the lobby to the mezzanine.

'Anybody with her?' I asked him.

'No, she was all by her lonesome,' John said, shaking his head.

'What's she done now?' Ethel asked, coming up close and half whispering in my ear.

'She didn't do nothing,' I said. 'I just can't find her. She didn't come back to the room last night and nobody's seen hide nor hair of her since, well, since John saw her, as far as I can tell.'

'Did you ask you-know-who?' Ethel half-whispered to me.

I gave her the stink-eye. 'Don't,' I said.

'Who's you-know-who?' John Blevins asked.

Nancy Perrin, another soprano, chirped in, 'Yeah! What do y'all know that we don't?'

'Is something going on?' Elmer Estes, a baritone, asked, wiggling his eyebrows.

Well, this is just getting way out of control, I thought to myself. 'Y'all behave!' I said. 'This is serious. We gotta find her.'

Just then three more members of the choir joined us. 'Any of y'all seen Rachael Donley?' Elmer Estes asked.

All three shook their heads. 'Is she missing?' asked Ruthie Lane, a contralto with a beautiful voice. She does a lot of solos.

I reiterated my tale of woe. Ruthie Lane, who hadn't heard the stuff earlier, was concerned. 'You think she's all right?' she asked me, touching my hand. I sure didn't mind *her* touch, as opposed to the preacher's earlier. She's a nice lady I've known since our children were in the church nursery together. And, besides, I could listen to her lift her voice to Jesus any day of the week and twice on Sunday.

'I just don't know,' I said to Ruthie. 'But I'm getting worried.'

'Oh, she's gonna show up,' Elmer said. 'I'm betting she went to visit some kin or somebody who lives around here and just forgot to tell anyone.'

Everyone nodded, and let it go. That was the best excuse I'd heard. I could live with that.

The girls checked the windows on the first floor, then headed upstairs. Alicia volunteered to check the windows in Graham's room. Strangely enough, although she'd lived in this house for almost two years, she'd never been in Graham's room. He'd never invited her in and she'd never attempted to go near it. She figured if she totally ignored him, Graham might never know how much she loved him. Sometimes it hurt, especially now with him gone away to college, but it was really better that he was out of sight. He certainly wasn't out of mind, but it was easier. A little easier.

No one knew, not even the girls. For all the love and affection, all the 'mom' and 'dad' stuff, she was still a guest in this home. She'd been in a lot of foster homes over the years, and had to admit this was the best one, but being a foster kid, she knew not to depend on the apparent loving feelings coming from a foster family. There was an unspoken issue of trust between the two parties – foster child and foster family. And she would not betray that trust by going after their son. Not that she knew how to 'go after' a guy. She'd never done it, and wasn't quite sure how it was done. She'd seen Megan try, like today with that guy who tried to rescue her, but, as usual, it was a fiasco. Bess never had to 'go after' a guy. They came after her. Little and pretty and sweet, guys were drawn to her. Big, gorgeous and loud-mouthed, it would take a certain kind of guy to go for Megan. Medium and

mousy? Alicia figured that, standing between those two, she never
had a chance with anybody.

But Graham? When she'd first met him, he had a girlfriend, Lotta,
a beautiful Latina with clear olive skin, big brown eyes, and boobs.
Guys always went for boobs. At sixteen hers still hadn't come in,
as if they were ever going to. She hid her bras from her 'sisters'
so they wouldn't know she still wore a 30A. Megan probably hadn't
worn a 30A since kindergarten!

She went in Graham's room and was surprised how much stuff
was still there. She'd seen the boxes of things he'd taken with him,
but he'd certainly left high school behind – except, of course, for
Leon. He had a bunk-bed arrangement with a top bunk along the
wall, and the bottom bunk sticking out into the room. Under
the half of the top bunk not being used by the bottom bunk was a
desk. It was cleared, but the walls could talk. Posters of punk bands
from Austin, a few national bands, some of Dallas Cowboy players,
and high-school calendars, one for each of the four years. She
touched them, wanting to peruse them at her leisure, but knowing
she couldn't stay in his room for long. The drapes matched his
bedspreads, dark red and green plaid, more a mom's choice rather
than a teenaged boy's choice. She went to the window and made
sure it was locked, then stood for a moment just soaking it in. Then,
sure that the door was shut, she went to the lower bunk, leaned
down, uncovered the pillow and stuck her face in it. It didn't smell
like Graham at all. He must have taken his pillow with him, she
thought. This is just an extra. She put the spread back up over the
pillow and left the room.

Once in her own, she sat down on her bed to put her books back
in the satchel. First, though, she reached inside to make sure the
chief hadn't been mistaken about there not being a secret bottom.
She felt around, trying to find a spring, a catch – anything that
would release a hidden compartment. Instead she found something
in the lining. It wasn't low enough to be part of a release for a
secret compartment at the bottom of the bag, but maybe something
up higher? She got her fingers around it, trying to feel with her
fingers what it was. Not being able to, she got her manicure scissors
and snipped a small hole in the lining. Sticking her finger in,
the hole stretched and she was able to take hold of the object inside.
She pulled it out. It was a flash drive, maybe. What the hell? she
thought.

Then a voice called from downstairs, 'Alicia! The sketch artist is here!'

She put the object on her desk next to her computer and hurried downstairs.

'You shoulda just grabbed her! You dumbass!' Mr Smith said.

'You wanted me to *kidnap* that girl? Are you crazy?' Mr Jones said.

'Do you have the satchel? Huh? Do you?' Mr Smith screamed as he drove the panel van through the streets of Black Cat Ridge, trying to find the main street to the freeway.

'Just shut up!' Mr Jones said.

'Shut up? You want me to shut up?' Mr Smith said. He reached for his gun in its holster inside his coat.

Seeing that Mr Smith was about to flip again, Mr Jones grabbed his arm, and the two began to wrestle. The panel van had reached the highway and Mr Smith should have taken the ramp to enter as the feeder ended shortly beyond the ramp. Instead the panel van swerved as the two fought and ran off the feeder into a grove of mesquite trees. For those not familiar with mesquite trees, they tend to have long thorns and sharp, skinny branches, and are good for only two things: rifle stocks and making smoke for some serious barbeque. The panel van took out a few of the lesser trees but slowed enough to come to rest against a slightly larger mesquite.

Mr Smith was the first to speak. 'What did you think you were doing?' he asked quietly.

'Keeping you from shooting me again!' Mr Jones said.

'You're right. I was going to shoot you. But not in the foot this time. I would have aimed for the head.'

'OK, then,' Mr Jones said. A few seconds later he added: 'Are you better now?'

'Yes, yes I am. Thank you,' Mr Smith said.

'No problem,' Mr Jones said.

'Of course, now we have a new problem. We're stuck out here in the woods,' Mr Smith said.

'You wanna try backing up?' Mr Jones suggested.

'That's a good idea, Mr Jones,' Mr Smith said, surprised to hear the words escaping his mouth. 'I'll try that.'

The engine had died upon impact with the small tree, so Mr

Smith turned the key. Nothing happened. He turned it again. Still nothing happened.

'Well,' he said, 'looks like this one's dead.'

'Guess we gotta steal another one,' Mr Jones said.

Looking straight ahead into the crowded forest of mesquite trees, Mr Smith said, 'You know I'm really going to kill you this time, don't you?'

Mr Jones smiled and said, 'I know you're going to *try.*'

VERA'S STORY
WEDNESDAY

That first day of the meeting was crazy busy. I heard a couple of sermons that were pretty good, went to a panel discussion on creationism vs. the big bang theory (no contest there), and had another choir practice that afternoon about four. Still no word on Rachael Donley. By the time I got to choir practice, the word had traveled around all our people and some of those from the other choirs (especially the altos – they tend to stick together, you know). There was a lot of chatter, but as far as I could tell, John Blevins was still the last one to see her. And no one, far as I could make out, had been up on the mezzanine level – where Rachael was last seen heading – at all.

I talked to Brother Joe, and told him what I'd found out.

'She must have run into someone she knew,' he said, 'and left for some reason. I'm sure she meant to come back, but something came up. Hopefully she'll call soon and let us know.'

I agreed with him and, after practice, headed to my room to get ready for dinner. It was then I noticed that Rachael's suitcase was gone. As were her toiletries from the bathroom and her hang-up clothes from the closet. On my bed was a note:

> *Dear Vera,*
> *So sorry I just ran off, but I saw a friend who I haven't seen in a long time and she's going through a divorce and is having a rough time. I couldn't leave her alone. I hope you understand. Please tell Brother Joe and the rest of the choir how sorry I am to have just walked out like that, but it was an emergency. Have a wonderful meeting!*
> *Best,*
> *Rachael*

Well, that's rude, I thought. She could have at least called. And since she came back to the hotel, why didn't she come talk to someone? If not me, then Brother Joe? Whatever, I thought, remembering that I hadn't liked her that much anyway before this trip. I just hoped she didn't try to get her money back on the room.

The sketch artist was gorgeous. I wasn't the only one to notice it. Megan forgot about her new short bob and kept trying to flip her hair. Bess had the hair and was flipping it like mad. Only Alicia seemed impervious to Calvin Hedley's charms.

Yes, Calvin Hedley. Horrible name for such a stud. Well over six feet, more like six and half, broad shoulders, round bottom, black hair, olive complexion and blue eyes to die for. And a smile that . . . Well, it was a heavenly smile.

Calvin and Alicia sat in the formal dining room, working away at the sketch, while we three 'girls,' and I use that term loosely, sat in the formal living room and watched. They'd been at it for an hour when I heard Willis's truck pull into the driveway. I sighed and left the living room. I wasn't up to giving my husband ammunition with which to tease me for the next ten years. 'Drooling over a kid half your age,' etc., etc., ad nauseum.

While he nestled his truck all snug in the garage, I got out a pan and some food and pretended I'd been cooking. 'What are we having for dinner?' he asked, kissing me and looking down at the assortment of crap I'd removed from the refrigerator. I looked too. Not good. The meat I'd had on the top shelf defrosting was fine. Even the bag of unsnapped green beans was OK. But how I would manage to make something tasty out of those two ingredients mixed with marshmallow fluff, lemon curd and hummus I didn't know.

Willis raised an eyebrow at me. 'The sketch artist is here,' I said, having already filled him in by phone on the latest catastrophe. I got the desired effect. His mind was off the mess on the counter and onto the activity going on elsewhere.

'Where are they?' he asked.

'Dining room,' I said and followed him out – after putting away everything except the chicken and the green beans.

Megan and Bess were still on the sectional sofa, gazing dreamy-eyed at Calvin, who had yet to notice them. Alicia was busy saying take this out, add this, etc.

'Hi,' Willis said, extending his hand. 'I'm Alicia's dad.'

Calvin stood up and shook hands. 'Nice to meet you, Mr Brooks,' he said.

'Ah, the name's Pugh. Willis Pugh. I'm Alicia's foster father.'

'Oh, sorry,' Calvin said and showed a terrific smile with dimples and oh-so-white teeth. I heard sighs from the living room. 'We're almost finished here, I think,' Calvin said, turning to look at Alicia. 'What do you think, Alicia?' he asked.

She looked at the sketch. 'That's as close as I can get,' she said. She nodded. 'Yes. I think that's him. Megs, Bess, come look.'

They didn't really need an invitation. They were off the sofa and in the dining room in a flash, elbowing each other to get closest to Calvin.

'At the picture, y'all,' Alicia said and grinned.

Bess blushed but Megan just tossed her invisible hair again. Bess looked at the photo. 'Yeah, that's the tall one, right?'

Megan looked. 'Yeah! He's always riding shotgun.'

'Did you get a decent look at the short one?' Willis asked.

'Yes, sir,' Alicia said. 'I think between us we can do him. If Calvin has time?'

Calvin smiled and I sighed. When Willis turned my way I coughed to cover up. 'All the time in the world. My wife has taken the kids to her mom's in Dallas for a week, so I'm free.'

The temperature in the room fell by several degrees. Shoulders slumped. Hair did not get tossed.

With very little enthusiasm, the three girls got to work on a sketch of the shorter stalker.

They could have walked back to BCR; they were very close to it. But since the BCR police were hot on their tails, they decided to walk to Codderville instead. Mr Smith's shirt was torn in several places and his skin ripped on his right arm near the elbow and on his left arm near the wrist. The knee had torn through his jeans on impact; all the other injuries, to both body and attire, had come from the mesquite. Mr Jones had a scratch on his hand. And, of course, the divot in his foot, but that wasn't from this accident – or the mesquite trees.

'I hate walking,' Mr Smith said.

'Who hates walking?' Mr Jones asked.

'Me! I hate walking! That's what I just said!'

'I meant, what a dumbass to hate walking!' Mr Jones clarified.

'Shut up!' Mr Smith said.

'*You* shut up!' Mr Jones said.

'God, I'm gonna kill you first chance I get!' Mr Smith said.

'Not if I kill you first!' Mr Jones said.

A blue-and-rust pickup truck pulled in front of them as they walked down the shoulder of the highway.

'Hey, you boys need a lift?' the old man inside the truck asked.

Mr Smith and Mr Jones both smiled at the old man. 'Thanks! Our car broke down,' Mr Smith said. He and Mr Jones jumped into the bed of the pickup.

'I'm only going as far as Codderville,' the old man said.

'That's fine,' Mr Smith said. 'Thanks!'

As Calvin Hedley left, Willis turned to us and said, 'How 'bout I take my favorite girls out for dinner?'

'You don't have to ask me twice,' I said, going to the kitchen and putting away the chicken and the green beans.

'Mexican!' Megan shouted.

'Pizza!' Bess shouted.

'Why don't we go to the cafeteria so we can all get what we want?' I suggested.

The gagging sounds coming from all three girls were a bit nauseating.

'How about Mike & Mary's?' Willis suggested. 'Y'all can get burgers or tacos or pizza, and Mom can get a salad.'

'And you're going for red meat, right?' I asked as we headed out the back door for the minivan.

'Sixteen-ounce T-bone, slap it on the ass and call it done,' he said, going to the driver's side.

'Uh uh!' Bess said, shooing him away from the door. 'This is our car! You don't get to drive! You and Mom have to sit in the back seat, too!'

Alicia called shotgun before Megan did, so Willis and I had the joy of listening to her bitch the entire way to Mike & Mary's, a local café owned by the parents of one of Graham's friends.

I myself am not adverse to a little red meat every once in a while, so I ordered the filet mignon, with the house salad and the vegetable medley. Willis, of course, got his T-bone, plus the house salad and a baked potato all the way. And I saw the twinkle in his eye when he spotted the dessert tray. Yes, I know. He's going to make me a young, and beautiful, I might add, widow.

By the time we got home, it was time for baths and bed. Luckily the girls had not been assigned any homework that night, so we were all out by eleven.

WEDNESDAY
VERA'S STORY

As I was getting ready for bed, I realized my hands were very dry and, rather than go all the way back to the bathroom to get my hand cream, I decided to open the bedside table drawer to see if Rachael had left any behind.

She hadn't. But what she had left was all her contact lens stuff, and her glasses. That didn't seem right, not after what she'd told me. Of course, lots of people say they're as blind as a bat when all they really mean is they just don't see as well as they used to. I picked up Rachael's glasses. The lenses were as thick as the bottom of a Coke bottle. OK, I believed her. She *was* blind as a bat.

Then why would she pack up all her stuff but leave this very important part of her daily wear behind? Answer? Well, I *am* E.J. Pugh's mother-in-law, you know. The answer was simple. She didn't. Someone else packed her stuff up for her. And the note? I was going to find an answer to that question first thing in the morning.

THURSDAY

'So, Bert, is it?' Mr Smith said to the old man. The old man nodded. 'This should teach you not to pick up people off the side of the road. We weren't even hitching, Bert!' Mr Smith shook his head as Mr Jones wound the duct tape around Bert's legs and the ladder-back chair he was attaching him to. 'We're not going to hurt you, OK? You're gonna be fine. We just need to borrow your truck tonight, OK? We'll bring it back safe and sound in a couple of hours and, if all goes well, we'll be out of your hair in no time flat. Sound good, Bert?'

Bert nodded his head as speaking was pretty much discouraged by the duct tape covering his mouth.

'You've got a nice little place here, Bert,' Mr Jones said. 'How many acres?'

Bert shrugged. Mr Jones laughed at his own stupidity. 'Oh, man, I'm sorry!' He uncovered half of Bert's mouth.

'Three hundred,' Bert said.

'Wow, that's great! What do you grow?'

'Feed corn mostly, some cotton, and some soy beans – that's a new crop. Trying it out.'

'Well, good luck to you,' Mr Jones said and refastened the tape over Bert's mouth.

'OK, you got all the information you need about acreage, there, Mr Jones?' Mr Smith asked, his tone sarcastic.

'Don't start!' Mr Jones said, heading for the front door.

'Who's the one dragging this out asking stupid questions?' Mr Smith said.

They went down the steps and climbed into the pickup truck, Mr Smith driving.

'So what's your dumb plan this time?' Mr Jones asked Mr Smith.

'We're going after that satchel. Into the house this time. Even if we gotta kill every last one of them, we're taking it!'

There was a mist in the air, caressing the grass, making the pavement shine. The blue-and-rust pickup truck chugged through the night, through empty streets, under the umbrella of illumination from the street lights. As the old pickup hit the highway and sped up, darkness swallowed all but their headlights as they crossed the blackened river that separated Codderville from Black Cat Ridge.

The windows on the old pickup were down, and the men inside could hear the chirping of insects and the crunch of their tiny bodies as the pickup's tires smashed them into the pavement. BCR was as quiet as Codderville. Security lights were all that could be seen – in stores, in homes. Streetlights shown down on the wet pavement, a siren's song to the crickets that would meet their death under the pickup's tires.

Mr Smith doused the headlights as he turned onto Sagebrush Trail. Second house in, that's where the prize was. Fifty thousand dollars' worth of a prize. He would get the whole amount if he killed Mr Jones *after* they got their money from Mr Brown. Something to think about, he told himself. If Mr Jones would stop getting on his nerves for a while, he might be able to keep him alive a little bit longer.

He drove down the street, made a U-turn, and came back, parking two doors down from the house they wanted, on the side away from that crazy broad that claimed to be a cop. That was freaky, Mr Smith thought.

He sat in the pickup truck, lights off, staring up at the second story of the house in question.

'What are we doing?' Mr Jones asked. He was sick of watching the Pughs' house.

See? Mr Smith thought. That's why he wanted to kill him *now*. Anybody would under the circumstances!

'We're scoping out the place,' Mr Smith said as calmly as possible.

'For what?' Mr Jones asked.

'I wonder which room is the brown-haired girl's room?' Mr Smith asked, ignoring him.

Mr Jones shrugged. 'Does it really matter?'

'Yes, Mr Jones, it does matter,' Mr Smith said, gritting his teeth and turning in his seat to stare at his partner. 'If we're going to break in and steal the satchel, we can only assume it's with the brown-haired girl, and that the brown-haired girl *and* the satchel will both be in her room!' He added, 'Dumbass,' under his breath.

'Don't call me a dumbass!' Mr Jones hissed. Mr Smith was getting on his last nerve, and that was the goddam truth, he thought to himself.

'I'll call you worse than that, you dumb moth—' Mr Smith started, but Mr Jones's fist came out of nowhere and landed on that little space between Mr Smith's upper lip and his nose, managing not only to bust his upper lip, but start a nosebleed to boot.

Mr Smith jerked backwards for a beat, then came bursting forward, his hands going for Mr Jones's neck. There commenced a quiet struggle with both men whispering epitaphs at each other, and flinging each other's arms about. The only sound was the squeaking of the shocks on Bert's pickup truck.

'Stop!' Mr Smith hissed, quite out of breath.

Mr Jones reluctantly sat back in his seat, as did Mr Smith.

'OK, we'll finish that later. Right now we need to go in there and find that satchel,' Mr Smith said, breathing hard.

'How are we gonna do that?' Mr Jones asked.

'Break a window, crawl in, go upstairs and find the right girl. The satchel will be with her.'

'OK,' Mr Jones said, reached under his seat and brought up a tire iron. 'Think this'll do for smashing the window?'

Mr Smith shrugged. 'Should do the trick,' he said getting out of the truck. 'Let's do it.'

Alicia awoke, not sure what had awakened her. She sat up in bed. Mr Jones saw her sit up at the same time she saw him standing by her desk. She opened her mouth to scream but Mr Jones was on her in a flash, a large hand over her mouth.

'Jesus!' Mr Smith whispered. 'What the hell?'

'Get the satchel!' Mr Jones whispered back.

'Now we've got to kill her!' Mr Smith said.

'No!' Mr Jones said. 'We can leave her—'

'To scream her head off before we even get out of the house?'

'So we take her with us?' Mr Jones suggested.

When Alicia heard Mr Jones's suggestion, she managed to arrange her mouth under the pressure of his hand so she could bite his palm. Mr Jones instinctively pulled his hand away, and Alicia sucked in air to scream, but Mr Smith's hand was over her mouth before the air or the scream came out.

'Take the bag!' Mr Smith hissed at Mr Jones. 'I'll take the girl.' Mr Smith, shorter, and though stocky, still lighter than Mr Jones, attempted to lift the sixteen-year-old, who was mostly all legs, off her bed. Her arms were hitting him, her legs kicking him. It was therefore hard to keep a hand over her mouth.

'OK,' Mr Smith said, rethinking, 'I'll take the bag, you take the girl.'

The two men switched places and Mr Jones easily lifted Alicia while still able to keep a meaty palm over her mouth. They went quietly down the stairs and out the front door.

VERA'S STORY
THURSDAY

I woke up at eight a.m., which is my habit, did my morning ablutions, got dressed for breakfast, then sat down between the two queen beds, picked up the phone and called my son's house. Early as it was, all I got was their silly machine and its silly message. I left a cryptic one of my own – serves E.J. right for all the cryptic ones she's left me – and headed out the door for breakfast.

There was only one of our group in the dining room, Mr Norris – Gerald Norris – a lovely tenor who'd moved to Codderville three or four years ago. He was a widower and had joined our church right off the bat. He'd always seemed like a good man.

As he was sitting at a table for four, and all by himself, I asked if I might join him. I don't think that was inappropriate, but no matter, tongues will wag.

He half stood but I waved him back down. Such chivalry no longer seems the norm, which is unfortunate. He said, 'I'd be delighted.'

After I'd perused the menu and gave the girl my order, Mr Norris said, 'You were rooming with Mrs Donley, right?'

'Yes, I was.'

'Any word from her?' he asked.

'Well,' I started, but hesitated. Is this the person to confide in? I'd like to talk this over with E.J., but I was still waiting for her to call me back. 'When I got back to my room earlier yesterday, her bags were gone and she'd left a note saying she'd gone to be with a friend who was distraught about her pending divorce.'

Mr Norris smiled. 'Well, then,' he said. 'All's well that ends well.'

'That's not quite the end of it, however,' I said, then quieted as the server brought my breakfast – oatmeal with strawberries, wheat toast, a glass of orange juice, and a cup of coffee.

When my meal had been placed before me, Mr Norris leaned forward. 'What?' he said, eagerly.

So I explained about what she said about her contacts, and how I'd found the whole lot still in the bedside table.

'Somebody else packed her up,' he said, 'but didn't know about her contacts and glasses. Somebody who obviously didn't know her all that well. Did you compare the handwriting on that note to something else of hers?'

I shrugged. 'I don't have anything to compare it to.'

'Well, surely we can find something,' Mr Norris said.

I smiled at him. He smiled back. The teeth may have been false, but the dimples were real.

Bess made it downstairs first, clad in an Indian-print mini-dress with black leggings and ankle boots. She looked adorable but I knew better than to say so. 'Where's Alicia?' she asked.

'Probably in the bathroom,' I said, setting out juices and cereal.

'No, I just came out of the bathroom. She's not in her bed, either, and it's not made. Which is a first,' Bess said.

Megan wandered down the stairs. She'd managed to pull on jeans, a bra and a top, but her shoes were in her hands, as well as her make-up bag. And by the bags under her eyes, she looked like she needed it.

'What's wrong with you?' I asked her.

'God! I hardly slept a wink last night,' she complained, throwing her body onto one of the bar stools. 'Something woke me up.'

'Did you see Alicia upstairs?' Bess asked her.

'I wasn't looking for her,' Megan said.

'But did you see her?' Bess insisted.

'No! Jeez. I just said I didn't sleep a wink last night! Get off my back!'

I left the kitchen and went to the bottom of the staircase, calling up, 'Alicia! Time to get up! Breakfast is ready!'

There was no reply.

'You don't want to be late on your second day of school!' I called up the stairs.

Still no answer.

'Oh, for God's sake. You're supposed to be the good one,' I said under my breath and headed up the stairs. I went to her room first and, like Bess had said, the bed was unmade. She wasn't in it, or anywhere else in her room. Not only was her bed unmade, but her desk chair was tipped over and papers from her desk were on the floor. Very un-Alicia-like. I moved down the hall to the bathroom. The door stood open. It was a mess – towels on the floor, hair-care products littering the sink counter. But no Alicia. I looked behind the shower curtain, just in case she was playing a joke. Alicia didn't joke much, but hey, it could happen. She wasn't there.

I looked inside both the open doors of the girls' rooms. No Alicia. I opened Graham's door and looked in. She wasn't in there either. With a sinking heart, I went back to Alicia's room, in search of the satchel. It wasn't in there.

I rushed down the stairs. She wasn't in the formal living or dining rooms. She wasn't in the master bedroom or bathroom, and I already knew she wasn't in the kitchen and family room, where I'd already been.

'Mom?' Bess said, seeing me rushing around.

'Is the minivan out there?' I asked.

Bess jumped down from her stool and looked out the window of the back door. 'Yes. Mom?'

Willis came out of the bedroom. Megan was down from her stool too. And the three of us, Bess, Megan and myself, were staring at each other.

'What's wrong?' Willis asked.

I turned to him quickly. 'Alicia's gone.'

'What do you mean, gone?'

'As in she's not here, Dad! Jeez! But her bed was slept in.' Bess turned to me, panic on her face. 'Mom?'

'Did you check—' Willis started.

'Everywhere!' I said. I didn't add 'duh' but I wanted to.

'The utility room? Your office?' he offered.

OK. He got me. The two places I hadn't checked. I moved fast, Willis and the girls right behind me. My office was under the stairs, down the hall from the formal dining room. She wasn't in there. Across from my office was a combo utility room and half bathroom that shared the plumbing of the master bath we'd added when we'd had the extension made a couple of years ago. It ran the length of the dining room and had a window. Alicia wasn't in there, but the window was broken.

The girls both screamed and burst into tears. Willis and I ran for our phones.

Luna called the school, giving vague excuses for all three girls' absences. She was in our house with Chief Donaldson, arguing about whether or not to call in the FBI. I'd tried to get the girls to go back to their rooms and lie down, but neither of them were having it.

'We're here for the duration, Mom,' Megan said. 'We'll do whatever is necessary to get her back.' She had her arm around Bess's shoulders. Bess, usually the stronger one, was still gulping back sobs, tears running down her cheeks.

'I think right now it would be good if you'd take Bess upstairs—' I started.

'No!' Bess all but shouted. 'I'm staying down here!' She wiped at her tear-streaked face. 'I'm OK.'

I pulled the girls to me and we hugged for a moment.

Together we went into the living room where Luna sat on the sectional with Chief Donaldson and Willis.

Stealing myself, I told those present, 'I checked Alicia's room again when I was pretty sure she really was gone – and so is the satchel.'

Chief Donaldson nodded. 'I'm not surprised,' he said. 'But thanks for checking, E.J. Meanwhile, it's protocol to call in the FBI when there's a kidnapping, which this obviously is,' the chief said.

Bess left the embrace of her sister and me and moved further into the room. 'The FBI only comes in if it's across state lines or there's a ransom, right?' she asked. She didn't wait for a response. 'There won't be a ransom and I'm sure they're around here some-where. All they wanted was the satchel, and they have that. And Alicia . . .'

She turned her back on them and came back into our huddle, tears leaking again.

'She's right, Barry,' Luna said. 'We're on our own on this one.'

'What's this "we" shit?' he said, then turned to me and my girls. 'Excuse my French, ladies.'

'Chief Polk is lending me to you,' Luna said, stating the name of the chief of police of Codderville, her boss. 'Until this thing is over.'

Barry nodded. 'Well, that's good,' he said. 'I'll have to thank him.'

'Thank me. I'm the one who talked him into it,' Luna said.

'Well, OK, then. Elena, thank you.'

'You're welcome, Barry.'

'Jesus Christ!' I said, stepping out of our huddle. 'Skip all this "Cumbiya" shit and let's find Alicia!'

Willis stood up and took my arm. 'Calm down, baby—' he started.

I pulled away from him. 'You calm down!' I said. Turning to the two professionals sitting there, I said, 'Do you have any leads on these assholes? You said they rented the car under the name Brown, right?'

Luna answered. 'That's what we found out,' she agreed.

'So what are you doing to track him down? This Mr Brown? Surely we can do something—'

'Mrs Pugh,' Chief Donaldson said, standing up. 'Lieutenant Luna and I will do everything in our power to bring your foster daughter home. Until then, you and your family need to stay put and let us do our work.'

He and Luna left by the front door, and all I could think as they departed was, Fat chance, Chief.

The rest of the night had gone decidedly downhill, as far as Alicia was concerned. The two men, who called themselves Smith and Jones, which she told them was extremely derivative, if not a

little clichéd, found duct tape in the truck, which she could only
conclude was not theirs since they had no idea where anything was
and since it was neither the blue car nor the white car they'd been
in earlier, and taped her mouth shut. The old truck did not have a
back seat, so the three of them rode on the front bench seat,
Alicia in the middle. At one point she managed to get a foot over
the hump in the middle to the driver's side, with hopes of slamming
on the brakes and killing the pair of bookends, but unfortunately
she hit the accelerator instead, only managing to throw them all
back against the seat.

'Grab her foot, for Christ's sake!' Mr Smith had yelled at Mr
Jones. Mr Jones grabbed both her legs and put one of his larger
legs over them, thus trapping her. She vowed never to wear shorty
pajamas again. She felt violated by the man's touch on her thigh.
When this was over, she had every intention of taking a bath in
hand sanitizer.

Meek Alicia was gone. She was channeling Megan and doing a
good job of it. At least she was pissing them off. But she had every
intention of busting out and heading home, with or without their
heads in her satchel that was sitting on the floor board beneath her
trapped legs.

They hadn't blindfolded her, which she thought of as possibly
a bad sign. If she knew where they were going, would they want
to silence her? Within fifteen to twenty minutes, Mr Smith turned
into a driveway, the headlights picking out barbed-wire fencing,
a few trees, and some cattle whose sleep was disturbed by the
bright light. She felt the old truck roll over a cattle guard, and
within minutes Mr Smith had stopped and turned off the engine.
They were parked in front of an old, two-story-frame house that
leaned just a little to the right. Cement steps that didn't connect
to the front porch nevertheless led to it, and Mr Jones had her
by the arm, leading her up the steps, across the porch, and into
the barren front hall. Off to the right was a room with a light on
and they took her in there. An old man sat in a ladder-backed
chair, tied to it with duct tape. She nodded her head at him and
he nodded back.

'My, aren't we polite!' Mr Smith said sarcastically.

'They're just being friendly. I think, under the circumstances,
they should both be commended for it!' Mr Jones said.

'I've decided I'm going to kill you with a knife, rather than a gun,' Mr Smith said to Mr Jones. 'It's slower. I'll have more fun.'

Mr Jones rolled his eyes. 'Don't listen to him,' he said to Alicia and Bert. 'I think he has a problem with low blood sugar.'

He sat Alicia down on the sofa, an old beat-up affair, held together with duct tape, possibly from the same role as the tape decorating Alicia and Bert.

'If you promise not to be mean, I'll take the tape off,' Mr Jones said. Alicia nodded her head and Mr Jones removed the restraint.

'What about that man? You know he could choke, or even get his nose stopped up and die because he can't breathe out of his mouth,' Alicia said, as sweetly as possible.

Mr Smith, having heard Alicia's comment, turned quickly to Bert. 'Take it off him,' he said to Mr Jones.

'You take it off!' Mr Jones said, even though he was up and moving toward Bert. He removed the tape and Bert stretched his mouth in different ways, then tried his voice.

'Excuse me, but I really gotta pee,' he said.

Mr Jones looked at Mr Smith, who was on the phone, talking to Mr Brown, he assumed.

'OK,' Mr Jones said to Bert. Taking out his pocket knife, he knelt beside Bert and began to cut the tape. When he was finished, he helped the old man to stand up.

Mr Smith waved at him frantically. Then mouthed: 'The girl! Tape!'

Mr Jones sighed and sat Alicia in the ladder-back chair and, only using enough tape to go around her body twice, adhered her to said chair.

'This is ridiculous!' Alicia said loudly.

Mr Smith looked at her and put his finger to his lips, asking for silence. She did not comply. She felt Megan was alive and well in her brain.

'You can't tie me up like this! I'm an American citizen! Help!' she screamed.

Mr Smith left the room with his cell phone and Alicia started to scream.

'Shame on you!' Mr Jones said, and taped her mouth shut again. 'This poor old man is gonna pee himself because you're acting like a baby!'

With that, he asked Bert to lead him to the bathroom.

Alicia sat in silence. She looked around the room, scoping it out. She hadn't lived with E.J. Pugh for a year and a half for nothing! She was going to get out of here if she had to bite an arm off to do it. Hopefully, someone else's arm.

THURSDAY
VERA'S STORY

Gerald was a smart man. It didn't take that long for us to go from Mr Norris and Mrs Pugh to a first-name basis. We were both of an age, and had known each other for several years, so it seemed fairly natural when we slipped into using first names. I really don't think I need to explain myself here. His first suggestion was to go to my room and find the note Rachael left me, which we did. I, of course, left the door open while he was in my room.

'She would have had to sign things to go on this trip, right?' I suggested.

'A couple of problems with that,' Gerald said. 'One, anything to do with the hotel she probably did over the Internet.' True enough, I thought. I'd made all my arrangements with the hotel over the Internet – or rather my granddaughters had. 'And two,' he said, 'anything she would have signed for the choir would probably be with Sharon and not Brother Joe.'

Damn! I thought, but didn't say out loud. A lady never cusses in mixed company. 'Then we're out of luck,' I said. 'I can't think of anything else she could have signed or written.'

'Did she sign for anything here? Like dinner? Had it billed to her room or anything?' he countered.

I thought. Hard. That first night we were too late for dinner when we got here. But breakfast the next morning? Damn, I signed for that! Then there was the luncheon, but that was part of the package . . . 'I don't think so, Gerald,' I said, shaking my head. 'I can't think of a time when she would have.' Then I remembered! 'She said she was going to get her nails done right before the luncheon! She forgot to get 'em done at home and saw they had a beauty shop here that did nails!'

'And the beauty shop will have that ticket with her signature,' Gerald said. He stuck out his hand like one of my grandkids going for a high five, so I got on tiptoe to hit it, then we were out the door.

And no, I didn't feel strange having a man in my hotel room. I've known him for several years, he's a nice man, and it was strictly business, so get your mind out of the gutter. Besides, as I said before, I'd left the door open.

I had just gotten off the phone with Lacy Kent, the woman from the junior orientation who was supposed to be coming over for coffee this morning. I had no desire to explain the entire convoluted mess to her – I lied and said one of my girls was sick. We postponed for the following week. I just hoped my life would not have been destroyed by then. The girls and I were sitting on the sofa in the family room when we heard the front door open and close. Willis came in the room.

'What are they going to do?' I asked, knowing my voice was weak and tired. Why was this crap affecting my kids? Again? What did I do wrong that this crap followed me around like a lost puppy, then morphed into a badly trained pit bull when I least expected it?

Willis sat down on the other side of the girls and put his arm around them. Our hands met behind Bess's back and our fingers entwined. 'They're putting out an APB – all points bulletin – on the white car.' He shrugged. 'Meanwhile, I guess we wait for a call.'

We heard a car in the driveway, the slamming of a door, and Megan jumped up and rushed to the back door. Graham walked in and Megan hugged him. He took her by the hand and walked into the family room.

Willis jumped up. 'What are you doing here? You're supposed to be in Austin!'

'Megan called me,' Graham said. 'I came as fast as I could. Is she all right? Have you found her? What the hell is going on?'

'Megan!' I said.

But Bess grabbed her sister's hand. 'Good thinking, Megs.' And she too got up and hugged Graham. He sat down between the girls.

'No, we haven't found her yet—' Willis started, but Graham jumped up.

'Then why aren't we out there looking for her?' my son demanded, and I thought maybe it wasn't such a good idea – him being here. When a young man is as in love as my son was with Alicia, reason and good sense were not always readily available.

I took his hand and pulled him down next to me. 'Where would you suggest we go look? Luna and Chief Donaldson are checking out all the hotels and motels in Codderville and Black Cat Ridge, and looking for the car the girls saw them in. We have that license plate, but it was stolen.' I rubbed his back. 'Everything that can be done is being done.'

'So tell me everything!' Graham said, taking both my hands in his. 'From the moment you dropped me off. Don't leave out a detail.'

So I started, telling him about not being able to eat dinner at the Driscoll – leaving out the part about not being able to have sex either (some things they don't need to know) – about his dad eating a healthy breakfast but me not being able to, at which point Willis tried to jump in with some denial, but Graham and I both shushed him, and getting home and Willis bringing in the luggage, finding the satchel.

Between the four of us – Willis, Bess, Megan and myself – we got the rest of it out.

'Where the hell did this satchel come from?' Graham asked.

'We don't know,' I said.

'When did it get put in the truck?' he asked.

Willis and I looked at each other. Willis said, 'The only time I can think of was when it was in the parking garage at the Driscoll.'

'OK, why would someone put that satchel in your truck?'

I had a brain fart. 'Scenario,' I said. 'Suppose a man is running through the parking garage, two guys are chasing him, he's carrying a satchel, he stuffs it in the first place he finds – Willis's clown truck – then runs up to the top level of the parking garage—'

'As in the two guys who've been stalking us?' Megan asked.

'Yes, and then the two guys chasing him shove him off the top!' Willis said.

'Oh my God!' Bess said. 'That guy at the Driscoll! The one who fell off the roof! You think this is about him?'

'Not so much about him,' Willis said, 'but more about what was *in* the satchel.'

'But there was nothing in there!' I said. 'We checked it out! Remember? You got the Dopp kit, I took the clothes to Goodwill and Alicia got the satchel as a backpack.'

Willis jumped up and headed to the master bedroom, the rest of us following and hanging out at the bathroom door while Willis checked out the Dopp kit. Dumping his razor, shaving cream, and

deodorant in the sink, he brought the Dopp kit itself to the bed. I
sat down next to him and, with the kids looking on, he took his
Swiss Army knife out of his pocket and began to tear the lining and
the bottom out of the kit. There was nothing there. Several shoulders
slumped.

'OK, so where were we in my scenario?' I asked the room in
general.

'The guys shove him off the top of the Driscoll parking garage,'
Graham said.

'But only one guy chases him up there,' I said. 'The other one
had to be near our truck, going for the satchel. Then we show up—'
I started.

'And they get the license and follow us home,' Willis finished.

'What guy at the Driscoll? What are y'all talking about?' Graham
pleaded.

'Tell you later, son,' Willis said, grabbing his phone out of his
pocket. 'Gotta call Luna!'

SIX

We found the beauty shop, or as they called it, 'The Salon' in fancy script. We went in and I talked to the girl at the reception desk.

'Hi,' I said. 'My name is Vera Pugh and my roommate Rachael Donley had her nails done here on Tuesday, but she had to leave the hotel for a family emergency.' I'm not big on lying, but this was for the greater good, and pretty much close to the truth. 'She asked me to pick up a copy of her charges here so she could pay me back when I see her.'

And I was right, I was going to be responsible for her manicure, too, along with her half of the room! This was costing me a fortune.

'Sure,' the young woman said. 'Donley?'

'Yes. D-O-N-L-E-Y,' I said.

She went on her computer, hit a couple of keys, then smiled. 'Here it is.' She hit another key and said, 'It's printing. Let me go get it for you.'

She was back in less than a minute – it was a small shop – and handed me the bill. Fifty-two dollars! I almost choked on my own spit! I looked at it closer and saw that, hey, it was only forty-two for the manicure – the rest was tip!

Since I wasn't able to speak, Gerald thanked the girl for me and we headed off to the lobby.

Dad called Luna and filled her in. She said she was going to call the detectives in Austin covering that case and get back to him. Graham and his sisters sat in the family room, side by side on the sofa, not watching TV for a change. They just sat there, not even talking much. Finally, Mom came in and told Graham the details of the man – James Unger – who had, as was now suspected by the police, been pushed from the top of the Driscoll's parking garage.

Graham nodded, taking in all the strange happenings since he'd left home only a few days ago. It could have been a year for all that had happened. Back in Austin, not so much. He'd registered, gotten some classes he wanted and a couple he didn't, at times that were scattered all over the place, making no rhyme or reason. He'd been very careful when designing his schedule to put all his classes in the afternoon so he could sleep late and study before he had to get ready. He'd also planned them according to the U.T. map he was given, so he could walk to all of them and leave enough time to walk from one side of the campus to the other. He had no intention of wasting what little money his parents allowed him on student parking on campus. But now he had one class in the chem building on the west side of campus immediately followed by engineering in another building on the northeast side of campus, then back to the chem building for lab. With ten minutes to traverse the famous forty acres twice.

He'd made one day of classes so far – English 101 and American history 101, both taught by TA's who didn't have English as a first language and with accents so thick he only understood every fourth word or so. Every day his stomach had been tied up in knots and he'd puked his guts out just the day before. So far, college had not been the magical experience his mother had claimed it to be. And then he gets the phone call. Megan telling him Alicia had been kidnapped. Right after lunch. He puked *that* up.

He excused himself and headed upstairs. He needed to lie down. Once in his room he realized something was different. He didn't know what it was until he laid down on his bunk. He could smell her. Putting his nose to the pillow his mother had put on his bed, he sniffed. Alicia had been in his room, on his bed. He could smell her. For the first time since he was eleven years old, Graham Pugh began to cry.

Alicia woke up to angry voices. At first she had no idea where she was or why her arms and legs wouldn't move. Then it all came rushing back to her. The sun was coming up. She could see it through the window. The sky was lightening, the trees and shrubs and cattle becoming clearer. Across from her on the sofa, the old man, Bert, lay asleep, his feet tied, his wrists bound in front of him. They had offered her the sofa last night but she'd declined, saying Bert should have it. Right now all she wanted to do was stand up and stretch. Everything ached.

The angry voices were coming from the kitchen, which she couldn't see from her vantage point.

'There's nothin' in here!' screamed an angry voice that she didn't recognize. Maybe this was the Mr Brown Mr Jones had spoken of?

'There was nothing in there when we got it!' Mr Smith said. That voice she'd never forget.

'Look!' the other voice said. 'See this hole you made? You don't think I can see this, asshole?'

'I didn't make that hole! Jones, come here!'

A third voice entered.

'Yeah?' Mr Jones said.

'Did you put this hole here?' Mr Smith asked him.

There was a short silence, then Mr Jones said, 'No.'

'Do you know who did?' Mr Smith asked.

'I dunno. Did you?' Mr Jones asked. To which Mr Smith answered with a resounding, 'No!'

Then there was silence. Alicia knew who had put that hole in the bag. And now she knew for sure what they were after. The flash drive. Of course, she'd known that somewhere in her psyche as soon as she'd found the damn thing. Now they were going to want to know where it was – and she wasn't about to tell them she'd left it in her room. They'd go back to her house and God only knows what they'd try to do to her family! Alicia felt the first twinge of panic since the entire ordeal had begun. She tried to take deep breaths, in and out, in and out, trying to conjure up yet again the might of her sister Megan. Her new mantra was WWMD – What Would Megan Do? And she knew exactly what Megan would do.

Mr Smith charged into the room, followed by Mr Jones and another man. The new guy was smaller than even Mr Smith, who was much smaller than Mr Jones. The new man had wispy blond hair and deep-set black eyes that did not sparkle or even gleam. He wore a snug T-shirt that showed off muscular arms, and even his jeans showed off overly-muscled thighs. After so much time with the beautiful Calvin the day before, she found herself describing the new guy in her mind: Roman nose, medium-to-dark complexion, yellowish teeth, firm jaw. He looked nasty.

Mr Smith was carrying her satchel. 'What'd you do with it?'

'With what?' Alicia asked.

'The thing that was in this hole!' he shouted, spittle flying across the space between them and landing on her face. With her hands secured behind her she couldn't wipe it off. She was rethinking that hand-sanitizer bath – maybe it should be Clorox.

'I don't know what you're talking about. That hole was there when I got the satchel,' Alicia said.

The new man knocked Mr Smith aside and leaned in to Alicia, his muscled hands resting on the arms of the ladder-back chair, his face only an inch or so from hers.

'Bullshit, little lady,' he said, his voice no longer screaming. It was worse. It was soft, quiet, and quite chilling. 'You cut that hole when you felt something in the lining, am I right? And then you did what with it?' He looked deep into her eyes, then smiled. 'You put it on your dresser in your bedroom, didn't you? Or on your nightstand—'

'She has a desk,' Mr Jones supplied.

'Now that makes sense,' the new guy said. 'I bet you have a computer, don't you, honey? And you put it near your computer because you were going to see what was on there. Did you? Did you stick that flash drive into your computer?'

Alicia remained silent. The new guy picked up her chair with her in it, held it about thigh high, then dropped it. Alicia thought some of her innards might just flop out.

He leaned in again. 'So where is it?' he asked.

Alicia refused to answer.

He shoved her chair away from him and turned to Smith and Jones. 'It's back at her house. In her bedroom. Probably on her desk near her computer.' He headed for the front door. 'Smith, you're coming with me. Jones, kill them.'

'I hope she knows we're looking for her,' Willis said. He and I were in the living room, sitting on the sectional, holding hands, away from our kids who were in the family room, trying to make their own sense of this mess.

'Why would she ever think we're not?' I asked, squeezing his hand.

'That business last summer—' he started.

I rested my head on his shoulder, my arms around his middle. 'That's behind us, honey. She knows.'

'If they do anything to her—' he started.

'Shhhhh,' I said. 'Don't go there. Please don't go there.'

We saw Graham come down the stairs. I wiped a tear off my cheek. 'Hey, honey,' I said. 'I didn't know you'd gone upstairs.'

'I thought I could rest.' He shook his head. 'Not gonna happen. I'm going for a drive.'

'Don't,' Willis said, getting up. 'You need to stay here.'

Again my son shook his head. 'That's not gonna happen either, Dad. I've got to be out there. I know it probably won't do a damn bit of good, but I've just got to . . .' His voice trailed off. Then he turned and headed into the family room to the back door.

Willis and I followed. 'Graham,' I said. 'Please stay with us.'

He shook his head. 'Gotta go.'

'We're going with him!' Megan said, jumping up, followed more tentatively by Bess.

'No—' Graham started, while at the same time Willis and I were both giving vehement negative responses.

'We'll keep an eye on him,' Bess said and, with his sisters flanking him, Graham left the house and headed for his car.

This mess was really affecting all my kids – my entire family. And I was getting mad. I wasn't sure exactly what Luna and Donaldson were doing to find my daughter; all I knew was it wasn't enough. Obviously they needed my help.

Mr Jones stood in the doorway to the living room, alternately staring at Alicia and Bert and then at the gun in his right hand. He'd been given his orders, and orders were orders, but . . . A kid and an old man? Jeez, he was a criminal, not a barbarian!

'Mr Jones?' Alicia said, trying at this point to channel her smart sister, Bess. Bess wasn't just smart, she knew people, knew how to reach them, and not in a smarmy way, but with understanding and empathy. But Alicia wasn't sure she could figure out how to empathize with a stone-cold killer, which she assumed to be an accurate description of Mr Jones.

'Don't talk to me,' Mr Jones told her.

'Do you really want to do this?' Alicia asked him. She was thinking quickly, wondering what she could say for Mr Bert. 'Look at Mr Bert, here. He's spent his whole life working this farm. It's been in his family for generations. His wife died right here in this house, the same house where she bore him three beautiful daughters. He's trying to hold on to this land for his grandson, to keep it in the family. Can you really just snuff out his life? Not to mention me, Mr Jones; up until a year and a half ago I was a foster kid, thrown from one rotten foster home to another. Given up at the age of three by a junkie mother. Too old to be adopted. But now I have a family. A real family, for the first time in my life. Please don't take that from me, and please don't take me from them,' she finished, tears in her eyes that were mostly genuine.

She noted with satisfaction that there were also tears in Mr Jones's eyes. He put the gun down on the table by the door. 'I don't wanna kill y'all,' he said, sinking down onto the sofa next to Bert. 'I really don't. But what am I supposed to do?'

'Untie us and let us go?' Bert suggested.

Mr Jones nodded his head. 'I suppose I could do that. But then I'll be in a heap of trouble.'

'Well, let's think of a way you can let us go and save face, shall we?' Alicia suggested.

It was the middle of the day; the girls should have been in school. Graham should have been in Austin to deal with his second day of classes. His 'B' day classes that he hadn't been to yet – chemistry and engineering. At this point he wasn't sure if he was ever going back to Austin – not for anything more than to pick up his stuff.

The sky to the east was darkening, storm clouds gathering. They seemed to fit his mood. He saw a lightning strike in the clouds then heard the clap of thunder. The clouds clapping, that's what Mom used to call thunder. Just the clouds clapping. And then he and his sisters would clap their hands just like the clouds. Jeez, things used to be a lot easier. Back then there hadn't been anything that Mom and Dad couldn't fix. Not a boo-boo they couldn't heal, not a bad grade they couldn't help you change.

He'd been a smart-ass kid, and sometimes he felt bad about that. Mom had her hands full, especially after Bess came to live with them. He'd been six years old then, and he knew what had happened next door. He remembered it all, quite vividly: his mom carrying Bess in from her house next door where, he eventually learned, Bess's entire birth family had been killed; Bess, covered in blood and gore from her mother. And then Bess coming to live with them, so traumatized by what had happened that she had been unable to speak for weeks. But eventually it was easy for her to become his sister. It had taken no time at all for him to want to knock her lights

out, just like he wanted to with Megan. She was his sister through
and through.

But that had never happened with Alicia. Neither of them were
kids, like he and Bess had been – she had only walked into his life
a year and a half ago. And of course, part of that time he'd been
with Lotta, his old girlfriend. But even then, after Megan and Bess
gave Alicia that make-over and he saw for the first time what was
under that mass of hair covering her face and that awful gray wool
jumper she wore every day, even with Lotta still in his life, he was
amazed at how the new Alicia made him feel. And it wasn't just
the attraction part of it, although that was definitely there. It was
much more. He wanted to protect her. Not in the way he wanted to
protect his other two 'sisters,' (as if he could ever think of Alicia
as a sister) but to keep her safe in every way possible. He wanted
to take away her past, change it from the horror it had been to
something that she deserved, but there was no way he could do that,
and it bothered him.

Graham was still trying to figure out what manhood was all about.
How much of the world he could control. And every day it seemed
as though fate was telling him how little control he had over anything.
He knew he couldn't change Alicia's past, but he'd be damned if
someone else was going to change her future.

They'd taken the old man's pickup truck. Parked on the side street,
they could see the house where the brown-haired girl lived, and the
driveway. They watched as a tall young man and two girls came
out and got in a Toyota.

'Who are the players?' Mr Brown asked.

'The two girls are the brown-haired girl's sisters. I don't know
who the boy is,' Mr Smith said.

'Which leaves who in the house?' Mr Brown asked.

'The mom for sure, and maybe the dad because of the missing
kid. One of my kids goes missing, I don't think I'd go to work,
know what I mean?'

Mr Brown did not respond. If Mr Smith had children, which he
found difficult to imagine, he really didn't want to know about it.
They ducked down as the Toyota turned their way, came to a stop
at the end of the street then turned left, right by the old truck. Mr
Brown listened for the car to pass, then sat up.

'OK,' he said to Mr Smith. 'You carrying?'

'Absolutely,' Mr Smith said, pulling a revolver from its resting place at his back, stuck in the waistband of his jeans.

They exited the pickup and started down the street, turning into Sagebrush Trail. Just as they did, a car passed them, turning into the corner house. Mr Smith made an about-face and headed back to the pickup.

'What the fuck?' Mr Brown hissed to Mr Smith's retreating back.

'She's a cop!' Mr Smith hissed back.

Mr Brown quickly joined his colleague and both climbed back into the pickup. Mr Brown started the engine and they drove away, just as the sky opened up and spilled the rain.

Mr Jones removed the bonds that held both Alicia and Bert. Alicia stood up and stretched. Bert sat on the couch and rubbed his wrists and ankles.

'Sorry about all that,' Mr Jones said.

'You only did what you had to do,' Bert said, shivering a bit at a huge clap of thunder outside the window.

Mr Jones nodded his head. 'I didn't mean for all this to happen. I mean, Max – ah, Mr Smith says he's got a job, gonna pay me twenty-five grand, and I need the money, you know? I got an ex-wife and two kids, and I'm behind in my child support, and I've been out of a job for more than six months! But I didn't count on all this stuff going on. I mean, I've done some stuff I'm not proud of, and I've done time, but I never killed anybody and I don't wanna start now! And Mr Smith keeps threatening to shoot me! All the time!'

Alicia walked over to where Mr Jones sat on the sofa next to Bert and patted him on the shoulder. 'I know this can't have been easy for you,' she said.

'Not at all!' Mr Jones said, tears in his eyes.

'OK, scoot,' she said, getting between the two men on the sofa. 'Now we need to come up with a scenario that will pass Mr Brown's inspection. One where Bert and I get away, but you're not blamed for it.'

'Anybody else notice it's storming out there?' Bert asked, his eyes focused on the window where a bolt of lightning had brightened the storm-darkened sky.

'We have to do it, Bert,' Alicia said. 'Do you have any raingear? Like umbrellas or slickers or anything?'

'I got one umbrella,' he said apologetically, 'but it's in the truck.'

'Well, we'll manage somehow,' Alicia said. 'Meanwhile, back to the problem of getting out of here and saving Mr Jones from Mr Brown.'

'I can only think of one thing,' Bert said. 'We bash Mr Jones here over the head with something and tie him to that chair there,' he said, pointing at the ladder-back chair, 'and then you and I take off.'

Alicia grimaced. 'I don't want to hurt Mr Jones,' she said, having realized he wasn't quite the stone-cold killer she'd assumed.

'It's the only way to do it, like Bert said,' Mr Jones said. 'But first you tie me to the chair, then hit me on the head. Y'all wouldn't be able to move me if I was unconscious.'

'Good point,' Bert said. He stood up and began looking around the mostly empty living room. 'I just don't see nothing here to bash your head in with. I mean, I got a cast-iron skillet in the kitchen, but how're we supposed to get that and come in here and bash your head in if we're both tied up?'

'Yeah,' Alicia said, 'and how are you going to explain to Mr Brown how Bert and I got you in that chair?'

Bert looked at Alicia. 'He'll have to be sitting in the chair when we hit him,' he said.

'Wait!' Alicia said, jumping up. 'Mr Jones, are you hungry?'

'Ah, now? Well, I could eat—' he started.

'Of course you could. And you'd order me to cook for you, wouldn't you? Me being a girl and all—'

'Oh, no! I've been cooking for myself a long time now—'

'Noooo,' Alicia said. Then succinctly, 'You ordered me to cook you breakfast. I got out the cast-iron skillet to cook eggs and—'

Both men grinned at her. 'Good one!' Mr Jones said, standing up and high-fiving Alicia.

'I love it when a plan comes together,' Bert said.

They drove aimlessly around, with no idea where to go. 'They wouldn't keep her here in BCR,' Megan said. 'They'd either take her to Codderville or someplace else.'

No one responded. 'I'm just saying,' Megan tried.

Still no response. Megan, riding shotgun, turned to look at Bess in the back seat. They both shrugged their shoulders.

Suddenly Graham slammed on the brakes. Megan, who'd been

turned in her seat, slammed her head against the passenger-side window. 'Ow!' she yelled.

'Sorry,' Graham said, but his tone said he couldn't care less. 'You think Codderville?' he asked Megan.

'I just think they'd try to go further than just here – BCR, you know?' she said.

He nodded his head, put his foot down on the accelerator and made a U-turn in the middle of Black Cat Ridge Blvd., only losing traction for a moment due to the slick road.

Alicia had tried to hit Mr Jones in the head with the cast-iron frying pan, but her effort had been weak and only managed to elicit an 'Ow' from Mr Jones. Bert had to take over. The ladder-back chair from the living room was one of a set of four that went with his kitchen table. He had Mr Jones sit in one of those, then whacked him a good one on the side of the head. Mr Jones started to say something, then his eyes rolled up in his head and he fell out of the chair.

'Oh my God!' Alicia yelled. 'Is he breathing?'

They both knelt beside Mr Jones and felt for a pulse. Alicia found one, beating strong. She sighed with relief. 'OK,' she said, 'let's tape him up.'

She and Bert managed to get Mr Jones taped up, grabbed a couple of granola bars out of the cupboard and some bottled water out of the fridge and headed outside.

The deluge had trickled down to a light sprinkle. As they walked, Bert said, 'I like that story you told Mr Jones. You know, about the farm being in my family for years and all that. Truth is, I just rent the place. Somebody else works the fields. And me and my wife, well, she up and left me like twenty-something years ago. And I don't have daughters. Got one son, and last I heard he was in prison up in Huntsville for manslaughter.' He sighed. 'Wish I'd had me a grandson, though. Carry on the name.'

'What is your last name, Bert?'

He laughed. 'Funny you should ask. It's Smith.'

Bert led her off the driveway and through the thick brush that paralleled the dirt road she'd come down the night before with Mr Smith and Mr Jones. They made their way through that to the farm to market road, when they saw the old blue-and-rust pickup truck coming toward them. They hid in the wet bushes and watched it turn onto the now muddy road that led to the old farmhouse.

'Should we make a run for it?' Alicia asked.

'Honey, you go. You're young. No way I can make a *run* for anything,' Bert said.

'I'm not leaving you,' Alicia whispered and settled down in the little hollow they'd formed in the weeds and grasses. A weeping willow shielded them from the dirt road and a small grove of oaks shielded them from the farm to market.

'What if they come looking for us in the bushes?' Bert asked.

Alicia looked around her, found a nice-sized stick, and hefted it. 'Let 'em come,' she said.

Bert laughed quietly. 'That's what I like about you, kid,' he said. 'You got balls.'

They were there for no more than twenty minutes when the blue truck came roaring back down the dirt road and turned on the farm to market road, heading back to Codderville.

'Glad we waited,' Alicia said.

'Yeah, no kidding,' Bert said and stood up, stretching his legs. 'Hard to get up off the ground when you get to be my age.'

Alicia bounced up like a young colt. 'I guess we should start walking,' she said.

'What the fuck? A goddam cop?' Mr Brown hadn't stopped yelling since they'd driven off from Sagebrush Trail, and kept slamming his fist repeatedly on the steering wheel. 'You forget to mention the little bitch lives next door to a fucking cop?'

'You missed the turn,' Mr Smith said, his voice relatively quiet, at least in comparison to his companion's.

Mr Brown's right arm shot out sideways, his fist colliding solidly with Mr Smith's jaw, throwing his head against the side window of the old truck. The window cracked. 'Shut up!' Mr Brown yelled.

Stunned, Mr Smith straightened up. 'Jesus!' he moaned, rubbing his jaw. 'What'd you go and do that for?'

'Because you're an idiot! And I hate idiots!' Mr Brown yelled.

Mr Smith wished Mr Jones had been in the truck with him so he could have shot him again. The thought alone seemed to relieve a lot of tension, and, truthfully, he was feeling quite tense. Maybe Mr Brown would shoot Mr Jones, and save him the job. If he hated idiots, he sure as hell would hate Mr Jones.

'So now what?' Mr Smith asked, feeling a bit woozy.

'We go back tonight. Late. And we kill everybody! Including that bitch cop!'

Mr Smith nodded his head, which hurt like the devil. It was a plan, he thought, then felt a very sharp pain in his head, followed by his vision blurring as he slumped in his seat; the only thing keeping him upright was the seatbelt.

Without the ceremony of knocking, Luna burst in our back door, cell phone pressed to her ear. 'I want an address and I want it now!' she yelled into the phone. 'Call me back and make it quick!'

She closed her phone and fell on the sofa.

'What's up?' I asked.

'Don't ask,' she said.

'But I just did,' I said.

'When I turned onto Sagebrush there were two men walking toward your house. One of them was the short guy from the other day. When he saw me he turned tail and ran. I don't know who the other guy was. It wasn't the big one though, that's for sure—'

Willis jumped up. 'Why aren't you chasing them? Jesus Christ, Luna—'

'I saw the vehicle they were in. An old blue-and-rust Chevy pickup truck. I got the license number.' She held out her cell phone. 'I'm waiting on a call now.'

Willis sat down in his chair, slumped over, hands clasped between his legs. He looked dejected. I don't suppose I looked much better. The three of us were quiet. The minutes felt like hours and I was ready to crawl out of my skin when Luna's cell phone finally rang.

All three of us jumped to our feet. Luna opened her phone. 'Hello?' She motioned to me for pen and paper. I obliged. She began to write. 'Got it!' She stuffed the phone in her pocket and looked at us.

'Get in my car,' she said and, again, without ceremony, went back out the back door as flamboyantly as she'd come in and jumped in her car.

We followed her, Willis riding shotgun, me in the backseat behind Luna, still not sure where we were going. She put her flasher on top of her car, turned on her siren and we sped out of BCR, over the river to Codderville. She didn't speak and Willis and I just stared straight ahead. A few minutes later, Willis finally asked, 'Where are we going?'

'Wait,' was all she would say.

She got off the highway just south of downtown Codderville, and followed a farm to market road to the west for about five miles. By then we were in deep country, passing empty fields of corn and cotton that had been recently harvested. The heavy wind produced by the speed of the car blew clouds of cotton bolls in the air. Luna slammed on the breaks, coming to a complete stop.

In front of us was our daughter Alicia, holding the arm of an old man, as the two limped toward us.

I burst into tears as I exited the vehicle.

I grabbed my daughter and held her tight, almost as tightly as she held me. Luna had taken the arm of the old man and was leading him to her car. Willis was behind Alicia, one arm on her shoulders, the other holding his cell phone to his ear.

I heard him say, 'We've got her. We're going home.'

Mr Brown drove back to the farmhouse, noticing that Mr Smith was being pretty quiet the entire way back.

'Hey,' he said, 'we're here.'

Mr Smith did not reply. 'Hey, Smith! Wake the fuck up!'

Mr Smith did not move. Mr Brown shook him, and Mr Smith's head rolled in Mr Brown's direction. The right side of Mr Smith's head had been bleeding. A lot. But it seemed to have stopped. Mr Brown knew that wasn't necessarily a good sign. He felt for a pulse in Mr Smith's neck. There wasn't one.

'Well, shit!' he said, pushing Mr Smith's body away from him. 'Goddamit! This sucks!'

He got out of the truck in disgust and went in the back door of the old farmhouse. It wasn't Mr Brown's day.

'What the fuck?' Mr Brown yelled. Mr Jones was lying unconscious on the floor of the kitchen. He walked up to the still body and kicked it. Then kicked it again. Feeling some relief of anxiety by that action, he kicked him a couple of more times. Then he walked to the sink, grabbed a pot, filled it with water, and threw it on Mr Jones's head.

Mr Jones sputtered, choked, and attempted to move, only to find himself taped up. He struggled against the tape that bound him, but anyone who knows duct tape knows that is for naught. Finally his eyes fell on Mr Brown, who was sitting in the ladder-back chair Mr Jones had been sitting in before he fell to the floor.

'Hey,' Mr Jones said.

'Hey,' Mr Brown said, fuming.

'Can you get this tape off me, man?' Mr Jones asked.

'Maybe in a minute,' Mr Brown said.

Mr Jones looked around the room as best he could from his position. 'Where's Mr Smith?' he asked.

'Funny you should ask,' Mr Brown said. 'He appears to be dead.'

'Huh?' Mr Jones said.

Mr Brown kicked Mr Jones in the stomach. 'Idiots! Nothing but idiots!'

'Stop that!' Mr Jones said, attempting to move his body away from the reach of Mr Brown's foot.

'Where are the girl and the old man, Mr Jones? Or should I ask, where are their bodies?' He lifted his head to look at the ceiling, then brought it back down to look at Mr Jones. 'Aw, no, now, if they were dead, as I instructed, then who in the world knocked you out and taped you up, Mr Jones?'

'Look, it wasn't my fault— Did you kill Max – I mean, Mr Smith?'

'No, I didn't. He hit his head against the side window and I guess something inside his brain just went flewy,' Mr Brown said, and then laughed. 'Who would have thought a tough guy like Mr Smith would have such a fragile head?'

'How come his head hit the window?' Mr Jones asked.

'Is that really the important question here?' Mr Brown asked in return. 'Isn't the really important question here how did the girl and the old man get away? Oh, and here's a good one: why aren't they dead?' Mr Brown stood up and walked up to Mr Jones, still helplessly taped up on the floor. 'LIKE I TOLD YOU TO DO!' Mr Brown screamed and kicked Mr Jones in the head.

Luckily for them both, and for Bert, Mr Jones did not have a fragile head. However, the steel tip on Mr Brown's steel-toed boots caught Mr Jones at the lower base of his eyebrow, splitting it open and gushing blood. Mr Brown lifted his left jean pants leg and removed a hunting knife. Mr Jones flinched, but Mr Brown went for the tape, not parts of Mr Jones's anatomy.

After Mr Jones was freed and standing, a paper towel from the kitchen counter sopping up the blood from his eye, Mr Brown said, 'We're leaving. Gonna steal another ride. Get in the truck.'

The two men walked out the back door of the old farmhouse and went to the pickup truck parked nearby. Mr Brown went to the driver's side, while Mr Jones went to the shotgun side. He opened the door and Mr Smith's head rolled toward him, his body still in place from the seatbelt.

'Just unbuckle it and toss it on the ground,' Mr Brown said.

Mr Jones was offended by Mr Brown's use of the 'it' pronoun. If Mr Brown couldn't see fit to call him Max or Mr Smith, at least he could have called him 'him,' for crying out loud. They might not have got on, but Mr Jones knew that Mr Smith had his own loved ones and would have needed the money too; he didn't deserve to die. Mr Jones unbuckled the old-fashioned seatbelt and grabbed Mr Smith's body under his arms, gently releasing him to the ground. 'Bye, ol' buddy,' he said to the body. 'I'm glad you didn't kill me.'

We ended up having a confrontation with Luna, who heard Willis say we were headed home.

'No,' she said.

'No what?' Willis asked.

'Just wait a damn minute!' Luna said. 'Alicia, where were you being kept and how did you get out?'

'At my place,' the old man said, pointing toward a dirt road maybe half a mile away.

'We made a deal with Mr Jones—' Alicia started.

'Who's Mr Jones?' I asked.

'He's the tall one. He's really nice,' Alicia said. 'He untied us and let us knock him out with a frying pan and then tie him up so we could get away and so Mr Brown won't kill him.'

We all just looked at her. Alicia pointed in the same direction the old man had pointed in only moments before. 'He might still be there. When the truck left again—'

'The truck came back here?' Luna demanded.

'Yeah, there were two of 'em in it,' the old man said. 'When they left again, like, what, Alicia, twenty minutes?'

'Yeah, Bert, that sounds right,' Alicia answered.

'Yeah, twenty minutes later there were still two of 'em in the truck. Or there coulda been three. My eyesight's not so good anymore.'

Alicia laughed. 'Bert, do you have anything that works anymore?'

'Not so's you'd notice,' he said in a sad voice. Alicia patted him on the back.

'I think we should go check on Mr Jones,' Alicia said. 'I sure hope Mr Brown didn't kill him.'

Luna looked at me, then Willis, then back at me. Willis and I shrugged. 'Sure,' she finally said. 'Let's go find Mr Jones.'

We all piled in Luna's car and headed down the dirt road, directed by Bert. Bert suggested we pull up to the back of the house. When we did, we saw the body. Luna turned off the engine of the car, and we all sat there staring at the dead man.

'Well, the good news is that ain't Mr Jones,' Bert said. 'That's Mr Smith. Mr Smith was a rotten SOB and pretty much needed killing, so everything's copacetic.'

SEVEN

THURSDAY

'We need to get Alicia home,' Willis said as we stared at the body.

'No, she can't go home,' Luna said. She got on her cell phone and made a call. She told the person on the other end to send out a crime-scene tech and a squad car to take us back to the station. 'Alicia needs to be debriefed. I'm sending y'all to BCR police station to talk with Chief Donaldson. He's expecting you.' She looked at Bert Smith sitting in the back seat of the car. 'Mr Smith, do you need to go to the hospital first?'

None of us quite understood why Alicia and Bert both were shaking their heads. 'Call me, Bert, ma'am. I don't think I'm gonna let anybody call me Mr Smith again. And no, ma'am, I don't need no doctor.'

Luna nodded her head. 'OK, I'll call you Bert if you don't "ma'am" me again, deal?'

'Yes, ma'am,' he said, then grinned at her.

'Everybody in the car,' Luna said. 'There are plenty of seatbelts back there. I'm going to drive you to the point where the dirt road meets the farm to market. We'll wait for the squad car there. No need to sit here staring at the dead guy.'

Willis was on his cell phone before Luna got the car started. 'Meet us at the BCR police station,' he said to his son and hung up.

I had Alicia in my arms in the back seat, stroking her hair. 'I was so worried,' I said.

'I know, Mom.'

Willis turned around in his seat. 'We both were,' he said.

Alicia reached out for his outstretched hand. 'I know you were, Dad. I know that.'

He squeezed her hand and I could see a tear in his eye. 'Never forget it,' he said. 'Ever.'

'Never ever,' Alicia said and squeezed back.

We waited for less than fifteen minutes and heard the squad car coming miles off, sirens blazing away.

Once the patrol person got there, Luna said, 'No siren going back. Speed limit, got that, Rookie?'

'Yes, ma'am,' the fresh-faced former boy scout said.

It took about twenty minutes to get back to BCR and to the police station. Like everything else in Black Cat Ridge, the police station had been part of The Plan. Although it took a couple of years to get it built and running, the urgent care area had been set out in the original town plans. Several acres earmarked for police, fire, and ambulance. It was all up and running now and close to the White Rock shopping center so, ta-da, it was all made of white rock, fitting the locale beautifully, with as few trees slaughtered as possible.

Inside, the waiting area had comfortable seating, good lighting, and piped-in music. There was reading material – *Ladies Home Journal*, *Time*, and *Men's Health*. It was more like an upscale doctor's office than a police station. There was even a little sliding glass window, behind which sat what in a doctor's office would have been the receptionist, but instead of scrubs, this young woman was wearing the black and gold uniform of the Black Cat Ridge Police. (The high-school teams' colors are also black and gold. Coincidence? In a place called Black Cat Ridge? Hardly. And yes, the football team is called the Alley Cats.)

There was a door to the left and a door to the right. The young cop led us through the door to the left. We went down a hall and ended up in what looked like a boardroom. Polished hardwood floors and table, twelve chairs, whiteboard, chalkboard, and a large flat-screen TV. He told us to take a seat and we did, then he said, 'I'll go get the chief.'

There was a large window that looked out onto the hall, and we watched as he started down the hall, then stopped. Turning, he pointed toward the room we were in. Then we saw them – our kids – Graham in the lead.

Seeing Graham, Alicia stood up and ran to the door, just as he ran to the door. The two stopped for half a minute, staring at each other, then they embraced. I was hoping they'd hold off a couple of years, but I still couldn't help crying at the beauty of it.

Mr Brown slammed his fist down on the steering wheel, making Mr Jones jump in his seat. They were in a fairly old Toyota Celica, old enough anyway to be able to hot-wire. Mr Brown had insisted that Mr Jones steal the car out of the parking lot of the Wal-Mart in Codderville, but since Mr Jones did not know the intricacies of hot-wiring, Mr Brown was forced to get out and do it himself. It was at this point that he first wished he hadn't hit Mr Smith so hard as to cause his death. He was sure Mr Smith would have known how to hot-wire a car.

They were parked across the street from the house where the brown-haired girl lived, and where the flash drive presumably still resided – upstairs in her room next to her computer.

'All the cars are still there!' Mr Brown yelled.

'Oh, no! That's not all of 'em,' Mr Jones said. 'That minivan is the girls' – the brown-haired girl and her two sisters – and that little sporty car, that's the mom's, and the dad has a really cool truck but it's in the gar—'

'Shut up,' Mr Brown said quietly.

'—age,' Mr Jones finished.

Mr Brown was down with the fact that he was going to have to kill Mr Jones. Either now or, if he behaved, later. But Mr Brown was fearful that Mr Jones did not know *how* to behave.

'And that boy, he had another car, like this one—' Mr Jones started.

Mr Brown drew his arm back and was about to cold-cock Mr Jones when he wondered what the tinsel strength of the Toyota's side windows might be. He didn't want Mr Jones dead now, like Mr Smith. Instead of hitting Mr Jones and knocking his head into the side window, causing yet another death by window, Mr Brown got out of the car.

'You got a gun?' he asked Mr Jones, who got out on his side.

'Yeah, sure do,' he said, drawing it out of his pocket.

'Put that goddam thing back, you idiot!' Mr Brown hissed. 'God only knows who's watching! But keep your hand near it. We break down the back door and rush in and kill anybody standing in our way.'

'But, Mr Brown, these are like, you know, innocent people,' Mr Jones said.

'If they're so goddam innocent, why do they have the flash drive and we don't?' Mr Brown countered.

Mr Jones couldn't answer that so he let it go. Instead, he went in another direction. 'What about that police lady who lives next door?'

Mr Brown stopped in his tracks. 'Do you see her car?'

'No, but I didn't see her car when she stopped me and Mr Smith that time either,' Mr Jones said.

'Which house?' Mr Brown inquired.

'That one,' Mr Jones said, pointing at Elena Luna's house, which shared its driveway with the Pugh house. Mr Jones had never worked with Mr Brown (or whatever his real name was) before, and he was coming to the conclusion that he wouldn't work with him again. He seemed even more temperamental than Mr Smith, and that was saying a lot.

Mr Brown squared his shoulders. 'She comes out, we kill her,' he said, his voice much steadier than his insides. Mr Brown was not thrilled with the prospect of killing a cop. As a matter of fact, Mr Brown wasn't thrilled about killing anybody at all, but he was even less thrilled about being killed himself. And that's what was going to happen if he didn't get back to Houston with that flash drive.

'Come on,' he said to Mr Jones as he headed across the street. They walked up the driveway, unaccosted by the cop who lived next door. They went up to the back door and found it unlocked. They walked in. There was no one in the kitchen or the big room with the large flat-screen TV. Mr Brown and Mr Jones looked at each other.

'This place is empty,' Mr Brown said. 'I can feel it. You know how you feel if someone else is in a room with you?'

Mr Jones said, 'No.'

'It was a rhetorical question, dumbass. I'm just saying, this place is empty.' They both stood in the same spot right inside the back door. Neither moved.

'You sure about that?' Mr Jones asked.

'I'm positive,' Mr Brown said, and finally took another step into the room. And another. 'Where's the staircase?' he asked.

'Toward the front of the house,' Mr Jones answered.

'Show me,' Mr Brown said.

'Uh uh,' Mr Jones said, shaking his head. 'I'm not going first! You go first!'

'Oh, for Christ's sake!' Mr Brown muttered, and went to a doorway toward the front of the house. A hallway lead straight to the front door, with a formal dining room on the right, with an arch into a formal living room. On the left of the hallway was the wall that supported the staircase that came straight down toward the front door, but curved toward the living room for the last three steps.

'See the way the staircase curves before the front door?' Mr Jones asked.

'Yeah, so what?' Mr Brown replied, heading for said staircase.

'That's fung shia,' Mr Jones said, oblivious to his mistake. 'If the builder hadn't turned the stairs like that, all the luck in the house would have gone right out the front door!' Mr Jones smiled brightly at his companion.

Mr Brown stopped on the third step and stared down at Mr Jones. 'You know, you're a real piece of work, Mr Jones,' he said.

Still smiling brightly, Mr Jones said, 'Thank you, Mr Brown.'

Heading back up the stairs, Mr Brown said, 'It ain't a compliment, dumbass.'

As Mr Brown resumed his upward trajectory, the house phone began to ring, stopping him in his tracks, as it did Mr Jones. Both stood on the stairs and listened to see if anyone would answer it. There was an audible click after the third ring. Then a voice said, 'You've reached the Pugh family. We're not answering the phone at the moment because we're having more fun playing without you. So leave a message if you want to join in.'

Then another voice said, 'I still say that's a rude message! Look, something funny is going on here and I need to talk to you about it. I found something I shouldn't have found.' Then there was a click, as if the old lady, because the voice was definitely that of an old lady, had hung up.

Mr Brown flung himself around to stare at Mr Jones, almost losing his balance. 'Who the fuck was that? And what does she know?'

Mr Jones's eyes were huge. 'I don't know! You think she found the flash drive?'

'Fuck!' Mr Brown swore, flung himself back around, and raced up the stairs.

There was a lot of hugging going on, then Chief Donaldson came in and my kids settled down, Graham and Alicia sitting side by side, holding hands, I presumed. We were definitely going to have to have a talk.

'Glad to see you back, Ms Brooks,' he said to Alicia.

'Glad to be back, Chief,' Alicia said, smiling at him. For a girl who'd been held hostage overnight, she looked pretty good. Her color was bright and her eyes sparkled and, even with uncombed hair and still wearing her shorty nightgown from the night before (although covered now by a BCR police sweatshirt), she looked as fresh as a daisy. I think all that might have more to do with my son than her return to the arms of her family. If you know what I mean.

'We're gonna need to go over everything that happened from last night on,' the chief said. 'It might get pretty dull for the rest of you,' he said, looking at Willis and me. 'I'd advise y'all to go on home and I'll call you when she's ready to be picked up. Y'all can get her some clothes and bring 'em back then.'

'We're not leaving,' Willis told him and I nodded my head in agreement.

Graham reached in his pocket and got his car keys, which he tossed to Megan. 'Y'all go back to the house and get her stuff. We'll wait here,' he said, and the authority in my son's voice gave me a chill. God, he was so grown up!

Without a word, my girls got up, went to their sister and hugged her, then were out the door on their brother's errand.

'So,' the chief said. 'Tell me what happened.'

'I woke up and saw two men in my bedroom. I started to scream, but one of them, I think it was Mr Jones, put his hand over my mouth . . .'

'Which one's her room?' Mr Brown asked Mr Jones.

'That one,' Mr Jones said, pointing at the end of the hall to the left. 'Should we check the other rooms?'

'Nobody's here,' Mr Brown said. 'Trust me.'

Mr Jones shrugged, wondering if he *should* trust the man who killed Mr Smith. Mr Smith could be quite irksome, Mr Jones thought, but certainly not enough to kill him. Unless he tried shooting Mr Brown in the foot like he'd done to Mr Jones. Mr Jones looked down at Mr Brown's feet. He could see no damage. Looking at his own, his white sock was still quite visible in the toe of his black motorcycle boot. He was still miffed about that. Those boots were leather and had cost over fifty dollars. And it wasn't like Mr Jones was made of money. Hell, if he was made of money he wouldn't be here in this house trying to steal something from a sweet teenaged girl's room. He wouldn't have been involved in this at all! *If* he was made out of money. And this, of course, made Mr Jones wonder how a person *could* be made out of money in the first place.

'Are you coming?' Mr Brown said, breaking into Mr Jones's reverie.

'Huh?' Mr Jones said.

'Shit,' Mr Brown said under his breath, and opened the door to the brown-haired girl's room.

The first thing he noticed was that it was a mess. Bed clothes scattered hither and yon, desk chair turned over, bedside lamp on the floor. 'You and Smith do this when you abducted her?'

'Couldn't be helped,' Mr Jones said.

Mr Brown went to the desk and saw the flash drive sitting at the base of the computer stand. He picked it up and put it in his pocket. 'Let's get out of here.'

The girls got in Graham's car, Megan in the driver's side. 'Oh, shit,' she said. 'I forgot! It's a stick!'

'Uh oh,' Bess said, staring at the gear shift. 'Do you know how to do this?'

'No! Do you?'

'No,' Bess answered.

The two girls looked at each other. Finally, Megan said, 'We can't go back in there without Alicia's clothes. So what do we do?'

'I've watched Mom with her Audi,' Bess said. 'Let me try.'

The girls got out and switched places. Bess got in and pulled the car seat up as close as she could get it. 'OK,' she said, and turned the key in the ignition. It sputtered and failed. 'Oh, wait!' she said. 'Maybe it has to be in neutral.' She pushed in the clutch and wiggled the gearshift to the neutral position, then turned the key. The engine sprang to life. 'What's first gear?' she asked her sister.

Megan shrugged. 'I dunno.'

Bess found a gear and then let the clutch slowly rise as she gave the car gas. The car died. 'I don't think that was first.' Bess put the gearshift back in neutral, started the car again, then once again attempted the clutch/gas routine. Again the engine died. Twice more and the car began to move. Both girls were so surprised and so thrilled that Bess removed her foot too quickly from the clutch, the car shot forward, and the engine died.

They finally made it to the house, turned off Graham's engine, and sat in their seats, Bess breathing hard, as if she'd pushed the car the entire way there and, truthfully, she felt she had.

'So what do you think?' Megan said.

'About driving stick? I hate it!' Bess said.

'No! About Graham and Alicia!'

Bess laughed. 'I think those two were the only ones who didn't know it was mutual.'

'You think Mom and Dad knew?' Megan asked.

'Yes. Don't you?'

Megan shrugged. 'I dunno. You think it will last? I mean, is she going to become our sister-in-law? Maybe it's a good thing Mom and Dad never legally adopted her.'

Bess shrugged. 'With Graham off at college, I just don't know.'

Megan let out a snort. 'Ha! He's not going back.'

'Says who?' Bess demanded.

'Says me, that's who!'

'You're wrong. There's no way he'd stiff Mom and Dad like that!'

'Betja,' Megan said.

'Bet me what? And it can't be money. That's gambling,' Bess said.

'You know, your goody-two-shoeness is tiresome,' Megan said. 'How about dishes for a month?'

'Make it two months!' Bess said and the two shook on it, then headed out of the car and upstairs to get Alicia some clothes. Alicia's room was a mess and Bess set about straightening it. 'Are you gonna help?' she asked her sister indignantly.

'Alicia should clean up her own room! I have to clean mine myself.'

'Ha! You've never cleaned your room in your whole life! That's why no one goes in there except you! We're afraid we'd get lost!' Bess said. 'Besides, Alicia's room is never a mess. This happened when those men took her.'

Both girls stopped for a minute and looked around. 'Jeez,' Megan finally said. 'How sick would that be? Wake up to someone in your room and then they drag you out?' She shuddered and crossed her arms over her chest.

Not noticing what Megan was doing, Bess ended up in the same position, arms across her chest, just thinking about the scene. Finally, she shook herself. 'Let's clean it up. There's no way she should come home to this.'

'Right,' Megan said, and actually began to make things right.

All in all, it took them forty-five minutes to go the two miles to their house, go in and get Alicia's clothes, straighten her room, and go the two miles back to the station. Most of that time was spent on the road.

'But I do know what this is about, sorta,' Alicia said to her audience.

Luna, who had joined us late, said, 'What's that?'

'That satchel, Mom, that you gave me? There was something in the lining. I cut it out and it was a flash drive—' She looked around at nothing but blank stares, mine included. I'd heard the phrase, but I didn't know what it meant. I know very few things about computers: how to turn them on, how to turn them off, how to get a Windows screen, and how to retrieve email. I don't peruse Facebook. I don't Twitter. I don't Snipe or Snope or whatever. I don't have a website, and I'm not even sure what one is. I write romance novels. My editor emails me changes. I email them back. That is my entire source of knowledge about a computer.

Graham said, 'It's a doohickey you stick in a port – a hole in the computer – that has information on it. Usually a download from another computer. That means—'

'I think we all understand download, son,' said the chief, 'but thanks for the mini-lesson. So, Ms Brooks, what was on that flash thing?'

'Flash drive. And I don't know. The sketch artist showed up and I just left it on my desk, and then forgot about it, what with all that was going on.'

'So it's still there?' the chief asked. 'In your room?'

'I don't know. That Mr Brown person kinda worked it out. That it was on my desk. They may be going to the house—'

Willis and I both jumped up. 'The girls!' we said in unison.

We were answered by voices from the doorway. 'What about us?' Bess said, and, 'You talking about us?' Megan said.

Willis and I sank back in our seats. 'Took you long enough,' Graham said.

'You know we don't drive stick!' Megan said.

Graham stood up. 'What did you do to my car?' he demanded.

'I drove it!' Bess said. 'It just took a while.'

The girls had only been driving for a few months – Alicia, the oldest, for six months, Megan for four, and Bess, who's sixteenth birthday we celebrated less than a month ago, not even a month.

One thing I was adamant about was that the girls learn to drive a stick shift. I don't think any driver – especially a female – should be out in the world and not know how to drive just about any vehicle she might encounter. I might have a little difficulty with an eighteen wheeler, but I think I could probably get it from point A to point B. To me, it's a safety precaution. But as so often happens, I just hadn't gotten around to teaching my girls – yet. Looked like there would be lessons while Graham and his car were here. Because, God forbid, I wasn't about to let them near my Audi.

'I swear if you stripped the gears or messed up anything—'

'Sit down, young man,' the chief said. 'Don't threaten your sisters, at least not in my presence. I don't want to have to arrest you.'

'Yes, sir,' Graham said, sitting back down. Alicia's hand was on his arm, stroking it. Oh, boy, did we need to talk.

'Lieutenant Luna, you wanna go to their house and see if the flash thing is still there?' the chief asked.

Four voices said, 'Drive,' in what would have been a round if we'd sung it.

'Yes, sir,' Luna said.

'Oh, and Luna, I got a call from the chief of D's in Austin. He's sending a couple of detectives over this way. Should be here shortly.'

'What are we supposed to do with them?' Luna asked, frowning.

'Keep 'em fed and watered, I suppose,' the chief said.

As Luna headed for the door to the room, the chief said, 'Don't you need to get a key?'

'I have one,' she said. 'We're neighbors.'

'The door's unlocked anyway,' Megan said.

I looked at Willis. 'Maybe we should stop doing that,' I said. 'Leaving the doors unlocked.'

There have been times since we've lived in Black Cat Ridge when we've locked our doors, like right after our friends and neighbors the Lesters, Bess's birth parents, were murdered, or when we were being stalked that time. Oh, and when Willis disappeared once, and that time Bess was kidnapped, but we always end up forgetting to lock up within a month or two of such incidents. Basically, all in all, Black Cat Ridge is a safe community. But then again, we do seem to attract the unsavory element to our door. Best it was locked when they came a'calling.

*   *   *

'We got it!' Mr Brown was saying into the phone.

'Then get back here immediately!' the heavily accented voice on the other end of the line said, and hung up.

Mr Brown started up the Toyota and put it in gear. 'We're off to Houston,' he said to Mr Jones.

'OK,' Mr Jones said. 'Can we get something to eat first?'

Mr Brown rolled his eyes. 'We are in a stolen car, Mr Jones,' he said, pronouncing each word succinctly. 'It would not be a good idea to stop by a restaurant or even a drive-thru in a stolen car. Do you see my point?'

'Oh, yeah, you're right,' Mr Jones said. 'Maybe once we're on the road?'

'We'll see,' Mr Brown said, and got on the highway to Codderville that would eventually lead to Interstate 10, that would take them all the way to Houston.

Clarissa Mayfair hated her partner. Absolutely hated him. Davis DeWitt felt the same way about her. Theirs was a match made in hell, or, to be more exact, in the homicide division of the Austin Police Department. The two had been assigned the homicide case of James Unger, the man who was pushed off the roof of the Driscoll Hotel parking garage. After several days of absolutely nothing, they got a lead that, unfortunately, led them out of town to a jerkwater place called Black Cat Ridge, located somewhere along the twisting, winding rope of a river called the Colorado.

They knew the river well – it flowed through Austin, in the guise of Lake Austin on the west end, and Lady Bird Lake in the center of town, bisecting the city, resulting in the common destination of south of the river and/or north of the river. A lot of the festivities in the city were located on, by, or near the river, or the Lady Bird Lake part of the river. The fourth of July fireworks were fired from a barge in the middle of the lake/river, the Austin City Limits TV show's annual ACL Fest was held on the banks of the river, the annual trail of lights was near the river, and the largest Christmas tree on earth has a view of the river, making the Colorado River an important part of the Austin lifestyle.

But driving for two hours to this Podunk town somewhere near the river they both loved, in each other's company, was not going to be fun. Actually, neither of them could think of something they'd rather not do more than spend two to three hours in a car with each other. Their mutual dislike had nothing to do with looks. They were both pleasant-looking people – Mayfair a petite blonde with green eyes and large breasts; DeWitt a large, dark-haired man with washboard abs and dark blue eyes. No, it had to do with personalities. And theirs didn't mesh. Within the first hour of meeting him, Mayfair was blessed with a peek at DeWitt's washboard abs when he pulled up his shirt and said, 'Look!' From that moment onward she thought he was vain and slightly stupid. When she replied to his offer of a peek at his abs with the response, 'Cover yourself up, you dumb fuck,' he considered her rude, aggressive, and not very nice.

Nothing had happened in the eighteen months since to change the opinions of either.

The first hour of the drive went something like this:

Clarissa Mayfair: 'You wanna drive, or should I?'

Davis DeWitt: 'I'll drive.'

Clarissa Mayfair: 'OK.'

The second hour went more like this:

Davis DeWitt: 'Is that it?'

Clarissa Mayfair: 'Yeah. Turn left.'

Davis DeWitt: 'Fuck! I *am* turning left!'

Clarissa Mayfair: 'Don't start with me!'

Which brought them to the parking lot of the Black Cat Ridge police department.

Inside, the Pugh family had just finished up and were heading for the front door of the station. They met the detectives from Austin on their way out.

'You the chief?' DeWitt asked Donaldson.

'Yeah. You the guys from Austin?'

'Yeah,' DeWitt answered. 'This the family?'

'Yeah,' Donaldson said.

'We're leaving,' Willis said.

'We need to talk to y'all,' Mayfair said.

'Not now! My daughter has been through hell and back and we're taking her home to get some rest. We'll call you when she's up to being questioned. Again,' Willis said, and walked his family past the Austin detectives.

'Hey, now!' DeWitt started, but Chief Donaldson put a restraining hand on his arm.

'Let 'em go,' he said. 'The girl's exhausted. She needs to rest.

Come on into my office and I'll tell you what we know so far.
Then, if you still need to, you can go talk to Alicia when she's
rested.'

'This is highly unorthodox,' Mayfair said.

To which her partner replied, 'Shut up.'

Which elicited a 'Don't you talk to me like that!' from Mayfair.

The exchange continued, letting Chief Donaldson know the flavor
of their relationship.

We got home, all stuffed in Graham's Celica, sans seatbelts. All the
other cars were still in the driveway as they were when we'd left
the house with Luna. Once we got everyone out and into the house,
Alicia said, 'I want a shower.'

Bess and Megan took an arm each and Megan said, 'We'll go
up with you.' Alicia let them lead her upstairs.

Willis and I looked at each other, then at our son. What the hell
were we supposed to do now?

Willis said, 'Son, sit down.'

'Dad, now's not the time.'

'I can't think of a better time,' Willis said. 'Please sit down.'

Graham reluctantly sat on the sofa. I sat down next to him, while
Willis took to his big comfy chair, like the king of the house on
his throne.

'Son, we've known for some time how you and Alicia felt about
each other—'

'How could you?' Graham said jumping up. 'I didn't know—'

I pulled him back down to the sofa. 'It's OK, honey,' I said. 'She
didn't know either. But the rest of us could see it.'

Graham turned pink around the ears. Willis went on, 'That's all
well and good, boy. I'm glad you two care about each other, but
there's a problem here. You two can't get physical—'

'Jeez, Dad!'

'I'm just saying, Graham. She's sixteen, you're eighteen. There's
a law.'

More than Graham's ears were pink this time. 'I'm not gonna
do anything,' he said, his voice barely a whisper.

'You're right,' Willis said, 'you're not. And to make absolutely
sure, Alicia will sleep with your mom in our bedroom, and you and
I will be upstairs. You in your room, me in Alicia's.'

'Oh my God! You don't trust me?' Graham said, on his feet yet again. I pulled him back down.

'It's not that I *dis*trust you, per se,' Willis said, 'it's that I don't trust your hormones. And I don't trust hers. This will just be until you go back to college.'

'I'm not going back,' Graham said.

'Now wait just a goddamn minute!' Willis said, jumping to his feet.

It was going to be a long night.

Mr Brown exited the freeway at a town called Columbus. It was eight o'clock in the evening and for the last forty miles Mr Jones's belly had been rumbling loud enough for Mr Brown to hear it over the engine noise of the stolen Toyota. Only a short way from the freeway they found a restaurant, Jane's, that was still open. The restaurant had a dinner buffet that was closed, but they were told they could order off the menu.

'I'm really hungry,' Mr Jones said.

'I know,' Mr Brown said.

'I think I'm gonna get the chicken fried steak. You think the chicken fried steak would be good here?' Mr Jones asked.

'I really wouldn't know. Ask the waitress.'

Mr Jones waited until the waitress came for their drink order. After ordering a Diet Coke, Mr Jones asked her, 'How's the chicken fried steak here?'

'Best in Texas,' she said in a deadpan voice.

That was when Mr Jones noticed that in the description on the menu of the chicken fried steak, it said, 'Best in Texas.' Duh! If he'd only seen that he wouldn't have had to ask! 'OK, then, I'll have the chicken fried steak, cream gravy on the side, mashed potatoes with some brown gravy, and the house salad with ranch dressing. Oh, and the sweet potato pie here?' he said, pointing at the dessert section of the menu. 'How's that?'

'Gone,' she said. 'Big lunch crowd today.'

'Oh. Whatja got left?'

'Chess pie, seven-layer chocolate cake, and banana pudding,' she said.

'You wanna split something?' Mr Jones asked Mr Brown.

Mr Brown, clenching his fists under the table, said, 'No.'

'I guess I'll have the chess pie. It any good?' he asked the waitress.

'Best in Texas,' she said. Turning to Mr Brown she said, 'You?'

'BLT and a Coke,' he said.

The waitress gave him a disgusted look and headed toward the kitchen.

EIGHT

THURSDAY

'You wanna ring the doorbell?' DeWitt asked his partner.

'No, you go ahead,' Mayfair answered.

Davis DeWitt rang the Pughs' doorbell.

It was seven o'clock at night and, like peace officers everywhere, if they had to miss dinner, *everybody* had to miss dinner.

Willis Pugh came to the door, napkin in hand. 'Detectives?'

'We need to interview Alicia Brooks, Mr Pugh,' DeWitt said.

'We're having dinner,' Pugh said.

'We'll wait. Inside or out. Your choice,' Mayfair said.

Pugh sighed. 'Come on in.' He pointed toward a room with a sectional sofa. 'Y'all can wait here until we're finished.'

Something told Mayfair this man wasn't one to be intimidated and nobody in this house would be rushing through their meal on account of DeWitt and herself.

She was right. Fifteen minutes later, Mr and Mrs Pugh, their foster child, Alicia Brooks, and a boy who Mayfair figured to be Pugh, Jr., from his resemblance to Willis Pugh, came into the room where they were sitting. She was taken aback to see her partner, DeWitt, stand up when the two females entered. She'd never seen him do that before. And he sure as hell never did it for her!

'Mrs Pugh,' DeWitt said, shaking her hand. Mayfair stood up and did the same.

Introductions were made around the room, and Mayfair was proven right when Mrs Pugh introduced the boy as their son, Graham, just in from college.

Everybody settled on the sectional sofa, and DeWitt said, 'Alicia, Chief Donaldson gave us all the information you gave him in his interview, and I hate to go over it again, but we have some questions. Are you OK with that?'

'Yes, sir,' Alicia said, and Mayfair couldn't help noticing that the girl slipped her hand into the hand of the heir to the throne – so to speak.

'OK. These two guys, they talk a lot while they had you?' DeWitt asked.

'Yes, sir, they talked some. Mostly sniping at each other. They didn't seem to get along. And Mr Jones told us later, after Mr Smith and Mr Brown left, that Mr Smith had shot him in the foot!'

'Did he say why?' DeWitt asked.

'He said Mr Smith seemed tense,' Alicia answered.

Mayfair shrugged. 'I guess being tense is *one* reason to shoot your partner.'

DeWitt snuck a quick look at her, but she wasn't making eye contact.

Sighing, DeWitt said, 'The dead guy's been identified as Max Serling, aka Mr Smith—'

'Aka?' Alicia asked.

'Also known as,' the Pugh's son answered.

'Right,' DeWitt said. 'He's a Houston resident with a pretty long rap sheet. Mostly B&E, car-jacking, and burglary. Never anything violent, if you can call car-jacking non-violent, which, personally, I don't think it is.'

'No one's asking for your personal opinion,' Mayfair said under her breath.

'Do we really have to do this here?' DeWitt whispered out of the corner of his mouth.

'I didn't say a word,' Mayfair said aloud.

'Yeah, you did!' DeWitt whispered louder.

'So, Miss Brooks, we faxed the sketch you had done of Mr Jones back to Austin to run against our facial recognition software,' Mayfair said, 'but it will take a while and there's a good chance nothing will come of it. So, can you think of anything he said or did that could help us identify him?'

'I'm thinking I could probably give a better description of him now. Maybe we should have Calvin come back out here,' Alicia said.

Inexplicitly, the other two girls, who'd been with the family coming out of the police station, appeared and the redhead said, 'Good idea!'

'Redhead' was a point Mayfair and DeWitt would discuss later – Mayfair insisting the mother was a redhead, but the daughter was a strawberry blonde, while DeWitt countered with red was red and why didn't she just shut the hell up. That issue, like so many between them, would go unresolved.

'But I'll tell you now,' Alicia said, 'I won't say a word against Mr Jones in a court of law. If it wasn't for him, Bert and I would be dead right now. Mr Jones saved our lives, at great risk to his own. Now he's off someplace with Mr Brown, and I'll tell you this, I think Mr Brown is the head guy! He's the one they called when they got the satchel. Mr Jones is a good man!' At this point, the girl burst into tears. The boy put his arms around her, patting her back. At one point she looked up, red-eyed and said, 'And I want my satchel back!'

But that was the last word they were going to get out of her that night.

Willis was true to his word. He came into our room, got his pillow and his new Dopp kit and headed upstairs, sending Alicia down.

As Alicia and I got ready for bed, the inevitable conversation arose.

'Mom, we don't have to do this,' she said.

'Do what, honey?' I asked, although I knew exactly what.

'Keep Graham and me apart at night. Mom, I'm not ready to . . . You know . . . do it.'

Well, if she couldn't say it, maybe she wasn't ready to *do it*.

'I think your dad just wants to keep the temptation to a minimum,' I said.

'But Graham and I haven't even gone on a date! Much less . . . you know.'

I sat down on the bed, pulling her down with me. 'Honey, how do you *feel* about him?'

The poor girl turned scarlet. She shrugged. 'You know,' she finally got out.

'No, honey, I don't. I have an idea, but I need you to tell me,' I said.

Alicia sighed and the extra color in her face began to fade. Finally, she looked at me and said, 'I've been in love with him since before I moved in here. Maybe it was just a crush at first, but it wouldn't go away. Even with Lotta in the picture. I love him, Mom. I can't help it.'

I hugged her. 'And you shouldn't have to. The problem is, he loves you, too—'

She grinned big. 'I know! I can tell!'

I laughed. 'And it doesn't matter if you've ever been on a date

or not, the feelings you have . . . Well, sometimes . . . often times
. . . that is . . .'

'If we're close to each other at night without supervision, we're
liable to do it,' she said.

I let out my held breath. 'You said it, honey.'

'But, Mom, he said he's not going back to school, and if he
doesn't, I can't stay down here forever. You and Dad need to be
together.'

I hugged her again. 'We'll have to work something out, sweetie.
And we will. I promise. Now, go brush your teeth.'

Megan slipped into Bess's room, making sure her dad didn't see
her. He'd left the door to Alicia's room open, but he was a heavy
sleeper, and the truth was they could have an orgy up here and
he'd never be the wiser. But she was pretty sure that wasn't going
to happen. Graham, for all his faults, had a lot of respect for their
parents, and, seeing how he felt about Alicia (of course, she'd
known about it for a long time, but to actually see it was something else!), she knew he would respect that. Maybe, she bet,
somewhere deep in his heart, he was glad Dad had done this.
Even Graham, a boy (and you know how *they* are), had to see
that Alicia wasn't ready for that. And Dad's move had taken that
temptation away.

Bess was awake, reading her world history homework, of all
things. 'What?' she said in a not unfriendly tone, but not a friendly
one either. She didn't take her eyes off her book.

'We need to talk!' Megan said, jumping on Bess's bed and
crossing her legs.

'Huh?' Bess said, acting like she was *so* engrossed in freaking
world history!

Megan put her hand on the top of the textbook and pulled it
down, thus exposing her sister's eyes. 'You really think we're not
going to talk about this?'

Bess sighed. 'I suppose you mean the whole Graham and Alicia
thing.'

'Ah, duh!' Megan replied.

Bess smiled. 'I think it was really sweet the way he came running
to the rescue like that. It was a good idea for you to call him.'

'Again, I say "duh!" If I hadn't called him, he never would have
forgiven either one of us.'

'True,' Bess said. 'I don't know why I didn't think to call him. I guess I was just so overwrought by the kidnapping.'

'Overwrought?' Megan picked up the world history book and shook it.

'What are you doing?' Bess demanded.

'Looking for the romance novel you have hidden in here. Overwrought? Only Mom uses that word, and then only in her historical romances.'

Slightly embarrassed, Bess took the offensive. 'I was worried, OK? I happen to like Alicia a lot!'

'Are you saying I don't like Alicia?' Megan demanded.

Holding her head high and not looking at her sister, she said, 'I didn't say that, but obviously you must think it, or why else would you go there?'

Megan hit her with the world history text. Bess grabbed it away and hit her back with it.

'Ouch,' Megan said.

'Yeah, ouch! Stop hitting me!' Bess said.

'I just came in here because I'm worried about the family dynamic,' Megan said.

Bess laughed. 'And you made fun of me saying "overwrought"? "Family dynamic" my ass!'

'I'm serious,' Megan said, 'and tease me all you want, but that is *exactly* what I'm worried about! Graham said he's not going back to Austin, Dad won't let him and Alicia be on the same floor at night, because of, you know,' she said, using a fairly descriptive and unpleasant hand gesture that used the index finger of one hand and a circle made of the index finger and thumb of the other. 'So does Alicia stay downstairs with Mom forever? You know Mom and Dad just made up after Dad leaving, so this can't be good for their marriage—'

'Mom and Dad will figure that out. They're tighter now than they've been in a while,' Bess said. 'Meanwhile, we still have those bad guys out there.'

Megan shrugged. 'But that's all over for us, right? I mean, they got what they wanted. We don't have to be involved anymore.'

'Ah, excuse me?' Bess said, sarcasm dripping off her tongue. 'Have you met our mother? No way is she going to leave this alone.'

'But that's why Dad left in the first place! Surely she won't get involved in this kind of thing again!' Megan said, distraught at the thought of her dad moving out again.

'Cheer up, Megs,' Bess said, playfully hitting her sister on the arm. 'At least we'll have Calvin the Beautiful again!'

Megan did immediately cheer up. 'Ooo, that's right! Yay!'

FRIDAY

It was after ten when they finally left the restaurant in Columbus, and Mr Brown figured he really didn't want to deal with the Houston problem when he was this tired, so they spent the night in a motel and, bright and early Friday morning, nine a.m., Mr Brown and Mr Jones were finally on their way. It was a long trip, about three hours total from Black Cat Ridge to Houston, if you counted the traffic in Houston, and who wouldn't count that? And as far as Mr Brown could tell, Mr Jones hadn't stopped talking once. Mostly he complained about his ex-wives. At first Mr Brown thought he was talking about just one, but then it dawned on him that – since Mr Jones complained about two different names – there might have been more than one wife. He wasn't really paying much attention, and he really didn't care how many wives Mr Jones had had.

He couldn't help thinking that since Mr Smith was dead, the fifty gees from his boss he was supposed to pay these two could easily come to him, especially if Mr Jones were to have an accident somewhere between where they were at the moment and their final destination.

It was a tad problematic, however. He couldn't shoot him and have it look like an accident. He wasn't big enough to strangle and/ or smother Mr Jones. And he didn't have any poison on him. For a while he fantasized about slamming Mr Jones on the head with something, then faking a car accident, but there were problems with that scenario, also. Like, what if the accident was worse than he planned and he got knocked out too? And, even if it went perfectly, how would he get the rest of the way to Houston? And wouldn't the Highway Patrol keep him around for questions, especially with a stolen car?

Mr Brown considered opening the passenger-side door and pushing Mr Jones out while going seventy-five miles an hour down the interstate, but there was the problem with reaching over Mr

Jones to do it, and then unlocking his seatbelt. As stupid as Mr Jones was, even he was liable to catch on to that.

Considering he still had some time, Mr Brown decided to keep thinking about it. A solution was bound to come to him.

It was a rough night. After almost twenty-five years of marriage, you get used to your partner's sleeping habits. Willis snored at about a medium decibel, and loved to throw his arm around me in his sleep and pull me close. Almost always woke me up. But sleeping with a teenaged girl was a whole different ball of wax. For one thing, she seemed to think her half of the bed was in the middle, and with those exceedingly long legs of hers, the middle became the entire bed. She didn't snore. What she did was grind her teeth and mumble. In my opinion, for what it's worth, that's much worse. I was exhausted when the alarm went off.

Even though it was Friday, we'd decided to get the girls back in school. As there apparently was no longer any danger to them, now those men had got what they wanted, there was no reason to keep them out. And I figured the sooner Alicia got back into a routine, the sooner her life could get back to normal. I'd called Luna the evening before and implored her to find Alicia's satchel. Personally, I never wanted to see the damn thing again, but Alicia loved it for some reason, and wanted it. I was determined to get it back for her.

As I came out of the bedroom to start the coffee, there was a knock on the back door. It was still locked, so I opened it. Luna stood there with the satchel.

'I had to promise Donaldson I'd bake him a cake, so you owe me. Specifically one homemade cake. You know I don't cook.'

'What flavor?' I asked, taking the satchel from her.

'Chocolate with cherries and pecans,' she said. 'Do I smell coffee?'

'Come in. It's almost ready.'

She came in and we interrupted the flow of the coffee machine to snatch two cups, doctored them, and went to the kitchen table.

'So I heard there was some drama at the station last night,' she said. 'The stars of which were Graham and Alicia.'

'Oh, God, don't start. We've got a problem on our hands. They're in love.'

Luna grinned. 'That's what you get for taking in cute strays, Pugh.'

'I heard that,' Alicia said as she shuffled in from my bedroom, hair disheveled, wearing a man's pajama top (Willis's, not Graham's), and panties. She poured a cup of coffee and came and sat down with us.

'Hey, I *said* cute,' Luna said.

'You did,' Alicia said, 'and I thank you.'

'You're welcome,' Luna said.

'Any word on the misters?' Alicia asked.

'Not a peep,' Luna said. 'But there was a possible sighting of the car on Interstate 10 headed for Houston.'

'That man, James Unger, the one who was killed at the Driscoll, he was from Houston, right?' I asked.

'Yeah. And that's where his company is.' She was silent for a moment, then pulled her cell phone out of her pocket. She hit a number and said, 'Donaldson, please, this is Luna.' She waited a minute then said, 'Chief? Hey, it's Luna. They're definitely headed for Houston. That's where James Unger lived, and where his company is. Maybe we need to be talking to his widow.'

She listened for a moment, then said, 'Yeah. I'm on my way. You call 'em, 'k?'

With the phone still pressed to her ear, she got up and walked out my back door, no goodbye.

'Goodbye!' I yelled as she headed for her car in our shared driveway. 'Rude!' I said as I took another sip of coffee. Damn, that was good. I probably needed to make another pot. This was definitely going to be a two-pot morning.

'Mom!' Alicia said and laughed, stretching those three letters to two syllables. 'She's on the hunt! Leave her alone.'

'Well, we're out of it!' I said, standing up and going to the fridge to start breakfast. But I still didn't know what was going on. And that's something that pisses me off. I really need to *know*, you know? 'Put on some pants and go upstairs and knock on your door. Tell Dad he needs to get up. I'm not sure he has his al—'

'I used my phone,' Willis said. Funny, I hadn't heard his heavy clomp on the stairs. 'Gotta take a shower.'

'Cereal or eggs?' I asked him.

'I'm starved. How about farmer's breakfast?'

'Ooo, yeah!' Alicia said. 'Do we have any tortillas?'

'I think so,' I said, checking out the shelves of the refrigerator.

'Yeah, then I can take a breakfast taco on the road!' Willis said.

I stood up. 'OK, then do you want just breakfast tacos or—'

'You have any of those canned biscuits?' he asked.

We were still in breakfast negotiations when Bess wandered in. 'We're having breakfast tacos!' Alicia told her.

Bess, who'd looked a little bedraggled, perked up. 'Really? On a Friday?'

I smiled. 'It's a celebration,' I said.

I got out bacon, cheese, eggs, a can of biscuits, the tortillas, a leftover baked potato, and the picante sauce. It was going to be a *fiesta*!

'Somebody wake up Megan,' I said.

'I'll do it!' Alicia said, running for the stairs.

I grinned at her back. 'Put on some pants first, then wake up Graham while you're up there,' I said.

'Oh, OK,' she said, as if that wasn't exactly where she was headed.

Before Willis left for work, he pulled me into the bedroom and gave me a superior kiss. Then asked, 'Did I hear you say to Alicia, and I quote, "we're out of it"?'

'Out of what?' I asked, thinking about maybe getting some more smooches.

'This Unger mess.'

'Oh,' I said. 'Yes, I said that. And we are.'

He looked at me, his head slightly tilted, like a dog eyeing something interesting. 'You're not dying inside to know what the hell's going on?'

'All I know is the girls are safe and we're well out of it,' I said, wishing I meant it, and headed to the bed to straighten the covers.

'If you're trying to ignore this for my sake—' he started.

'Not at all,' I said, keeping my back to him as I fixed the bed, afraid he'd see the lie in my eyes.

I guess he didn't need to see my eyes. 'You're full of crap,' he said, a smile in his voice. 'You wanna dive into this with both feet, don't you?'

'I have no idea what you mean,' I tried again.

He came up behind me and kissed my neck. 'You have my permission to get as involved in this as you'd like—' he started.

I swirled around. 'You're *permission*? Did you just say you gave me your *permission*?'

He backed away. 'Ah, maybe I misspoke,' he said, heading for the door. With his hand on the knob, he said, 'But you do have it!'

And then made a beeline out the bedroom door and through the kitchen to the back door, laughing his head off.

'OK, so what are we gonna do in Houston?' Mr Jones asked Mr Brown.

'Gotta meet with the big boss. Give him the flash drive,' Mr Brown said.

'I thought you were the big boss,' Mr Jones said.

Mr Brown snorted. 'Hardly. This is some big, hairy deal going down. I'm just the hired help, like you and Smith, except the big boss hired me and I hired you – which makes me, technically, your boss.'

'What's on that flash drive thing anyway?' Mr Jones asked.

Mr Brown shrugged. 'That's above our pay grade. Need to know basis only.'

'Huh?' Mr Jones asked.

Mr Brown sighed. 'God, you're stupid,' he said, rather good-naturedly for him. 'You ever serve?'

'Serve what?' Mr Jones asked, totally confused at this point.

'Your country, man! Your goddamn country! You ever serve?'

'Oh, you mean like the army or something?' Mr Jones asked.

Again Mr Brown sighed. 'Yeah, Jones, I mean like the army or something.'

'No. I tried once but I couldn't pass the test – you know, the written one?'

'Yeah,' Brown said, pretty sure he believed the truth in that statement. 'Well, I did. USMC. Served in the first Iraq war. Got a purple heart.' He pounded on his thigh. 'Schrapnal,' he said. 'Looked like hamburger for a while there. Had to put the skin of a pig on my thigh.' He laughed heartily. 'But don't try to throw me!'

Mr Jones said, 'Huh?'

'Pig skin?' Mr Brown said. 'Like a football? Don't try to *throw* me, get it?'

'Oh, yeah sure.' Mr Jones laughed. 'Funny,' he said.

'Not when you have to explain it.'

They drove in silence for a while, then Mr Brown said, 'Look, when we get there, I think it would be best if you stayed in the car, you know? This guy, he doesn't want that many people seeing his face and, fact of the matter, it's a pretty ugly face. I think you'd be safer staying in the car.'

'What about you?' Mr Jones asked. 'You've seen his face? Is that gonna be a problem for you?'

'Naw, I should be OK,' Mr Brown said, although there wasn't a lot of confidence in his voice.

'Well, just leave the keys, in case he kills you or something,' Mr Jones said.

NINE

FRIDAY

'OMG!' D'Wanda whisper-screamed. 'Is she OK?'

'She's fine,' Megan said. 'But guess what?'

'What?' Azalea asked breathlessly.

'I called Graham and he came home immediately, and he and Alicia have declared their love!'

D'Wanda looked at her twin, who appeared crestfallen.

Megan covered her mouth with her hand, then removed it and touched Azalea on the arm. 'OMG, Az, I'm so sorry! I've been so wrapped up in this whole drama—'

'That's OK,' Azalea said. 'It's not like he even knew I was alive.'

'Oh, that's not true—' Megan started, but D'Wanda interrupted. 'Don't, Megan. No way you're gonna make it better.' She punched her twin on the arm. 'Get over it, Azalea. He don't love you, never did, never will. But there's more fish than him in the sea.' She pointed with her head to the other side of the cafeteria. 'See Logan over there? He be watching you like a hawk, girl.'

'I don't even know Logan, and how do you know he's watching me and not you? We're identical!'

''Cause he be looking at you right now!' D'Wanda, who liked to pretend she came from the mean streets of Houston or Austin, or at the very least Codderville, rather than a forty-five-hundred-square-foot house on Storybook Lane in the affluent community of Black Cat Ridge, said.

Azalea looked over at Logan, who quickly looked away. Azalea's eyes went back to the tabletop and what was left of her lunch. 'He's not Graham,' she said in a small voice.

Megan patted her on the back and shared an eye-roll with D'Wanda over her twin's lowered head.

FRIDAY
VERA'S STORY

The lobby was teaming with people: some of them with our Baptist meeting and some of them not. You could tell the Baptists by their choice of attire. No fancy Armani suits on our men or those red-soled tramp heels for our ladies. We looked like normal Americans in polyester pantsuits and button-down shirts. Gerald and I found what they call a 'conversation nook' (I found this out on HGTV – so cable is good for something), sat down on a really soft leather sofa, and put the two pieces of paper side by side on the coffee table – the note left on Rachael's bed when her belongings were spirited away, and her signature on the bill at The Salon. And sure enough, they were not a match. Not even close.

Me and Gerald just looked at each other. Finally I said, 'Oh, goodness. I think something really happened to her.'

'I think you're right,' he said, staring at the two writing specimens. 'Should we tell Brother Joe?'

I shook my head. 'No,' I said, 'let me think on this some.'

He nodded and we headed off to choir practice. Our concert was to be tomorrow night and we still had a lot of rehearsing to do. Gerald had a duet with a woman from the Louisiana church, and they practiced that up to lunch. I tried calling E.J. again, and just when I started to hang up, she picked up the phone.

When she said 'hello,' I said, 'Well, it's about time you answered your phone!'

'Hello to you too, Vera. Hope you're having a lovely—'

'Not so much, no,' I said. 'I think my roommate's been murdered.'

Mr Jones sat outside in the stolen vehicle, waiting for Mr Brown. It was a great big house in River Oaks, where most of the Houston millionaires lived. Mr Jones, of course, was not aware that the house was an architectural mishmash of Greek revival, Georgian, and Federalist, with a touch of Beaux Arts. He only knew it was big and what he thought of as pretty.

Mr Brown had been inside for close to half an hour, and Mr Jones wasn't sure at what point he should move to the driver's side and take off. He thought it might take Mr Big (whoever he was) more than half an hour to kill Mr Brown, but he wasn't sure. On the other hand, he didn't want to be a sitting duck out here in the driveway if Mr Big's henchmen came looking for him. And, on the third hand, if he had one, he *was* sitting in a stolen car. Stolen out of Hicksville. He wondered how long it would take for the Houston cops to find out a car was stolen from the sticks. Then the front door of the mansion opened and Mr Brown stuck his head out. He motioned for Mr Jones to come to him.

Mr Jones wondered if it was a trap. But if he didn't go in, he wouldn't get his twenty-five gees, and God knew he needed that money. His kids needed braces. His ex-wife was gonna sue if she didn't get back child support, and he saw this sweet ride he could get for less than ten grand, and God also knew he needed a new ride.

So Mr Jones got out of the stolen vehicle parked in Mr Big's driveway and headed to the front door of the house. Those front doors were the first of many affluent impressions Mr Jones received on his way to meet Mr Big. The doors were ornately carved and half a foot thick. The entry where Mr Brown received him was black-and-white-checked marble with an ornately carved archway leading into a two-story-high rotunda with a stained-glass ceiling.

'Close your mouth, Mr Jones,' Mr Brown said. 'You're gawking.'

'Jeez,' Mr Jones said, 'this place is awesome!'

Mr Brown led Mr Jones to yet another ornately carved door to the right of the rotunda, and knocked. Not waiting for a reply, he opened the door and ushered Mr Jones in.

Mr Jones tried not to look at the room, but at the people in it. He thought that would be the polite thing to do, but his eyes seemed to go straight to the room itself – creamy marble floors with old but cool rugs, silky-looking fabric walls, brocade-covered sedans and love seats. He willed himself to look at the people. There were three in the room: a woman sitting on a love seat, hands in her lap clutching a wad of tissues, her eyes red and swollen; a big man, even bigger than Mr Jones himself, by the French doors leading outside, standing stiffly, legs parted, hands clasped in front of him, and a third man. He immediately identified Mr Big. He was the short guy by the fireplace, wearing blue jeans from the nineties with lots of strategic holes in them, a white Polo shirt and leather sandals.

He was bald as an egg with dark brown eyes and bushy black eyebrows. Mr Jones knew he was Mr Big because he was the only one who spoke.

'So, Mr Jones,' he said in a heavy foreign accent, 'we meet at last. Thank you for your part in completing this mission.'

'You're welcome,' Mr Jones said, suppressing a giggle. The guy sounded just like the villain in the last James Bond movie he'd seen.

'Now I suppose you expect me to pay you,' Mr Big said.

'Ah, well, yeah, I guess,' Mr Jones said, hoping that was the right answer.

Mr Big laughed and moved away from the fireplace, coming up to Mr Jones and hugging him. Since his head only reached Mr Jones's breastbone, it was a bit awkward.

'Of course you are!' Mr Big said, slapping him on the back.

Mr Jones smiled widely, glancing at Mr Brown, who smirked back at him.

'But that will have to wait,' Mr Big said, giving Mr Jones a sad look. 'Your work is not yet completed, I am sorry to say.'

'Do what?' I said.

'Murdered,' Vera repeated. 'At least, that's what me and Gerald think.'

'Gerald?' I said.

'Never mind that. Do you want me to tell you what's been going on?' Vera asked.

I wanted to say no. I really did. Wasn't it enough that my daughter had been stalked, our house broken into, and said daughter kidnapped? And I was beginning to wonder if it really was over. I felt I had a vested interested in helping to catch these assholes who kidnapped my daughter and put the entire family at risk. And besides, Willis had given me his permission. Don't tell him I said that. I didn't need my mother-in-law making up fairy-tale murders because she was secretly bored with the Southern Baptists. But on the other hand, Vera has been there for me so many times in the past, I couldn't blow her off.

'Yes, of course,' I said instead.

So then she told me all about her roommate Rachael Donley, how she came to *be* her roommate, what she thought she might be doing with Brother Joe, and how she – Vera – felt about Brother

Joe, about the trip to the Wal-Mart, and finally to Rachael's disappearance.

'I'm sure she'll show up, Vera,' I said. 'If she's as loose as you say she is, maybe she found some hot guy in the lobby—'

'I never did say she was loose!' Vera shot back. 'I said I thought she might be making time with Brother Joe, and her not even separated yet. I didn't say nothing about her picking up strange men in the lobby! Besides, that's not the end of it, if you'll stop interrupting me!'

'Sorry,' I said, and sat down in an easy chair. I had a feeling it was going to be a long call.

So then I heard about Rachael coming back without being seen and taking all her belongings and leaving a note about a friend being sick.

'So, then she's OK,' I said, trying to stop the flow.

'If you'd ever close your mouth for more than two seconds you'd have heard that no she's not OK!' Vera fairly shouted at me. Vera at times – and those times were usually around me – had a surly disposition, but this was over the top even for her.

'Tell me,' I said. And she did. By the time she was through I was itching all over.

It's a disease, this puzzle-solving business of mine. I get physical symptoms when something's up that I need to solve. I've been this way since I was a child. When my sister Cheryl – the one closest to me in age – would lie to me, which was whenever she opened her mouth, I had to find out the truth or I'd start itching, which would move into hyperactivity, followed by sweating, low blood sugar, and, I suppose – if I ever let it go that far – eventual death.

I was fairly certain something *had* happened to Vera's roommate – if everything Vera told me was the truth. Vera didn't lie, but she was getting up in years and there could be some senility-based confusion going on here. Not that she'd shown any signs, but this trip could have upset her mental balance. And besides, I had my own case to worry about – I had my own bad guys.

'So you need to go to the authorities,' I finally told Vera.

'What authorities? Brother Joe as head of our delegation? Or the hotel security? Or straight to the police?' she asked.

'I'd start with Brother Joe,' I suggested. 'Let him notify the police.'

There was such a long silence on Vera's end of the line that I finally said, 'Ah, you still there?'

'Yes,' she said, her voice clearly agitated. 'Here's the thing,' she said, then said nothing.

'Vera?'

She sighed. 'I just don't trust Brother Joe.'

'Why?' I asked.

'I don't know!' she all but yelled at me. 'He's just – I don't know. Untrustworthy-ish.'

'Untrustworthy-ish? Is there such a word?' I said, almost laughing.

'Don't you start with that "I have a degree in English so therefore I'm better than you" stuff you like to pull!' she said. 'I'm trying to convey my feelings to you, *Eloise*,' she said, pulling out the dreaded name card and actually emphasizing it. 'And my feeling is that I'm not sure I can trust Brother Joe. Like I said, he'd been making googly eyes at Rachael for several weeks now. So if he was, well, you know—'

'Doing the horizontal mambo with her?' I suggested.

'I was gonna say "involved," but you will take the low road whenever possible, won't you, Eloise?'

Again with the name calling. 'So what you're saying,' I suggested as lewdly as possible, yet staying within reason, 'is that if Brother Joe was banging Sister Rachael, then maybe he's not the one to go to with your suspicions because maybe they had a lover's quarrel and he offed her.'

Vera sighed heavily over the phone line. 'Something like that.'

'So who's Gerald?' I asked.

'He's in the choir,' she said.

'And you've taken him into your confidence?' I asked, trying to keep any signs of my inner thoughts to myself. My inner thoughts being: Vera and Gerald, sitting in a tree, k-i-s-s-i-n-g . . .

'I needed to talk to somebody, and my only real friend in the choir is Gladys – Mrs Cook – who was supposed to be my roommate, but she came down with that flu that's going around. Anyway, he had some good ideas, like going to the beauty shop to compare handwriting. That's all.'

The 'that's all' was said rather tentatively. I couldn't help adding to myself, 'First comes love, then comes marriage—' But then there was that whole 'baby carriage' business and that was just so wrong in so many ways.

'Now what do I do?' Vera asked.

That was a good question. I wondered how quickly I could fly to D.C.? Or was that just sublimation?

It was Bess's day to drive so she hoisted herself up into the driver's side of the minivan and buckled up, ready to head home. Megan had shotgun, and Alicia sat in the middle seat in the second row so she could participate in any discussion that might occur. It didn't take long for Megan to start up.

'Alicia, I want you to know that Azalea is grief-stricken over you and Graham professing your love for one another,' she said.

Alicia's entire body turned crimson. 'Oh my God! You didn't tell her, did you?' she screeched.

'How else would she know?' Megan asked in all innocence.

'God, Megan,' Bess said, turning to look at her sister, thus taking her eyes off the road. 'That's family business! You had no right to tell anybody!'

'Oh my God!' Alicia wailed yet again. 'Do you think she'll tell anybody?'

'Probably not,' Megan said.

Alicia let out a sigh and said, 'Thank God!'

'But D'Wanda was there and she's the biggest gossip in school, so it's probably all over the place by now,' Megan said.

Alicia burst into tears. 'I have to quit school now!' she wailed. 'Everybody's going to think I'm dating my brother!'

'Well, duh,' Megan said. 'You are!'

FRIDAY
VERA'S STORY

I met up with Gerald in the lobby at lunchtime. We sat at a table by the window, away from everybody else and I said, 'I talked to my daughter-in-law this morning.'

'Oh, right, she's the one who gets involved in all the murders, right?' he asked.

'How did you know that?' I said, surprised. It wasn't a secret, but it wasn't broadcast news either.

Gerald touched my hand where it lay on the table. 'People talk, Vera,' he said.

Not wanting to, I slowly removed my hand. 'Even more now, if they see that,' I said, and could feel myself blushing.

'Just you and me sitting here alone together's gonna have tongues wagging,' Gerald said with a smile. 'Might as well enjoy it.'

I'm not sure where it came from, but a giggle escaped my lips. I got myself together and said, 'Well, anyway, E.J. – that's my daughter-in-law,' I said, and he nodded. 'She thinks we need to notify the authorities but I'm not sure who to notify. I suppose we should tell Brother Joe—'

'Uh uh,' Gerald said. 'I don't trust him.'

I coulda kissed him I felt so good he agreed. I mean that figuratively. 'So the hotel or straight to the police?' I asked.

'Straight to the police,' he said. 'And I think we should go down there instead of calling them to come to the hotel. We don't want to make a scene at the convention.'

'Absolutely,' I said. 'And we can take the two notes, and her contact stuff.'

'Good thinking,' Gerald said.

I called Willis at work. It took me much less time to tell him about his mother's adventure than it had taken her to tell me. She does like to talk.

'So I thought I'd fly to Washington—'

Willis actually laughed. 'You're out of your mind,' he said.

'Why?' I shot back, hands on hip.

'Because the girls need you right now. Because we have Romeo and Juliet under our roof at the moment and I need you right now. Because Graham needs you right now.'

'You're right,' I said. 'And your mom really deserves some alone time with Gerald. I'm sure there's no way he can get his hands on Viagra away from home like he is.'

There was dead air for about half a minute, then my husband said, 'Was she on her cell phone or do I need to call the hotel?'

'Willis, your mother's a grown woman—'

'Uh uh!' he said, his voice rising. 'She's my mother! She's the grandmother of almost grown kids! She is *not* this Gerald person's plaything!'

I couldn't help it. I started laughing. The fact that he didn't understand my laughter made me laugh that much harder.

*   *   *

Clarissa Mayfair knocked on the motel-room door. Davis DeWitt opened it. Mayfair pushed past him and sat on a straight-back chair at the small table by the window.

'What do you want?' DeWitt asked her, sitting down at the end of his bed.

'Got a call from Lewis,' she said, naming another detective in Austin. 'He called Mrs Unger's house and left a message, but no response.'

'So why did you need to come in here to tell me that?' DeWitt asked.

'Because I wanted to jump your bones,' Mayfair said sarcastically. But not sarcastically enough. For a split second DeWitt seemed to be contemplating the offer. Jeez, men! Mayfair thought. 'In your dreams,' she said, to which he replied, 'You mean my worst nightmare,' to which she replied, 'Bite me,' to which he replied, 'It would probably make me sick.'

Mayfair got up from the table and moved to the door. 'I was going to ask if you wanted to go to Houston to talk to Mrs Unger directly, but I *really* don't want to be alone with you for that long. I might die of exposure to that much stupidity.'

DeWitt stood up, nodding his head. 'That's an idea. Did you run it by the Houston loo?'

'No! I'm not rude enough to do that without talking to you first, asshole!'

'Sure you are,' DeWitt said.

Mayfair opened the motel-room door. 'You call him. I'm gonna go find some lunch,' she said, and left the room.

VERA'S STORY
FRIDAY

'You think we can ditch the luncheon here?' I whispered to Gerald as we got up from our table in the lobby.

'You wanna grab something on the way to the police department?' Gerald asked me.

'You bet!' I said, more than ready to leave the hotel. I was getting cabin fever big time.

Outside it was a nice fall day, with some leaves on the trees beginning to change. We don't exactly have seasons back home. What we have is hotter than blazes, even hotter, a little less hot, then hey, it's freezing out there, and damn, here comes the heat again. And what's freezing to us and what's freezing to a Yankee can be really different. Although I've had enough schooling to know that freezing is anything under thirty-two degrees Fahrenheit, 'freezing' back home is anything under fifty degrees, and 'hot' is above ninety, and 'damn hot' is over one hundred. When we've had more than a month straight of over one hundred degrees Fahrenheit, it's called 'hotter than blazes.' Now think about that when you call us sissies for being cold at fifty degrees. Just saying. And then y'all have to put up with winter for months on end, while we just get a little dab of it every now and then. Now that I'm older, the heat doesn't bother me nearly as much as the cold. I like to know that it may actually *say* thirty-two degrees on the register by my bird feeder, but that it'll probably be in the sixties by mid-afternoon. So anyway, sorry, but I get sorta P.O.'d with my Facebook friends and their weather chauvinism.

I brought a light jacket with me, along with the notes and the contact stuff in a bag, and we got directions from the desk about how to get to the police station and, lo and behold! Those directions took us to the subway! It's called something else in D.C., but to me it's just a subway, which is what they got in New York and I've never been on one because, truth be told, this was only my third trip out of Texas and I've never been further east than New Orleans. So I was excited about going to the subway, until we got to the opening and there was this escalator going down so deep I couldn't even see the bottom! I couldn't help myself – I grabbed Gerald's arm.

'I'm not going down there! It looks like the bowels of Hell!' I said.

He laughed and patted my hand where it rested on his arm. 'I've been to this exact location before, Vera, and that's not the bowels of Hell. It's just where we buy our ticket cards for the metro. Then we'll go a little further down to the platforms.'

'Sweet Jesus,' I said under my breath.

'Just hold my arm and we'll step off together, OK?' he said.

So we tried that and I didn't fall and he was right, it wasn't the bowels of Hell. It was clean with tall ceilings so I didn't feel claustrophobic, and you bought the ticket cards through this machine and then used the cards to go through turnstiles to get to the stairs going down to the platform. That was a little scarier. Trains going this way and that really fast and, I gotta say, I just held on to Gerald like he was my lifeline.

It was an interesting experience and one I hoped I'd be more adept at on the way back. We got off two blocks before the police station with the hopes of walking there and finding a restaurant where we could eat. We found one not too far from where we came up that said 'Home Cooking' right on the sign, so we went in.

I knew right then how my friend Cecile felt that time I talked her into going to my all-white Baptist Church. Because this was an all-black restaurant. And boy, the stares we got. I could feel Gerald pulling a little on my arm, like he wanted to leave, but I was hungry and couldn't think of any good reason why I couldn't eat where I was.

So I said to a waitress who stood there staring at me, 'Think you might have a table for a little old white lady from Texas and her companion?'

And the waitress laughed. All the tension seemed to seep out of the room, and Gerald's hold on my arm relaxed. 'Sure, honey,' the waitress said. 'Y'all come on over here and sit.' She handed us some menus and said, 'What part of Texas you from?'

'Little bitty place called Codderville, 'bout halfway between Austin and Houston,' I said.

'Yeah? I got me a cousin who lives in Houston! I've been there a couple times. Rockin' good town,' she said. 'What j'all want to drink?'

'You ever heard of sweet tea?' I asked her.

She reared her head back and laughed. 'Honey, I was born and bred in the state of Maryland and I think we done invented sweet tea.'

'No, now, I think that was Texas, but this is your place so I'll let you have it. Gerald, you want sweet tea?'

Looking at the waitress, Gerald said, 'Yes, ma'am, thank you.'

'I'll go get those teas while you two check out the menu. Oh, and today's specials are on that board there,' she said, pointing at a small blackboard set atop the counter where single patrons were eating.

She went away and I tried staring at the board. 'Can you read that?' I asked Gerald.

'Not hardly,' he said, squinting.

'It's chicken and dumplings or fried chicken and waffles, with peach cobbler for dessert,' said a lady sitting a table over. 'I had to get Martha to read it to me earlier. Can't see that far no more.'

'I'm telling ya,' I said. 'If I could have one thing back from my youth it would be my vision.' I thought a moment, and added, 'That might be a close second to high boobs.'

The lady laughed. 'Ah, baby, I'd settle for an ass that didn't go around the block!'

I laughed with her, but couldn't help sneaking a peek at her behind. She was right.

'Well, I want the chicken and dumplings,' I told Gerald, and he replied, 'I'm gonna try the chicken and waffles. That sounds good.'

And they both were. I tried some of his fried chicken and waffles and he tried some of my chicken and dumplings, and then we both had peach cobbler for desert.

When Martha the waitress brought us the check, I asked her, 'You sure you don't wanna leave here and move to Codderville with us? Open a little restaurant there and I'd be your first permanent customer.'

'Oh, now, honey, I ain't movin' to no small town. I gotta be in the big city, 'cause I got the moves!' she said, and did something with her arms and hips and pelvis that seemed to prove she wasn't lying.

TEN

All Mr Jones wanted was his twenty-five gees and his own bed. But that's not what he got. He didn't get his money, or his own bed. What he got was a shared room with two queen-sized beds – just like a hotel room, he thought – and Mr Brown.

'Why we staying here? I really want to go home,' Mr Jones said to Mr Brown.

'Shut up,' Mr Brown said, and began looking around the room.

'What are you doing?' Mr Jones asked, following Mr Brown.

'Jesus! Will you sit down?' Mr Brown snarled, shoving Mr Jones down on one of the beds.

Mr Jones bounced right back up. 'Don't you go shoving me!' he said to Mr Brown, shoving *him* on the other bed.

Mr Brown bounced back up. The beds both had very good springs.

'You don't lay a finger on me, asshole! Never! You understand me?' Mr Brown shouted, his index finger digging into Mr Jones's chest.

In Mr Jones's defense, he'd had a rough couple of days. And it was really just a reflex that made him grab that index finger and bend it backward until he heard it snap.

Mr Brown's eyes grew wide; he grabbed his broken finger with his other hand, and sank to his knees. His mouth was open, but no sound was coming out, as he fell face first onto the lovely Oriental rug that covered the bedroom floor, out like a light. Mr Jones decided that Mr Brown actually had a very low pain threshold. Who'd have thought it?

Mr Jones, being basically a nice guy, pulled down the covers on the bed he designated as Mr Brown's – closest to the door, in case anyone came in shooting – and picked up Mr Brown and laid him on the bed. He took off his shoes and socks, although he did regret taking off the socks, and tucked him in.

Then *he*, Mr Jones, began to peruse the room. He checked out the one window, as a possible escape route. It was nailed shut. Mr Jones wasn't sure why, but he didn't like that. Not a bit. He had a Leatherman tool in his pocket, found a pry bar-type instrument, and proceeded to dig out the nails. Then he unlocked the window and attempted to raise it. With a little nudge from someone as large as Mr Jones, it began to come up, although it was sticking in places. Mr Jones had already taken note of the taper candles in cut-glass sticks on the dresser. He grabbed one and greased the inside frame of the window liberally with candle wax. He continued his work until the window was all the way up and would go up and down smoothly and without a sound. Then he shut it and went to the nearest bed, which he had designated as his own, and sat on it, wondering what Mr Big had in store for the rest of the day.

VERA'S STORY
FRIDAY

We left and headed the rest of the way to the police station. It was a rainbow collision the few blocks it took us to get to the police station. Whites, blacks, Hispanics, Asians, and all assortment of Middle Easterners. Never seen so many foreign-looking people in my whole life.

I gotta say this D.C. police station wasn't what I expected. The only thing I know about police stations is what I see on TV, and this surely didn't look like that place on *NYPD Blue*, which is as close as this lady has ever been to a police station. I've had to bail E.J. out of jail a time or two, but I've always done that over the phone. This place in the country's capital was not what I expected. It was modern. Well, modern when I was a young lady anyway. Very 1950s. Light wood and Formica, vinyl tile floors, and fluorescent lighting. It was very noisy and hectic. People in uniforms rushing around, some of them dragging handcuffed people with them, a lady sitting in a chair screaming for no apparent reason, two little children jumping up and down on visitors' chairs.

'Who should we ask for?' Gerald asked me as we approached the window. 'Missing persons or homicide?'

'Let's call it what we know it is,' I said. 'Homicide.'

When the man on crutches in front of us left the window, we stepped up.

'We'd like to speak to someone in the homicide department,' Gerald said.

The woman behind the window was looking at a computer screen, not at us, and said, still without looking, 'Has someone been murdered?' in a dead monotone.

'Well, we think so,' Gerald said.

'No thinking about it!' I interjected. 'She's dead all right.'

The woman looked up. 'Well, which is it?' she asked. 'Real dead or just a little bit dead?'

'A friend of ours is missing and we have reason to believe foul play is involved,' Gerald said.

'How long this friend be missing?' the woman asked.

'Two days,' Gerald said.

'Elevator's over there. Take it to the third floor, see missing persons. Next!'

'No, we want homicide—' I started, but the lady interrupted me. 'Then show up with a dead body. Next!'

I was muttering under my breath as Gerald took my arm and led me to the elevator. 'We'll see what they have to say,' he said.

'Hmph,' I said.

There was another window when we got to the missing persons department and we told the lady there – who was about twelve and didn't seem all that bright – about our problem. 'Have a seat,' she said. We did, and watched her. She didn't get up to go tell somebody we were sitting there; she didn't use the phone to tell somebody we were sitting there; all she appeared to be doing was texting on her cell phone. I tried to talk myself into believing she was texting somebody that we were sitting out there. I didn't fall for it.

Finally, after about fifteen minutes, another woman came to stand behind the girl at the window and actually looked at us. She said something to the girl, who glanced at us and blushed.

The other woman opened the door to the side of the window and said, 'I'm so sorry you've been kept waiting,' and came out to greet us. Me and Gerald stood up and we all shook hands. 'I'm Melissa Vernon. I'm a missing persons detective. How can I help you, Mr and Mrs?'

'Oh, no, ma'am,' Gerald said quickly. Maybe a little too quickly. 'This is Mrs Vera Pugh, and I'm her friend, Gerald Norris.'

'OK, Mr Norris. Mrs Pugh, is it?'

I nodded.

'Why don't you come back to my desk and we'll talk,' Melissa Vernon said, and held open the door for us.

She led us through a bullpen of sorts. All the desks were facing one direction, to the right as you come in the door – nine of 'em, three to a row, about five of 'em occupied at that moment. At the back of the room was a desk sitting all alone, turned toward the others. This was the one she led us to. There were two chairs flanking this desk – I noticed the others only had one chair each.

She was a pretty woman in her late forties, early fifties, maybe, about twenty to thirty pounds overweight, with graying blonde hair, amber-colored eyes, a strong chin, and a crooked overbite. She was wearing those high-top boy's tennis shoes with a nice polyester pantsuit in a muted lavender.

We got settled, denied the offer of refreshments, and then finally got down to business.

Graham burst into Megan's room. 'What the fuck were you thinking?' he yelled at her.

'Don't you come barging in here screaming at me! What are you talking about?'

'Telling those twins our family business!' Graham shouted.

Megan's shoulders fell. She understood now that she'd done a bad thing, but it hadn't even crossed her mind that she shouldn't tell the twins. She told them everything. 'Sorry,' she said, then stuck her nose back into her iPad.

Graham slapped the iPad out of her hand. 'Sorry's not gonna cut it!' he said, his words soft and kind of scary.

He'd left the door open and Alicia and Bess rushed in.

'Graham, please don't!' Alicia said, grabbing his arm. 'It just happened. I know she didn't mean any harm by it.'

'Ha!' he said, staring daggers at his sister. 'Don't bet on it. She's not stupid, but she is mean.'

Megan burst into tears, which made Bess run to the bed and put her arms around her. 'Graham! You leave her alone!' she shouted at her brother.

'I'm not mean!' Megan wailed. 'And I am too stupid!' She hid her face in Bess's hair.

'Graham!' Alicia said, tears starting up. 'Don't do this! I won't come between you and your sisters! I won't! I swear I'll leave!'

And she burst into tears, and with Bess already crying because of Megan, that meant Graham was standing in front of a bed full of crying women.

'My God, boy, what did you do?' said Willis from the doorway.

Graham turned to his father with wide, fearful eyes. 'Not enough to cause this,' he half-whispered.

'I just hope you didn't break them.'

'Dad!'

'Girls!' Willis said upon entering Megan's room. 'What's going on?'

Megan, between sobs, said, 'Graham hates me! And I deserve it!'

'No you don't!' Alicia, also between sobs, said. 'You couldn't help it!'

'Yes, she could,' Bess said, drying her eyes.

'Bess!' Alicia wailed, and Megan began to cry harder.

Their dad asked, 'OK, Bess, what's going on?'

She stood up and headed for the door. 'It's not for me to tell, Dad. This is between the three of them. I'm outta here.' She went down the hall to her room, and they could hear her door slam shut.

'OK, Graham,' Willis said. 'What did you do?'

'I didn't do jack-shit, Dad!'

'Obviously you did something! We have two crying women here.'

Megan stood up, almost knocking over Alicia. 'He didn't do anything, Dad,' she said, still sobbing, 'I . . . I did! I . . . did a terr . . . ible thing, Daddy,' she said, and fell into her father's arms.

Looking at Graham, Willis said, 'Call your mother up here. Now,' as he patted Megan's back and then said, 'There, there,' a lot.

VERA'S STORY
FRIDAY

It hadn't gone all that well with the missing persons lady, Melissa Vernon. She'd taken down the information all right, but I felt like she just thought we were a couple of senile old coots who, if they ever actually had a friend named Rachael Donley, had simply misplaced her. We left the police station, both of us depressed because we knew we'd get no help from them.

It was getting on toward late afternoon, but the sun was still out and it was warmish, so we found a little park on the way to the metro, and decided to rest our feet when, really, I felt we were resting our souls.

'Well, that was disappointing,' I said.

'She did seem to be a bit patronizing, didn't she?' Gerald said.

'A bit,' I said, trying to keep the sarcasm out of my voice.

'What do we do now?'

I shrugged. 'Don't rightly know,' I said. 'I guess I could call E.J. again.'

'Well, now, Vera,' he said, 'she's all the way back in Texas, and we're here in the nation's capital. I think we need to figure this out for ourselves.'

'And how do you propose we do that?' I asked.

'Well,' he said, frowning deeply. 'We got any suspects?'

'Only Brother Joe,' I said.

'Why do we suspect him?' Gerald asked.

'Because he was fiddling with her,' I said.

'And why would he want to kill her for that?' Gerald asked.

I looked him in the eye. He wasn't being mean; he actually wanted to know.

'Got a lot of possible reasons,' I said. 'One: she was breaking up with him; two: she wouldn't break up with him; three: she was gonna tell the deacons that he was a fornicator *and* an adulterer; four— Well, I don't have a four.'

'Four: maybe she found out something she shouldn't oughta have,' Gerald said, the frown gone from his brow.

'You got a five?' I asked him, grinning.

'Yes. Five: maybe they knew each other before,' he offered.

'OK,' I said, standing up. 'Which one of those should we tackle first?'

I heard Graham call me and went to the bottom of the stairs. 'What?' I said, slightly irritated. I hate it when the kids scream at me from upstairs rather than just come down and speak to me directly.

'We need you up here,' Graham said, standing at the head of the stairs.

That's when I heard the crying. Oh, shit, I thought. What now?

I made it upstairs and into Megan's room, where I found Megan clinging to her father and crying, and Alicia prone on the bed, also crying.

'Where's Bess?' I asked Graham. Where there were two crying girls, there was usually a third.

'She got disgusted with the scene and went to her bedroom,' Graham said.

Between Megan's sobs I could hear my husband saying, 'There, there,' as he patted her on the back. 'Go,' I said, shoving Graham toward the stairs. 'You, too,' I said to Willis, detaching him from a weeping Megan. 'Shut the door on your way out,' I said and pulled Megan to the bed.

I got Alicia in a sitting position, still sobbing, and sat between the two, one arm over each. I let them cry it out. Then, as the crying became less heated, I said, 'Somebody needs to tell me what's going on.'

Megan let out a shuddering sigh. 'It's all my fault,' she said.

'Megs, don't!' Alicia said, her lower lip quivering.

'It is, Alicia.' She turned to me like I was a French revolutionary and she was Marie Antoinette. 'I did a terrible thing. I told the twins about Alicia and Graham, and D'Wanda's a big gossip and it's going to get all over school, and everybody will think Alicia's dating her brother, for God's sake, and then she'll get ostracized and it's all my fault! I wasn't thinking!' At which point she fell on my lap, bawling.

'It won't be that bad,' Alicia said, her lower lip quivering a bit more than it had earlier.

'And Graham hates me!' Megan said to my nether regions. 'He came in here and I thought he was going to kill me, literally!' She lifted her face to look into mine. 'Mom, I was really scared!'

'He would never hurt you—' Alicia started, grabbing Megan's arm.

Megan pulled away and removed herself from my lap. 'Oh, hell he wouldn't!' she said. 'Anybody messes with his precious Alicia can just forget about it!'

Alicia stood up, too, wiping her eyes. 'OK,' she said. 'Then that's how it is.' Looking at me, she said, 'Mom, if I can borrow some money, I'll go stay in a motel tonight, and I'll move all my stuff out over the weekend.'

'Where do you think you're going?' I asked her.

'I have friends I can stay with,' she said.

'Name them,' I said.

'What?' she said, frowning.

'I want the names and addresses of these friends' – and, yes, I used air quotes – 'you'll be staying with.'

'It doesn't matter,' she said, walking to the door and opening it.

As she left the room, Megan looked at me. 'I wonder sometimes how differently my life would have turned out if the Lesters hadn't lived next door,' she said.

'Yeah, you and me both,' came from the door, where Bess stood. 'Girls—'

They both turned their backs on me.

I left Megan in her room, shutting the door behind me at her request. The doors to all three girls' rooms were closed. The door to Graham's room was open, and I peaked in. Graham was not in attendance. I stepped inside and sat on his bed, my head in my hands. How had the Graham/Alicia drama come back to the Lesters? Hell, it always did. Everything always came back to the Lesters.

I always thought Willis and I had done the right thing, keeping an open and free discussion about Bess's birth family going all these years. But maybe it had been a mistake. Then again, how could we have kept what happened a secret? The whole world – well, our world – knew about it. 'Massacre on Sagebrush Trail' had been the headline of the Codderville News Messenger. It had been in the paper for weeks, and in spite of our protests they had printed Bess's name.

We'd found the people responsible for the deaths of Bess's entire family – the Lesters – her parents and her brother and sister. I'd found out who'd killed my best friend, Terry, Bess's mom, and Willis had found out who killed his best friend, Roy, Bess's dad. It had been the very worst and hardest time in my life, but strangely enough a few good things had come out of those black days. I had met Luna, who was in charge of the investigation, and who, in her own surly fashion, has remained my friend to this day; and I had become closer to my mother-in-law, Vera, when she showed up the day after the bodies had been discovered with a gallon of bleach, scrub brushes, and a mop and pail. But the brightest, most sparkling thing to come of it was Bess. She became our daughter, just as surely as Megan was and just as surely as Graham was our son. We'd adopted her when she was five, so she'd been with us for twelve years, legally ours for eleven. But she and Megan had always been best friends, then sisters. I started to cry. I was losing my babies. In so many ways.

It had been a quiet ride. A very long, very quiet ride. Clarissa Mayfair liked to talk, but not around Davis DeWitt. DeWitt had three switches when it came to any response to a comment of hers: one, the scoff; two, the challenge; or three, the patronizing über-male bullshit. So she learned to just keep her mouth shut around him. She had decided long ago that this relationship wasn't like in the movies. There was no chemistry, no sexual magic that was going to change the fact that they despised each other and have them hopping in bed three-quarters of the way through. Nope, she couldn't stand the man. And because of that, she found nothing about him sexually appealing. Except for the fact that, like most men, DeWitt would screw anything, she doubted he found her sexually appealing either. One of these days the lieutenant was going to get serious about her weekly request for a change of partner.

They drove straight to the home of James Unger. As DeWitt turned off the car and started to open his door, Mayfair said, 'We need to check in with the Houston police. Did you call the loo?'

'Fuck that. We're just going to talk to her. We're not going to arrest her.'

'What if she's sitting there with a picture of herself pushing her husband off the garage roof?' Mayfair said.

DeWitt just looked at her, one eyebrow raised. Mayfair returned the look with a big, toothy, phony smile.

They opened their doors simultaneously and headed to the front of the house. And it was a nice house. Upper-middle-class nice. Maybe five thousand square feet. Two-story white brick with black shutters, and a double front door painted bright red. They rang the bell. The door had slim, beveled glass windows on either side. When no one came to the door, each took a window to look through.

'Overturned furniture,' Mayfair said, her hand on her gun at her side.

'Here, too,' DeWitt answered, also touching his gun. 'I'm gonna break down the door.'

'Yeah? Well, I'm gonna call the Houston PD.' She pulled out her cell phone and dialed 911.

DeWitt said, 'The wife could be bleeding out in there,' and applied his heel to the lock mechanism of the door. It actually worked, since the dead bolt had not been thrown. DeWitt stepped inside, gun drawn.

Meanwhile, Mayfair was trying to explain to the 911 operator who she was, why she was in Houston, and what was going on at the home of James and Elizabeth Unger. She finally ended the call by saying, 'For God's sake, just send some detectives out here!' And then followed her partner into the Unger home.

VERA'S STORY
FRIDAY

I wouldn't tell just anyone this, but Kelvin, Willis's father, and I were sexually ahead of our time. That is to say, Kelvin had a way about him that had me actually liking that part of marriage. I remember my mama telling me on the morning of my wedding that all I had to do was lie there and try not to cry. That never became an issue. I'm only telling you this because I have to admit here that I was beginning to think of Gerald the way I often thought of Kelvin. But then I'd stop myself, knowing that I could never know two men in my life that would make that worth the trouble. And wouldn't it be embarrassing if I seduced Gerald and he was bad in bed? Then I'd have to change churches and I'd been going to the Codderville First Baptist since before I could walk. But the more time I spent with him, the more times he slipped his hand into mine, the more I thought about it. I think, at heart, maybe I'm a trollop.

But the job we had before us was not frivolous. We had a murder to solve, or a body to find, or, hopefully, both. So we found a small room off the lobby called the library, where nobody ever went, and sat in there to talk. There was a computer in there, and we looked at each other and both grinned.

'This is gonna be a piece of cake!' Gerald said.

'We'll just Google Rachael's name, and then Brother Joe's name. See what we come up with?' I suggested.

'Sounds like a plan,' he said, and sat down in front of the computer. I was a little miffed about that. I mean, this was *my* investigation. He was *my* helper, not the other way around!

I just sighed – loudly – and pulled up a chair next to his.

He turned to look at me. 'I'm sorry, Vera. Did you want to do this?'

'No, no, that's OK,' I said. 'You're here now, let's just do it.'

He Googled Rachael's name and came up with absolutely nothing. 'Donley's her married name, right?' I said. 'Maybe we can find something under her maiden name.'

'What's that?' Gerald asked me.

I shrugged. 'I have no idea.' I thought for a moment. 'Tomorrow's Saturday. Linda' – the church's secretary – 'comes in a half day on Saturday. She should have that.'

'What would we give as a reason for asking?' Gerald asked.

'We'll think on that. Now, do Brother Joe,' I said.

Gerald put in the name Joe Logan, got nothing, put in Joseph Logan, got nothing – and by 'nothing' I mean not our Joe Logan. Just lots of people who weren't our Joe. Then we decided on Joe Logan, Baptist Preacher, got nothing at all, then tried Minister. Ditto.

'Facebook!' I said.

'You think he has an account?' Gerald asked.

'I know he does. I'm friends with him,' I said.

Gerald shook his head. 'I don't have Facebook,' he said. He stood up. 'You do it.'

We changed places and I pulled up my Facebook account. I hadn't checked it for more than a week, but Brother Joe's profile picture wasn't hard to find. I double-clicked on it and pulled up his page. I'm not sure what I expected to find. A confession? A declaration of undying love for Rachael Donley? There wasn't much there. I was vacantly staring at the page when Gerald said, 'What's that?' and pointed at something on the screen. It was the 'where you're from' question, and in that space were the words: 'Bethesda, MD.'

'He said he never lived outside Texas,' Gerald said.

So I typed in 'Joseph Logan, Bethesda, MD.' Still nothing. You heard of channeling? Shirley MacLaine does it. I think I sorta channeled a TV cop show. I typed in 'Joseph Logan, Deceased.'

There were three, and one was from Bethesda, Maryland.

ELEVEN

SATURDAY

The grandfather clock downstairs struck midnight, and Bess snuck out of her room. The arrangements were as they had been: Willis asleep in Alicia's room; Alicia downstairs with E.J. She didn't dare knock on Graham's door; she just opened it and walked in. He was awake, but reading.

'You ever heard of knocking?' Graham said with an attitude.

'Shove the attitude. All hell's breaking loose here and you're the one who can set it all straight,' Bess said.

'Oh? And how am I going to accomplish this magical thing?'

'Start by not being a smart ass.' Bess hit the covers over his feet and he moved them back, allowing her to sit on the end of his bed. 'And finish by going back to Austin.'

Graham threw his book on the bed. Bess noticed it wasn't a school book. 'I think it's a little late for that,' he said.

'You've lost a week of classes. The first week. You can make that up—'

'I'm not leaving Alicia—'

'Just finish the semester, then come home. Everyone will have cooled down by then. I'm not saying I think either of you two are going to fall out of love, I'm just saying the rest of the family will have settled down and come to grips with it.'

'No! I'm not leaving—'

'Alicia told Mom she's leaving the house, going to stay with "friends." You and I both know she doesn't have "friends" she can stay with. She's going to go live on the streets—'

Graham jumped up. 'Not if I can help it! We'll live in my car—'

Bess grabbed his arm. 'Graham! *You* need to get a grip! What are you going to do right now? It's after midnight! Are you going to run downstairs and wake up Mom and Alicia and start the drama up all over again? Just listen to me!'

Graham sank back on his bed. Bess sat next to him, her hand on his shoulder. 'You're my big brother, and I will love you always,

no matter what goes down with all of this . . . crap, for want of a
better word. I'm just saying, right now you've put the entire family
in a bind, Graham. Mom and Dad can't even sleep together. All
three of us girls are at each other's throats. Alicia can't think straight.
If you were out of the equation for a while, things could get back
on track, everybody could calm down. Please, just think about it,
please?'

'Yeah, OK, Bessie,' he said, using her childhood nickname and
pulling on a lock of her hair. He smiled slightly. 'Let me think about
it. Let me talk to Alicia.'

Bess stood up and kissed the top of her brother's head. 'Thanks,
bro,' she said and left the room.

It was seven a.m. and Mayfair and DeWitt sat in chairs facing
Lieutenant Buddy Nixon, the head of homicide for the Houston
police department. It had been three whole minutes and Lt Nixon
hadn't said a word. Mayfair and DeWitt were both twitching in their
seats.

The phone on Lt Nixon's desk rang and he picked it up and
identified himself. Then said, 'Yes.' Followed by, 'Uh huh.' With
an 'OK' thrown in, and finally, 'That's doable.' Lt Nixon punched
a button on his phone and the voice of Austin police's Lieutenant
of Homicide, Jack Hornsby, filled the small room.

'What the fuck did you two think you were doing?' Lt Hornsby
shouted. 'I gave you permission to go talk to the widow! And, AS
YOU KNOW, detectives, when one goes to another's jurisdiction,
one MUST CHECK IN. DID YOU CHECK IN?'

'Loo—' DeWitt started.

'No, you did not! You went straight to the widow's house, then
you decided to bust the door in—'

'Sir, I tried to tell him—'

'Shut the fuck up, Mayfair. Just shut the fuck up. Both of you
fucked this up royally, and if it wouldn't cost more than my budget
allows to send two more detectives over there and get your asses
back here to do paperwork for the rest of your lives, I'd do it. But
I can't. I have to deal with what I have, and unfortunately what I
have is you two fuck-ups. So listen. Lieutenant Nixon will use you
as he sees fit, and you will bring me anything he feels is germane
to our investigation. DO. YOU. UNDERSTAND.'

'Yes, sir,' Mayfair said.

'Yeah, Loo, right,' DeWitt said.

'Lieutenant Nixon?' Lt Hornsby said.

Lt Nixon turned his back on the two fuck-ups and took the call off speaker. Mayfair and DeWitt just sat there, not looking at each other, listening to this Houston top murder cop laughing with their own top murder cop, and they were pretty sure it was at their expense.

I woke up and saw that it was only seven o'clock on a Saturday morning! I didn't need to get up! Why did I wake up? I didn't have to pee, which was my usual reason for getting out of bed these days. I think it all boiled down to an inability to toss and turn. With Alicia taking up nine-tenths of the bed, it was hard to do. I got up and moved into the family room. I grabbed an afghan out of its basket next to the sofa and laid down, covering myself. Then I thought maybe I should have peed while I was up. So I got up, went back into the bedroom, used the facilities, and came back out. Alicia had managed to expand her skinny self to cover the entire bed. I went back out to the family room and laid back down on the sofa. A light came on behind me. I jumped to a sitting position, my hands in a position for what I thought might be a karate chop. It was my husband.

'What are you doing up?' I asked him.

'What are *you* doing up?' he countered.

'I have a teenager with colt legs in my bed.'

'I think I'm getting to that age where I can no longer sleep in,' Willis said with a sigh. 'Not to mention my feet hang off Alicia's bed.' He came and sat down on the sofa next to me. I covered us both with the afghan.

He touched my thigh under the covers. I looked at him and he looked at me, then we both looked around the room. It was definitely empty.

VERA'S STORY
SATURDAY

I met Gerald for breakfast that morning, energized and ready to find us a killer. I wasn't sure how we were going to get to the town of Bethesda in Maryland, but that was my plan.

I ordered an egg, scrambled hard, a biscuit with cream gravy, and an orange juice, and asked Gerald, 'So where's this Bethesda place and how do we get there? Do we need to rent a car?'

'Bethesda is a suburb of D.C. and we can get there by the metro,' he said.

'Oh,' I said. Was I ready to go back down into the bowels of Hell? Well, it hadn't really been that bad. 'OK. So eat up and let's go.'

'Brother Joe wants me to rehearse with that lady from Louisiana after breakfast – you know, for our duet tonight – and right after that we have the rehearsal for all three choirs,' Gerald said. 'You think we can put this off until tomorrow?'

'No, that's OK,' I said and sighed. 'I'll go by myself.'

'Now, Vera—'

'No, no, it's OK. I do most things by myself nowadays. I'm used to it.'

'I won't hear of it! You can't go down to the metro by yourself, you'll get lost!' he said.

Well, that got my goat. 'Are you calling me senile? Are you saying I can't go from this hotel, two blocks to the metro station?'

'No, of course not,' he said, falling back in his seat. 'I just don't want you to go without me, that's all. I think we work well together.'

If I were a younger woman, I woulda blushed. But I'm made of sterner stuff these days. 'When do you think our rehearsal will be over?'

'Could be pretty late. And we go on at eight tonight. And another problem,' he said. 'Tomorrow's Sunday, and if we need to get information from any state or local agency, they won't be open until Monday.'

'We leave Monday,' I said, almost in tears. Was I just gonna go home and forget all about Rachael Donley? How could I possibly do that?

'Well, I've been thinking about it. I've got a whole bunch of frequent flyer miles and I'll get us two tickets to fly back whenever we finish up. What do you say? Will you stay in D.C. with me?'

'We're gonna need to find another hotel. This one is way too expensive,' I said.

Mr Jones woke up to the smell of breakfast. Mr Brown was not in his bed, so Mr Jones could only assume he'd lived through the night. Mr Jones got up and went into the bathroom, used the facilities, washed his face, then headed downstairs. He followed the smell of bacon to the kitchen. It was a huge room with restaurant-style appliances that could have fed an army. Instead, sitting at a table in the middle of the room were Mr Big, his henchman, and Mr Brown. The crying lady was doing the cooking.

'Please! Mr Jones, join us! I hope you had a pleasant night?' Mr Big asked in his heavily accented English.

'Motherfu—' Mr Brown started, but Mr Big interrupted. 'God only knows what you did to provoke him, Stuart— I'm so sorry, Mr Brown.'

As Mr Jones took a seat at the large round table, as far away from Mr Brown as he could get, he couldn't help noticing the heavily bandaged right index finger. He decided to keep his smirk to himself.

'So now we discuss the next phase of our journey. Our journey that ends, Mr Jones, in you receiving your share of the money,' Mr Big said.

'Excuse me, sir, but I just signed on to get that thingamabob and get it to you. I really need to get my money now. I got mouths to feed, you know.'

'Actually, you have back child support to pay. I believe you are what they call in this country a deadbeat dad?' Mr Big said.

'No, now, that wasn't my fault. I got laid off—'

Mr Big clicked his tongue and shook his head. 'You Americans, always ready with an excuse for your failures. And yet your lives are so easy! Me? I was born in a gulag, yet look at me now!' He waved his arms around the room. 'I live in a mansion! I live like a czar! You? You are pitiful. And no, your job is not over, Mr Jones, and it will not be over until I say it is over. Do you understand?'

'Yeah, sure,' Mr Jones said sullenly, as the crying lady sat a plate of food down in front of him. He took a bite. Um, he thought, scrambled eggs with cheese and onions. And bacon. And fried potatoes! Oh, and look! Biscuits! Yummy.

'I don't understand,' Alicia said.

They were sitting outside on the covered deck, side by side on the porch swing, holding hands. 'It'll just be until Christmas – that's the end of the semester,' Graham said. 'This way I won't have wasted the money Mom and Dad put out for my tuition and books and the dorm and everything, *and* I'll get some credits behind me.

But most of all, it'll give everybody a chance to cool off. Get things back to as close to normal as they can get, considering.'

'Considering what?' Alicia said, her lower lip quivering.

'Considering that I love you and that you, hopefully, love me,' he said quietly.

'Oh, I do!' Alicia said, and threw her arms around Graham's neck. He laughed then sobered and kissed her for the first time. Then the two just sat there for a long time.

Finally Alicia said, 'I don't know if I can stand being away from you now.'

'Yeah, you can,' Graham said, kissing her hand. 'We know where we stand now. And we know it's just going to be a matter of a few months.'

Alicia sighed. 'I guess Mom and Dad really need to get back into the same bedroom.'

Graham laughed. 'Those two can make any place a bedroom.'

'What?'

'I started to come downstairs early this morning. I went straight back up,' he said.

Alicia covered her mouth. 'You mean?'

'Right there on the family-room sofa.'

'Ewwww . . .'

Elizabeth Unger was gone. When Mayfair and DeWitt finally got into the Unger home, they too (besides, of course, the Houston PD, who had already gone over every aspect of the house and its disarray) discovered that the greatest possibility was that Mrs Unger had been snatched. Nobody was that bad a housekeeper. Overturned chairs and tables, broken dishes, food on the floor. No, it was pretty obvious that someone had come in while Mrs Unger was fixing dinner for two and taken her. The kitchen table was set for two, and there was still food in pots on the stove, crusted over and dried out. Mrs Unger obviously put up a fight, but to no avail. It was also a good bet that she'd been snatched before her husband had been killed in Austin.

'Ya think we could get into her lab?' DeWitt said.

'Ya think HPD hasn't already done that?' Mayfair answered sarcastically.

'Ya think you could keep your opinions to yourself?' DeWitt replied.

'Ya think you could shut the fuck up?' was Mayfair's response.

'No. I mean it. We should go to the lab,' DeWitt said.

'Where is it?' Mayfair asked.

'Fuck if I know,' DeWitt answered.

'Call the Houston loo,' Mayfair said.

'You call him,' DeWitt said.

'You're a fucking idiot,' Mayfair said as she pulled her cell phone out of her pocket and hit the number she'd put in earlier that day. 'Loo, this is Mayfair from Austin. Yes, sir. We're at the house. We'd like to go by the lab, sir, if that's all right with you.' She listened for a moment then said, 'Yes, sir. I understand, but just as another pair of eyes, sir?' Again she listened. 'Thank you, Loo. Now if we could get the address?' She listened for a second then hung up the phone.

'So what's the address?' DeWitt asked.

'He wouldn't tell me. He said, "look it up."' Mayfair looked at her partner. 'Think you can handle that?' she asked and vacated the house, heading for their car.

Unger Laboratories was near downtown, very close to, if not actually in, Houston's infamous Fifth Ward. It was a cement block, one-story building surrounded by a seven-foot tall wrought-iron fence, bars at the one door and the windows. Considering the disrepair of the neighboring buildings – burnt-out shells, or those still standing with broken windows, and empty of life – it was a fair statement of fact about their location.

An unmarked car pulled up about the same time as Mayfair and DeWitt. The man inside showed them his detective's shield and leaned out the window, something in his hand. 'You Mayfair and DeWitt, Austin PD?' he asked.

'Yeah,' DeWitt said, dragging out his own badge and ID. He showed it to the detective, who then handed him a set of keys. 'This one,' he said, pointing out a key, 'opens the front door. This one,' he said, pointing out another, 'is for the lab, and this one opens the iron gate.'

'Thanks,' DeWitt said, reaching for the keys.

The detective held them just out of his reach. 'I'm parked right over there,' he said, pointing across the street at the one living thing on the entire block – a scrawny oak tree. 'Bring the keys back to me.' And with that he handed DeWitt the keys, did a U-turn, drove up half a block, did another U-turn, and nestled under the shade of the oak tree.

'Hell, he's not too obvious,' DeWitt said.

'Maybe he's just acting as a deterrent, rather than trying to catch someone,' Mayfair said.

Mayfair and DeWitt exited their vehicle and stood staring around them. It was deadly quiet. Most, if not all, the buildings on that block were abandoned – boarded up, or just left with broken windows and mounting piles of trash.

'Kinda spooky,' Mayfair said.

'Wow, you really are a girl,' DeWitt said as he moved toward the wrought-iron gate. Mayfair raised her leg and caught DeWitt's leg, making him lose his balance and almost fall, only catching himself at the last minute with a grip on the fence. 'My daddy always told me to never hit a girl. But you're pushing my limit, bitch!'

Mayfair sighed. 'Do you need extra time, or would it be easier if I used that key instead? I know it takes special skill.'

DeWitt glared at her and unlocked the wrought-iron fence's gate.

There was a knock on the back door and Luna entered the great room where Willis and I were watching Saturday morning cartoons. We got hooked when the kids were little – they got over it, we didn't.

'Got a minute?' she asked, sitting on the easy chair as Willis and I were cuddled on the sofa. She said this while simultaneously lifting the TV remote and turning off the new and seriously large flat-screen TV.

'Hey!' Willis opined.

'Hey is for horses,' Luna said. Then: 'Listen! I haven't told y'all this, didn't want to make a big deal out of it, but Eddie's being released from Leavenworth.'

'Oh my God!' I yelled, jumped up and threw my arms around her neck. We didn't touch much so she initially recoiled, but after a second hugged me back.

Willis was also on his feet and actually hugged her next. 'I can't wait to meet him!' he said, a big smile on his face.

Note of explanation: Eddie is Eduardo Luna, Sr., Elena's husband. While he and Elena were both in the Air Force, and Elena was pregnant with their second child, Eddie had words at a bar with an officer who was being an asshole. The asshole officer pushed Eddie, an enlisted man, and Eddie pushed back. The asshole officer fell down, hit his head and died. Eddie has been in Leavenworth for the past twenty years. Elena and her boys take a two-week vacation every Christmas and drive to Leavenworth, Kansas. I've never asked if Leavenworth – the prison – had conjugal visitation. We didn't talk about things like that. Actually, we very rarely talked about Eddie. I always got the feeling that was somehow not on the table for discussion.

'Anyway,' Luna said, shooing us away from her, 'I'm going to Houston to pick him up. Nearest straight shot from Leavenworth. The government doesn't pay for plane changes. And anyway, I sort of want the time on the road to, well . . .'

'Get to know each other again,' I said.

'Yeah, that.' She cleared her throat. 'So, anyway, I got a call a while ago from Detective Mayfair, the female APD?'

Willis and I both nodded.

'She and her partner are in Houston, initially to see the wife of James Unger, but it turns out she was snatched.'

'No shit?' Willis said. 'Who— Our guys?'

'Those guys were awfully busy – kidnapping the wife, then the next day chasing down the husband. Gotta be more people involved. I mean, who's holding the wife while those two dumbasses were here?' Luna said. 'So Mr Brown is working for somebody probably. Anyway, since Eddie's coming in on Tuesday, I thought I'd hop on over to Houston tomorrow. Thought you might want to tag along, E.J.'

I was more than ready. My whole body wanted to see this through. But I took a second to look at my husband. 'Hell, yeah, we'll come!' Willis said. 'Come on, Eeg, we've come this far with these guys, we need to see it through!'

'Willis Jerome Pugh!' I said, letting out the dreaded middle name he so abhorred. 'Are you actually encouraging me to get involved?'

'Sure. As long as I'm there with you – EVERY STEP OF THE WAY,' he said, emphasizing the last part with both his voice and his evil eye.

'But the kids – we can't leave Romeo and Juliet alone—'

'Really, Mom? Really?' came from behind me. 'Romeo and Juliet? Isn't that rather a cliché?'

'Oh, hey, Graham,' I said, ears, face, and neck burning. 'Didn't know you were there.'

'Obviously,' my son said.

Behind him someone giggled. Alicia peeked around. 'Don't worry, Mom. Y'all can go.'

'We were coming down to talk to y'all when we heard your conversation. And, truthfully, Mom, I'm kind of surprised you're not already in Houston hunting them down. But, here's the thing. Someone, and I'm not naming names – but she's short and her name starts with a "B" and ends with an "ess", suggested to me last night that I go back to school and finish the semester, so that y'all won't lose all the money you've already spent, and so that there can be a cooling off period for the whole family. Things have gotten out of hand, and I'm man enough to admit that some of that has been my fault—'

'Some of it?' Willis said sarcastically.

Graham ignored him. 'So I'm leaving tomorrow. I'll go before y'all leave and you can call Megan at any point to make sure I didn't turn around and come back – y'all know she'll spill her guts first chance she gets. How does that sound?'

I got up and hugged my son, then my daug— no, then Alicia. Can't call her my daughter anymore. It would just be too weird. 'That's a wise decision,' I told him. To Alicia, I said, 'Are you down with this, honey?'

She nodded. 'At first I wasn't, but it's the only thing that makes sense.' She smiled up at Graham, and for the first time since taking her into our home, I noticed she was absolutely beautiful. 'But he'll be home weekends,' she said.

OK, then, I thought. No more sex on the weekends.

'So what are we supposed to do now?' Mr Jones asked Mr Brown when they were alone in the kitchen.

'Don't even speak to me!' he snarled.

'Hey! You were poking me in the chest! And you got a fingernail on you! It hurt. I got a scratch!' Mr Jones said in his own defense.

'A scratch? You got a fucking scratch?' He held up his broken digit. '*This* is not a scratch! You broke my fucking finger!'

Mr Jones smiled at Mr Brown. 'Next time, don't poke me, 'k?'

'I don't know why Mr Smith just shot you in the foot! He should have shot you in the head! At the very least, in the nuts!' Mr Brown said.

Mr Jones shook his head. 'Don't you even mention Mr Smith. You killed him! You're not allowed to utter his name!'

'I'm not *allowed*? By who? You the name-calling police, fuckface? Mr Smith, Mr Smith, Mr Smith—'

Although not completely done with his breakfast – there were rashers of bacon left on the serving plate, half a biscuit on his own plate, and some fruit he hadn't even started on yet – Mr Jones got up and left the room.

He was wandering the halls of the big house, peeking into rooms, when he unfortunately peeked into the one containing Mr Big, his henchman and the crying lady.

'I don't want to hurt you, Elizabeth,' Mr Big was saying, 'or rather, have Misha hurt you.' A nod of his head indicated the henchman. 'But I will. You and your husband made a deal with me. Then your husband said no, after all the money I gave you for your research. Isn't that true?'

The crying woman, Elizabeth, said nothing. 'You owe me, Elizabeth,' he said softly.

'I'll pay you back, I promise,' she said, looking at her hands in her lap.

'Yes, you will. I have set up a very nice lab for you downstairs – better than the lab you and James had. Much better. And look!' he said, spreading his arms wide. 'The location is *so* much better, don't you think? And no commute. Well, only from your bedroom to the basement!' Mr Big laughed.

'I won't make those pills!' Elizabeth said, raising her head and staring at Mr Big. 'You can't make me!'

Mr Big barely moved his head, but Mr Jones saw it. And so did Misha. The big brute walked over to the woman, grabbed her hand and, taking a pair of pliers out of his pocket, yanked off the fingernail of her pinky finger.

Elizabeth screamed and so did Mr Jones.

Mr Big jumped up. 'Aw, Mr Jones, so nice of you to join us.'

'Hey, now, y'all don't do that to her! Stop!' Mr Jones said, coming into the room.

'Oh, we have, Mr Jones. We have stopped. Elizabeth?' he said, turning to the woman, who was again crying and holding her left hand in her right as blood dripped on the floor. 'Misha, please clean that up. Elizabeth? I asked you a question. Have we stopped? We could of course, go on. There is so much further we could go. Nine more fingers, ten toes—'

'Hey, Mr Big, I didn't sign up for torture—'

Mr Big took Mr Jones by his beefy arm and led him to the door. 'Of course you didn't, Mr Jones. And no one is asking you to torture anyone. That's just silly. Please send in Mr Brown,' Mr Big said as he pushed Mr Jones out the door and shut it behind him.

Having lived for thirty-odd years without an original thought, Mr Jones did as he was told and went to the kitchen, telling Mr Brown that Mr Big wanted him. Mr Brown left and Mr Jones sat back down at the kitchen table, idly eating the remaining food on the table – fruit last, of course. But thoughts did begin to swirl around in his head. He thought about the brown-haired girl, Alicia, and the old man. How he'd tried to save them, and maybe he had. Then he remembered: before the girl and the old man had knocked him out, he and Alicia had put each other's cell phone numbers in each other's phones. He took his out of his pocket and looked. Sure enough, there it was: Alicia Brooks.

'Hey, asshole,' said Mr Brown from the doorway. 'We've got an assignment. Get your ass in gear.'

Mr Jones put away his phone – for now.

TWELVE

Mayfair caught the cast-iron gate just before the heavy hinge slammed it shut, and followed her sulking partner to the front door. He used the key to open that door and they found themselves in a small reception area with a heavy door directly behind a reception desk. They went to the door and used the last key to open it. Inside was the lab, about a thousand square feet of nothing but machines and test tubes. Two desks were at the front of the room, near the entrance door, and were turned parallel to the door, facing each other. Each had a name plate saying 'Dr Unger,' but one was pink and one was blue. A joke, Mayfair thought. She sat down at the pink desk, while DeWitt took the blue desk, and they began to rummage through what was left. They figured the Houston police, and possibly the perps, had already done most of the rummaging, leaving little of any interest behind. There were no computers on either desk, so Mayfair assumed the HPD had already rescued them. She'd ask, but it was a given.

Giving up on the desk, Mayfair walked around the different stations, noting subtle differences – one had one kind of machine, along with test tubes and other crap, including binders, and the next another kind of machine, along with its paraphernalia. She checked out the first binder and found it full of numbers and symbols that meant nothing to her. But possibly would to another scientist? Why didn't the HPD take this with them? She put the binder under her arm and went on to other stations. Each had a binder – some were empty, and some had pages filled with the same kind of numbers and symbols. She gathered up the binders with writing in them, and left the empty ones.

'Why not take 'em all?' DeWitt asked her upon seeing her bounty.

'Because these have been written in and the others haven't,' she said, enunciating clearly as one would to a child.

'Fuck you,' DeWitt said. 'What's in 'em?'

'Stuff,' Mayfair said.

'I'll stuff you in a test tube, Mayfair! Give!'

Mayfair opened one of the books to let him see. 'So, what does it say?' she asked.

'Well, this is the symbol for aluminite, and this symbol means gestation,' he said.

Wide-eyed, Mayfair said, 'Are you shitting me? You can read this?'

DeWitt laughed. 'Naw, just having some fun at your expense. I have no idea what it means.'

'Jesus, you're a shit,' Mayfair said, and headed back the way they had come.

'Don't leave on my account,' DeWitt said, still laughing. 'Just leave!' Which cracked him up even more. By the time he got outside, their unmarked sedan was gone and his partner with it.

SATURDAY
VERA'S STORY

While Gerald was practicing his duet with the lady from the Louisiana church, I went back into the library room – that's what they called it, the library, even though there were only a few books in there and the spines on them looked like they'd never been cracked. I got out my cell phone and called Linda, our church secretary, knowing she'd be busy printing out the bulletins for tomorrow's service. Which made me wonder who Brother Joe had gotten to replace him. I'd have to ask Linda.

She answered on the third ring. 'First Baptist,' she said, her voice harried.

'Hey, Linda, it's Vera Pugh. You sound like you're busy,' I said.

'Busier than a cat covering up poop in a windstorm. What can I do for you, Miss Vera?' She only calls me that because I asked her to stop calling me Mrs Pugh. The woman's in her sixties – not that much difference in our ages that she needs to go and call me 'Miss Vera,' but I ignored it as usual. But before I could answer, she added, 'And how's everybody doing? Y'all having a good time?'

'How can you not have a good time at a Southern Baptist convention?' I asked back. 'And everybody seems to be enjoying themselves.' Getting back to business, I said, 'I need two things: first, who'd Brother Joe get to cover for him tomorrow?'

'Nobody! He told me to do it. Couldn't find a retired preacher available to save my life, so I got Brother Leeman Hodges to do a layman's service,' she said.

'Well, that'll be better than a lot of them retired preachers we got before,' I said.

'Don't I know it! Some of those old codgers can be long-winded, boring, and loud.'

'I hear ya. Listen, second question: what's Sister Rachael Donley's maiden name?'

There was a slight pause, then Linda said, 'I haven't the slightest idea.'

'Don't you have it written down somewhere?' I persisted.

'Why would I? She wasn't married in this church, was she?' Linda asked.

I sighed. 'Not that I'm aware of.'

'Well, now, let me look at her file. Sometimes women, specially these younger ones, like to use their maiden names as their middle names. So let's look. While I'm looking, how come you need it?'

'Well, she had to leave to go visit her mother. She gave me the number but I lost it, so I want to look up her mother's name – it's got to be the same as hers. Her parents were never divorced or anything.'

'That makes sense,' Linda said. 'Ah ha! Here it is and you're in luck! I'm pretty sure this is a maiden name, 'cause who would call their daughter this? Rachael Gregory Donley.'

'Gotta be the maiden name!' I said with a grin. Then had a new thought that might help with Monday's trip to Bethesda, Maryland. 'Could you fax me a picture of Brother Joe? We need the official church photo.'

'Goodness gracious,' Linda said. 'Brother Joe asked you to get this?'

'Ah, no, we – that is, the choir, thought we could use it.'

'Well, I hope to heaven he didn't ask for it! I've been trying to get him to sit down with the photographer for over a month and he keeps putting me off. We don't have any photos of him.'

'OK, then,' I said, then thanked her and said goodbye. No photo, huh? Curiouser and curiouser. I knew there was something about that guy I didn't like!

I couldn't wait to tell Gerald, but he was in rehearsal, which left me with the computer and Rachael Donley's maiden name. I powered up, plugged in Rachael's maiden name and anxiously awaited the four to five seconds it took to spew out this information. There were eight Rachael Gregorys, but only three of them spelled their first names with the second 'a' – Rachael rather than Rachel. One was a current high-school student doing quite well in athletics in Wisconsin, one was a housewife with a cooking blog in Indiana, and one was someone searching for a Rachael Gregory who graduated George Washington High School in Farmersville, Texas, in the year 2000.

OK, I thought, a person who graduated high school in the year 2000, would be roughly in their early thirties – depending on their age upon graduation. I would definitely put Rachael in her early thirties. I was pretty sure she was from Texas, although Farmersville wasn't familiar, but then again, I don't think she ever said where she was from in Texas, not that I ever asked. I should have thought ahead.

I clicked on that page and found a callout for the graduates of the 2000 class of George Washington High for a reunion this coming spring. She was on a list of people no one knew how to get hold of. There were three of those in a graduating class of eighty-five students, which seemed to me to indicate that Farmersville was a medium to small town.

There was an email address so I clicked on that and wrote the following: 'I too am looking for Rachael Gregory Donley, who disappeared from her hotel room three nights ago—'

No, that would just scare the bejesus out of whoever I was writing to, so I erased it. The 'To' line just said, 'Reunion Committee.' Have to be more subtle than that. 'I'm a friend of Rachael Gregory's and would be pleased if you could send me some info—'

OK, that didn't sound *too* stalkerish! So I sat there at the desk, staring at the blank email until I finally gave up. There was something I could do right now, but it didn't concern the email. I'd wait and have Gerald help with that. I had a feeling he could be more subtle than I. No, the thing I could do right now was get a picture of Brother Joe!

'So where we going?' Mr Jones asked Mr Brown.

'That's on a need to know basis,' Mr Brown said, 'and you don't need to know.'

'Yeah, I do!' Mr Jones said. 'If I'm supposed to do something, I need to know what it is, dumbass!'

'You'll do what I tell you to do when I tell you to do it. Is that clear?'

Mr Jones shook his head. 'You're not the boss of me,' he mumbled to the side window.

'Huh!' Mr Brown said. 'Yeah, I am, asshole. And don't you forget it.'

'If I killed people as easily as you do, you'd be a dead man, Mr Brown.'

Mr Brown laughed. 'Good thing I'm riding with a pacifist then, huh?'

Mr Jones continued to stare out of the side window as they left the beauty of River Oaks and in only minutes were in the ghetto. Ten minutes driving through the worst streets he'd ever seen, and they pulled up in front of a white cinderblock building with a high wrought-iron fence around it.

Mr Brown handed Mr Jones a bunch of keys. 'This one,' he said, pointing at one of the keys, 'opens the gate. So go do that.'

Mr Jones gave Mr Brown his version of the evil eye – which unfortunately wasn't nearly as evil as Mr Jones thought it was – and got out of the car. They were no longer in the Toyota; that had been dumped, but were in one of Mr Big's cars, a pristine 2010 Mercedes SUV.

Just as he stepped on the sidewalk, Mr Jones noticed movement behind him and to the right. He turned. A man was walking toward them. A white guy in a black neighborhood, cheap suit, gut, and an extra bulge on his hip. He threw himself back in the Mercedes. 'Cop!' he said.

Mr Brown looked in his rearview mirror, started the car and slowly drove away.

After Luna left, the four of us – Graham, Alicia, Willis and I – sat in the family room and discussed the situation, ad nauseum. Willis and I side by side; Graham and Alicia glued to each other.

'So, what do you think?' Graham asked us. I knew in my heart it didn't really matter what we thought. This wasn't a first crush like Lotta – young as they both were, this was the real thing.

'I think it's very mature of both of you to come up with this plan—' I started.

'Ha!' Graham said. 'The only mature one in this household is Bess. It was her idea. My gut reaction was hell no, but after thinking about it, I realize it's the only thing that makes sense.'

'I agree with your idea, but not your statement that Bess is the only mature one—' Willis started.

Graham grinned from ear to ear. 'You didn't see what I saw when I innocently came downstairs early this morning for something to eat. I didn't make it to the kitchen.'

Alicia giggled, covering her mouth with her hands, and I felt like doing the same, but restrained myself.

'We're adults! And we're married,' Willis said, obviously trying to hit all the bases. He cleared his throat and said, 'OK, so going back to school. That's a good idea. And I have an idea for after that. You know there's a junior college in Brenham,' he said, mentioning a town maybe twenty miles away where Blue Bell Ice Cream is made. Best ice cream ever – right up there with Ben & Jerry's and Häagan Dazs. Only shipped by order outside of Texas.

'Have you shared this with me?' I asked.

'I am now,' he answered. 'Anyway,' he gave me a withering glance, 'with your grandmother's permission, of course, and I can't see her saying no, you move in with her, which would put you even closer to Brenham, and you commute there. Then you and Alicia can date like normal people.'

'Move in with Grandma?' Graham said, eyes big. 'I don't think so!'

'Why not?' Alicia asked him.

He just looked at her for a long moment, then said, 'Hell, it's Grandma! Would you want to live with her?'

'Hey, now, that's my mother—' Willis started.

'She's a hell of a cook,' I interjected. 'She goes to bed at eight every night. And we just bought her that wide-screen TV.'

'And we could date,' Alicia said. 'And Mom and Dad can have their bedroom back.'

'So I can't live in my own home anymore?' Graham said.

Alicia stood up. 'Maybe I'm the one who should go live with Grandma, if she'll let me,' she said, and headed for the stairs, Graham on her heels, saying, 'No, now, Alicia, I didn't mean that . . .'

Later that night, Willis and I were alone in the family room. Megan and Bess had gone to a party, and Graham and Alicia were on their first date. And, for some reason I'm yet to fathom, the TV was off.

So I took that opportunity to turn to my husband and ask, 'Just what the hell do you think we can accomplish by accompanying Luna to Houston tomorrow?'

He shrugged and pulled me to him. 'Damned if I know,' he said. 'But we didn't get the weekend we wanted at the Driscoll, so I thought we'd make reservations for us and for the Lunas at the Four Seasons. And we'll pick up the tab for Elena and Eddie.'

I kissed him. What a guy, my husband. Of course, it was my book money he was spending, but hell, he'd supported me for almost twenty-five years, and still was. My new-found book booty just took care of the fun stuff, like a plethora of electronics – new iPhones, tablets, laptops, etc., large flat-screen TVs, new cars, and, in April next year, a two-week trip to Italy.

'What a wonderful idea,' I said.

'I'm a wonderful guy,' he said.

'Yeah, you are. But can you prove it twice in one day?' I asked with a grin.

He sighed. 'Well, I'm no longer the young stud that I once was, but, hell, I'll give it the old college try.'

And we went to our own bedroom – together.

SATURDAY
VERA'S STORY

I was able to sneak in a side door of the conference room on the mezzanine being used for choir practice, and with my new iPhone I took several shots of Brother Joe from several different angles. It was hard to get a picture of his face straight from the front, but I got enough side and partial full face shots to piece together a full face photo properly – if I could still remember what my grandson taught me about photo-shopping. I was sitting in the back of the room when Brother Joe called a lunch break. I waved at Gerald and he came with me for a quick lunch.

'I found Rachael's maiden name,' I told him as we sat down at the table.

'Really? How?' he asked.

So I told him. The waitress came and we gave her our order, then he said, 'How does this help us?'

So I told him about Googling Rachael Gregory's name and how I came up with three names and narrowed it down to the one closest to her age from Texas. Gerald smiled at me. 'You are so clever, Vera!' He reached for my hand and I let him hold it.

'So here's the thing,' I said. 'Rachael's high-school class is having a reunion and they're looking for her. I thought about emailing the reunion committee – even started to a couple of times – but I'm not as clever as you think. Couldn't come up with a darn thing.'

'First off, what do we want to know from these people? If they're looking for her, how can they help us?' Gerald asked.

He had a point. I thought about it for a moment. 'Well, maybe we can find out who her closest friend was back then. Maybe they're still in touch, or a favorite teacher or something.'

I could see him shrug his shoulders in the reflection of the monitor. 'If they knew that, wouldn't they have asked those people first, before they put it out on the Internet?'

I was beginning to think Gerald was too damn smart for his britches.

'We'll figure out something,' he said. 'We'll go to the library as soon as we finish here. We should have a little time before rehearsal.'

'You poor baby,' I said and squeezed his hand. 'Your poor vocal cords are gonna be plum tuckered out before this day is over!'

By the time we finished eating – as you get older, your eating speed decreases – we only had fifteen minutes to spare in the library. But Gerald was quick on his feet. 'OK, how's this?' he said, standing behind me real close, his hands resting on the back of my chair, his thumbs on my shoulders. '"Dear Committee Chairperson, my name is whatever, and I work for attorney whoever, who is currently searching for a woman named then put her whole name in there, married included. We wish her no ill; in fact, she has been mentioned in someone's will. Please contact me as soon as possible if you hear from Mrs Donley, née Gregory." How's that?' he asked.

I changed the 'whatever' to my name, and named the attorney after Gerald. 'You don't mind, do you?' I asked him.

He smiled. 'Not at all,' he said.

'And I think we should take out the "we wish her no ill" part. Don't give 'em any ideas,' I said.

He patted my shoulder. 'You're right! That makes perfect sense.'

So we hurried out of the library and back to the rehearsal hall, where all three choirs rehearsed together for the next few hours. After that, we all headed to our rooms to rest and get ready for our concert. We were gonna be singing at eight o'clock but nobody wanted to eat before the concert for fear of throwing up once on stage, so we made arrangements with the kitchen for a late seating for all of us – all three choirs – around ten.

We were, as my grandchildren would say, awesome! Not one bad note from all three choirs. But that was because we were just one choir that night! And we sang for His glory! And the duet Gerald did with the lady from Louisiana brought tears to my eyes, it was that good.

Afterward we were a raucous bunch in the dining room. The place was empty when we got there, so we sorta took it over, pulling tables together so we ended up sitting in one giant circle. It was nice that I was sitting next to Gerald. There was a certain faction that ordered alcohol, but they were on the other side of the circle from me and Gerald, and even though they got loud, so did everyone else. It was a fun evening and neither of us brought up Rachael Donley.

Mr Jones and Mr Brown spent a great deal of the afternoon spying on the Ungers' lab, to no avail. The cop sat in an unmarked car across the street from the lab, reading a Lee Child book. They got close enough to see that the second time they drove by. After that they just parked and watched him. They were not aware that he was watching them back over the top of the Jack Reacher novel and had already taken down the license tag number of the Mercedes SUV. Unfortunately the Mercedes was registered to a holding company, which would take the authorities on a chase through many layers before it finally hit at an account in the Cayman Islands simply called 'The Cars Account,' and that only had a number attached to it, which the authorities in the Cayman Islands were not allowed by law to reveal. Of course, the police officer didn't know this and, even if he did, would probably have taken down the license number anyway.

After two hours, Mr Brown called Mr Big and explained their situation. Mr Big said something in Russian that sounded bad and a little scary, then said, 'Come back. We wait,' and then he hung up.

Mr Brown didn't want to go back. There was something about Mr Big that scared the hell out of him, but he wasn't about to let Mr Jones know that. Mr Jones was already skittish – he'd panic and run if he thought Mr Brown was thinking about panicking and running.

It was after three in the afternoon when they got back to Mr Big's mansion in River Oaks. Mr Brown thought that this section of the city was the quietest he'd ever been in, and he'd lived in Houston for almost twenty years. But River Oaks – man, the only people he'd seen since he started working for Mr Big were Mexican gardeners and black maids. Even Mr Big had some of those – a whole crew of Mexican gardeners and three black maids who came to clean every other day. No cook – he and Mr Green, the henchman, took turns with breakfast and lunch, and dinner was usually delivered by fancy restaurants that brought you take-out. Pretty cool, Mr Brown had thought, eating T-bone steak and a baked potato out of Styrofoam. But since he and Mr Green had snatched Mrs Unger, she'd been doing all the cooking. And she was pretty good at it.

Once inside the mansion, Mr Brown and Mr Jones both squared their shoulders, went to the door to Mr Big's library and knocked. A brusque 'Come in' reply and they entered. All three were there – Mr Big, Mr Green, and Mrs Unger. Mr Big was sitting on his throne-like chair, Mr Green was standing at rest by the French doors, and Mrs Unger was tied to a Louis XVI side chair, her mouth taped with duct tape.

Mr Jones appeared to be the only one who noticed that Mrs Unger, who was again crying, was also trying desperately to breathe, as her mouth was taped shut and her nose was filled with snot from all the crying. She was turning bluish and rocking her very expensive chair.

'Hey, y'all!' Mr Jones cried and ran to the widow and pulled off the duct tape.

Mrs Unger gulped in mouthfuls of air.

'*Mister* Jones!' Mr Big said in a loud voice. 'May I ask what you think you are doing?'

'She couldn't breathe!' Mr Jones said.

'Then it would behoove her to stop crying,' Mr Big said.

Mr Jones just stared at Mr Big. Finally he said, 'You mean you were letting her suffocate as *punishment*?'

Mr Big looked at Mr Brown. 'Can you not control your hired hand, Mr Brown?'

Mr Brown looked at Mr Jones and jerked his head toward the door. 'Out!' he whispered with a menacing snarl.

Mr Jones bent down to Mrs Unger. 'Ma'am, you OK?' he asked.

She shook her head. 'No, not even a little bit,' she said, tears starting up.

'Don't cry,' Mr Jones whispered.

'Out!' Mr Brown snarled louder.

Mr Jones left the library and went in search of the kitchen. When he found it, he checked out the fridge, found a Dr Pepper and sat down with it at the large round table. He opened the soda and his cell phone simultaneously and pushed the button to call Alicia, the brown-haired girl. The phone rang four times, then her sweet voice came on the line asking him to leave a message. He did. 'Hi, Alicia, it's Mr Jones. I'm in Houston at Mr Big's house. He's Russian, I think. Anyway, they've got this lady here against her will and I think it's that guy's wife, the one who fell off the Driscoll? Anyway, they're torturing her! The house is in River Oaks, but I don't know what street—' Hearing footsteps, he turned off his phone and put it in his pocket.

Mr Big's henchman walked in the kitchen. 'He want peanut butter samwish,' the hulking henchman said.

Mr Jones nodded at him. 'Make it,' the henchman said.

So Mr Jones got up and made a peanut butter 'samwish.' 'Does he want jelly?' Mr Jones asked, while still in the assembling phase.

The henchman turned and walked out of the room. Mr Jones stood there for two full minutes before the henchman came back. 'Grape,' he said.

While looking in the refrigerator for the grape jelly, Mr Jones asked the henchman, 'So what's your name? Or rather, what do we call you?'

'I am Mr Green,' he said.

'Of course you are,' Mr Jones said under his breath, getting a little tired of all the aka's. He finished the sandwich, put it on a plate and handed it to Mr Green. Mr Green set the plate down, opened a cabinet and brought out a silver tray, upon which he sat the plate with the sandwich, reached in the fridge and brought out a Yoohoo, set that on the tray next to a crystal glass, opened a drawer and pulled out a monogrammed linen napkin, then, without a word, left the kitchen.

As Mr Green left, Mr Brown came in.

'What the hell did you think you were doing in there?' Mr Brown spat at Mr Jones.

'The woman was dying!' Mr Jones said.

'He wouldn't have let her die!' Mr Brown said. 'He needs her.'

'For what?'

'That's on a need—'

'Oh, fuck off,' Mr Jones said.

Mr Brown sighed. 'I'm not really sure, but I think he wants her to make something for him. He's got a whole lab set up in the basement.' He shrugged. 'That's all I know and, personally, I just want my money so I can blow this whole scene.'

'You and me both,' Mr Jones said, elbows resting on the table, and feeling more dejected with every passing minute.

The kitchen door opened and Mr Green came in with one beefy hand squeezing Mrs Unger's upper arm. She was untied and ungagged. Mr Jones stood up as they came in the room.

'Where you taking her?' he asked.

Mr Green held up an index finger and moved it from side to side. Then continued to a door at the far end of the kitchen.

'That's the door to the basement,' Mr Brown said. 'I guess she finally agreed to work for him.'

Mr Green and Mrs Unger disappeared behind the door as Mr Jones and Mr Brown listened to the footfalls going downstairs.

Mr Jones said, 'I never heard of a basement in Houston. I thought we were too close to the ocean or something.'

'Naw, it's the ground water. We're too close to that. Not having basements is more of a southern thing. But these big mansions, like buildings downtown and whatnot, they got basements.' Mr Brown shrugged. 'Don't ask me.'

Mr Jones squinted his eyes at Mr Brown. 'How come you're being nice to me all of a sudden?'

Mr Brown sighed heavily. 'Because I'm tired of being cranky, and, besides, what you did in there, with Mrs Unger in front of Mr Big, I'd say normally that took balls. But with you, I'm just not sure if you're too stupid to realize how close you came to death.'

'Well, Mr Nice Guy's gone back into hiding,' Mr Jones said.

'No, I admire what you did. Wish I had the balls to do it. This whole situation here stinks. How come y'all killed Mr Unger in the first place? All Mr Big wanted was that damn satchel.'

'We didn't,' Mr Jones said. 'Well, I didn't, but Mr Smith didn't mean to. Mr Unger was too close to the edge, and me and Mr Smith had been running after him for a while, and Mr Smith was out of breath and mad, so he poked the guy in the chest too hard, I guess, and he just went over backwards.'

'So it was a fucking accident?' Mr Brown asked.

'Yeah, I guess that's what you'd call it.'

Mr Brown sighed heavily. 'That's not what the courts will call it – they'd call it murder in the commission of a felony and you'd be just as guilty as Smith.'

'What felony?' Mr Jones asked.

'Snatching the bag – no, you didn't. Chasing Unger? Not a felony.' Mr Brown smiled. 'You might be OK.'

'You think I should turn myself in?' Mr Jones asked.

'Jesus! Just when I'm beginning to think you're not a stupid asshole! No, doofus, you don't turn yourself in. Ever! Shit.' Mr Brown got up and left the room.

They didn't see Mrs Unger again that evening. Not even for dinner. Someone delivered what Mr Jones thought of as a whole bunch of Greek food around eight o'clock, and he and Mr Green spread it out on the table in the kitchen. Mr Green again loaded the silver tray for Mr Big, and told Mr Jones to make a similar tray for Mrs Unger. Mr Jones couldn't find another silver tray, but did find a plastic one. He found the plates and served the lady a little of everything, eager to go downstairs and see this lab, and especially to check that Mrs Unger was OK. He was worried about her. Not knowing her drink preference, Mr Jones fixed her a glass of ice water and a Diet Coke, knowing ladies liked the diet stuff. He found one of the monogrammed linen napkins, placed the ornate silverware on the tray, and headed to the door to the basement.

Mr Green caught him halfway there. 'No,' he said. 'Give.' He held out his arms for the tray. 'Open,' he said, indicating with his head the door to the basement. 'Key,' he said, nodding at his pants pocket. A large placard, like one you'd see at a gas station for the men's room, hung out of Mr Green's left side pocket. At the end of it was one key.

Mr Jones used it to open the door. Mr Green just stood there. Mr Jones nodded his head at the door. 'It's open,' he said. Still Mr Green just stood there. 'What? Aren't you going down? I fixed all the food for her—' It was then that Mr Jones noticed the look on Mr Green's face. It wasn't pleasant. In fact, he had the distinct feeling Mr Green was contemplating doing harm to Mr Jones for reasons unknown to Mr Jones. And then it clicked. He put the key on the tray and Mr Green stopped looking at him and went down the stairs to the basement.

Mr Jones sighed audibly and headed for the table. That encounter had taken the steam out of Mr Jones. He wasn't even hungry any more. He grabbed a dolmas out of the bag and slowly ate it.

THIRTEEN

SUNDAY

I woke up at seven in the morning. Totally awake, not going back to sleep, no way, no how. I hated that. I love to sleep. I love to sleep late. I love to lie in bed on a weekend morning with my husband and spoon. I used to love it when the kids would barge in the room way too early on a weekend and jump in bed with us – all three of them plus us in the king-sized bed; this was before Alicia joined the family. Back when they were little. God, how I missed that.

I got out of bed, trying not to disturb Alicia, although I think an earthquake wouldn't disturb Alicia, and headed for the bathroom, hoping that what woke me was just the need to pee, and then I could go back to sleep. Of course I was able to pee – when am I not? But I was still wide awake. I wandered into the kitchen and put on the coffee, grabbed some orange juice and went to the front door to see if the Sunday Austin paper had been delivered. It had so I took it back to the kitchen with me, finished the OJ, then started on the coffee. Then it hit me: we were going to Houston today! That's why I couldn't sleep! I realized my face was hurting from the large smile. Why was I smiling? Because I was getting out of town? Because Luna was getting her husband back? Because Graham would be going back to school? No, in my heart of hearts, I knew the reason I was smiling was that I was back in on the chase.

God help me, that was it. I lost the smile. What kind of person was I that normal things went to the backburner when there was a crime to be solved? I wasn't in law enforcement – not police, or a bounty hunter, or a private detective, or even a lawyer (although the bounty hunter thing had possibilities – I would look good in black lycra with crossed ammo belts). There was the added bonus of a fancy hotel with piped-in movies and room service, and as much nookie as either of us could handle. I was going to try to be more mature about this. Take a back seat to Luna and her Houston brethren.

Try not to go crazy. Well, at least not bat-shit crazy. I have a tendency toward bat-shit crazy.

I opened the paper, ready to be dazzled by the daily mayhem.

'What do you mean, you called Luna?' DeWitt said around a mouthful of granola bar.

'Oh, I don't know,' Mayfair said. 'I think I mean I picked up my phone and punched in her number and said, "Hello, Luna, this is Mayfair."'

'God, I hate it when you try to be cute—'

'I never have to *try* to be cute. It's just who I am,' Mayfair said.

DeWitt slammed his fist against the steering wheel of their car. '*Why* did you call her? You think we need the help of some yokel cop who couldn't find these guys even in her Podunk town, much less a city the size of Houston, for God's sake!'

'I thought it would be nice to have someone around to bounce ideas off. You don't bounce. On you, they just fall flat.'

'Yeah? Well maybe it's not me – maybe it's your ideas!' DeWitt said.

'Whatever,' Mayfair said, watching the city flash by her side window, glad once again that her parents had opted to leave Houston when she was a kid and settle in Austin instead. Coming from the gateway to the Hill Country, all this flatness made her anxious. The only hills in sight were overpasses.

'So she's actually coming here?' DeWitt said.

'Yep. She'll meet us at HPD around noon.'

'Again, why?'

'Again, bite me.'

They were on their own for breakfast. Mr Jones still didn't see Mrs Unger, and he also didn't see Mr Green take a tray down to her. As he was alone in the kitchen, Mr Jones went to the door of the basement and turned the knob. He almost fell over from shock when it turned in his hand. As it was, he drew his hand back like the knob had been on fire. He touched it again, turned it, and pulled the door back. Looking down the stairs, he saw nothing but a black pit. Looking up, he saw a light switch on the door's inner frame. He flipped it on and the stairs lit up. Checking behind him to make sure no one else had come into the kitchen, he stepped onto the small landing, letting the door silently close behind him.

Gingerly he made his way down the stairs, holding on to the railings. At the bottom it was gloomy and dark. He looked around for another light switch and found one. Switching it on exposed an empty basement. Well, empty of any lab-type stuff, as far as Mr Jones could tell. There was a broken chair, some lawn furniture, and a few boxes, but definitely not a lab.

To the right of the stairs was a door that opened into a large laundry room. Straight across from the stairs was another door, with a padlock. Mr Jones went to this door and knocked. And again, shock: someone answered.

'Hello?' A woman's voice.

'Mrs Unger?' Mr Jones asked.

'Yes?' she said, her voice closer to the door now.

'Are you OK?' he asked.

'Please let me out of here,' she said.

'The door's padlocked,' Mr Jones explained.

'You're the big guy, right? The big American guy? Can you kick it in?' she begged.

'I probably shouldn't do that. Mr Big would get real P.O.'d if I did that.'

'Who's Mr Big?' she asked.

'You know, that Russian guy who runs this,' Mr Jones explained.

'Oh, Vlad,' she said, derisively. 'I'd call him Mr Bald.'

Mr Jones laughed. 'Yeah, he is pretty bald, huh? How come you know his name?'

'He was our financial backer. In case you get away and I don't, know this: his name is Vladimir Andronikov. This is his house—'

'What street are we on? I called my friend and left a message, but I didn't know what street to tell her.'

'Dalton Lane,' Mrs Unger said. 'Who did you call? Are they on their way? Did you call the police?'

'Well, now, no, I didn't call the police. I don't know any police. But I called my friend – she's this girl we kidnapped, but she likes me because I helped her get out of it, and she'll help us, I swear.'

'A girl? Are you being sexist or is it really a girl? How old?'

'Like sixteen, seventeen, hard to tell.'

'Shit! A girl! How can she possibly help?' Mrs Unger asked.

'She's real smart,' Mr Jones said.

Mr Jones heard the door open above. 'Gotta go!' he said and

scooted quickly into the laundry room, and hid behind one of the machines.

From above he heard someone say something in Russian. Then someone else answered him in Russian. Had to be Mr Big – Mr Bald! Ha! He liked that – and his henchman Mr Green. Mr Big's voice, higher in octave, was screaming at Mr Green, who's deep, throaty voice sounded defeated. Their voices grew louder as they came down the stairs.

Mr Big said something else in Russian and then Mr Jones heard the hasp of the lock being withdrawn and the door to the room where Mrs Unger was being held opened.

'Ah, Elizabeth,' Mr Big said in a bright voice.

Mr Jones moved to the door of the laundry room and opened it a crack to listen.

'How are you this morning?' Mr Big said.

Mrs Unger didn't answer.

'Are you hungry?' Still no answer. 'Mr Green, please fix our good doctor some breakfast. With a lot of hot, hot coffee, eh? You Americans love your hot, hot coffee. I prefer tea, but as you Americans say, "Different strokes for different folks."' Mr Big laughed.

'Actually,' Mrs Unger said, 'no one has used that reference since the mid-eighties. You're behind in your slang, Vlad.'

'Please, Elizabeth, don't try to make me angry. You know what I'm like when I'm angry. We don't want to see that again, do we?'

Mrs Unger said nothing.

'So, Elizabeth, how does it go? Were you able to accomplish anything last night? I hope that flash drive was all that you said it would be.'

'The flash drive is fine. What I *need* are those notebooks from my lab. Do you have them?'

'We'll try again today to get them for you. The police are watching your lab.'

'Too bad they weren't watching my house,' Mrs Unger said. 'Maybe then they could have killed all of you.'

'What is that word? Oh, yes! Spunk! You are showing spunk today, Elizabeth. What has changed that makes you feel you can disrespect me as you are now doing? Do I not still have you as my hostage? Do I not have the ability to tear off the rest of your finger-nails at my whim? Can I not still kill you with a wave of my hand?'

More footfalls on the stairs. Mr Jones nudged the laundry room door a little closer to totally shut, and watched as Mr Green came down with a tray and walked into the lab room. He never looked anywhere but straight ahead. Mr Jones opened the door a little wider.

'Ah, Elizabeth, see what we have for you! Scrambled eggs – Misha, did you use butter and cheese?'

'Yes.'

'Good. Doesn't that sound yummy, Elizabeth? And some bacon, and wheat toast! What a good breakfast! Oh, and look, Elizabeth, orange juice and a carafe of coffee. Is it the good kind, Misha? The kind with lots of caffeine so that our good doctor will have plenty of energy to work for us today?'

'Yes,' Mr Green said.

'There! You see, Elizabeth, I am still your friend. What happened to James was an accident, as I've told you so many times. And my Misha will handle getting your notebooks for you, right, Misha?'

'Yes,' Mr Green said.

'So, dear friend, eat up, and before you know it we will both be billionaires! Won't that be fun?'

'I don't want your blood money!' Mrs Unger screamed.

Mr Jones heard the sound of a slap and heard Mrs Unger cry out. It took all his strength to keep from leaping out of his hiding place and bashing in a few skulls. He was afraid that if he tried it, Misha, or Mr Green, or whoever, who was definitely bigger than Mr Jones, would be the one bashing in *his* skull. And what good would that do Mrs Unger? She'd be on her own.

'See, Elizabeth? You made my Misha nervous. When he's nervous he lashes out. Raising your voice to me is one thing that makes Misha very nervous.'

He saw them coming out of the lab room and pulled the door in, only leaving enough room to see the lab door itself. He watched as Misha reset the padlock and followed Mr Big up the stairs.

We decided to ride to Houston in Luna's car – me in the back seat, *of course* – with the plan for Willis and me to return by Am Track, which had a station in Codderville. I'd always wanted to take a train – it was just unfortunate that Houston is only a few hours away. I'd like to do the whole compartment overnight thing. Pretend Willis was Cary Grant and I was Eva Marie Saint, get a little *North by*

Northwest action. That would be cool. Elena and Eddie would drive her car back to Codderville.

Since this was half work and half vacation, Luna was driving her personal car and would turn in the mileage which would be half paid – a portion by BCRPD and a portion by Codderville PD. All the fractioning was boggling my mind. I am not a friend of math. Her personal car was a 2001 Lincoln Town car, in pristine condition. Since she usually drove her unmarked, the Lincoln had very little mileage on it and was gorgeous. It's interesting that as I age, cars I used to make fun of – like Cadillacs and Lincolns and those enormous Chryslers – I now look at and go 'ahhh.' Is it just me? Of course, I wouldn't trade in my two-seater Audi for all the big luxury cars in the world. But Luna's Lincoln had plenty of legroom in the backseat, which put me too far away from the front seat to hear clearly what Willis and Luna were discussing. So, after trying to pull my seatbelt up enough to lean forward and listen, I finally gave up and sat back in the plush seat and thought about the past few hours.

It had been a lovefest when Graham packed his car around ten this morning, ready to take off for Austin. There was a tearful scene at breakfast when Megan and Graham made up – she was crying, not my macho son – and as he packed his car, Megan and Bess were all over him, hugging and kissing him, telling him to buy them things that could only be found in Austin – what, I don't know. Then Willis and I took our turns, hugging and kissing him, and telling him to study, study, study. Then the four of us went back into the house by the kitchen door to leave Graham and Alicia alone. I'm not saying we didn't all peek through the window. Graham finally got in the car and started it, then, with one last long kiss from Alicia through the window, he took off. Alicia headed for the kitchen door and the four of us headed to the sofas, Willis quickly turning on the TV.

When she came in the door, she was crying. I'd decided it would look more natural if I was in the kitchen, which was my usual spot when not in my office, so I was closest to her when she came in. Seeing her face, I engulfed her in my arms, took her to the bedroom and sat her on the bed.

'You can cry here all you want. Either alone or with me.'

She reached up and pulled me by the hand down to the bed. And laid her head on my shoulder and we both cried. In about three minutes both my other girls poked their heads in the door to my bedroom, saw what was going on, and jumped on the king-sized bed, both bawling, and holding on to Alicia and me. And I thought maybe I shouldn't wish to go back in time like I had earlier. I was very uncomfortable physically – they weren't little kids anymore. Somewhere during all this musing my early morning rising got to me and I fell asleep.

When I woke up we were pulling off the freeway in search of Reasoner Street – home of the main Houston cop shop.

SUNDAY
VERA'S STORY

Today would be the close of the convention. A big breakfast event with a church service while we ate. I thought that was sacrilege, but I'm just an old woman and no one cares what I think. Gerald was going to do a solo, as was that Louisiana woman, and there was a quartet from the Atlanta choir also performing. And then we had to check out before noon.

Luckily none of the drinkers from the night before were going to perform today – I could see a few of them dotted among the tables, bleary-eyed, drinking coffee like crazy and holding ice water glasses to their foreheads. There's a reason we Baptists, as a rule, don't drink. And I was seeing it right before my very eyes. Not to mention it's a sin. And don't start with that old saw about how Jesus drank wine. That's all they had. I'm sure the water was polluted.

There were so many preachers at this convention that they had to take turns giving the sermon and everybody wanted to one-up each other. Luckily Brother Joe wasn't one of them. It might just be me, but he's a piss-poor example of a Baptist preacher. The first preacher to speak really knew his fire and brimstone, only he went on a little too long, like forty minutes, which left the second and third guys only ten minutes each, but I've never known a preacher who could say hello in less than half an hour. It was near on eleven in the morning before we got out of there.

Once in my room, I remembered I hadn't sent E.J. those pictures of Brother Joe. I glanced through them. Three pretty good shots. And one with Gerald in the background. I bet I could blow that up, crop out Brother Joe, and I'd have a very nice picture of Gerald. If I wanted one, and I'm not saying I did. It was just a possibility. I hit send on all three pictures and started packing up the last of my things – I'd packed most of them the night before – when there was a knock on my door. I opened it to find a bell hop standing there. As I hadn't called for one to help me with my bags – I'm perfectly capable of handling my own bags, thank you very much, and don't feel like it's worth a dollar a bag just to have them taken downstairs! – all I could say was, 'Yes?'

'Ma'am,' he said, flourishing an envelope addressed to Rachael Donley. I took it, smiled and said thank you. I didn't tip him. I suppose I should have, but I forgot.

After Mom and Dad left, Alicia headed for her room. 'No!' Megan said, grabbing her by the arm. 'You're not going to mope around all day, right, Bess?'

'Absolutely!' Bess agreed. They dragged her toward the back door. 'We're going to go do something.'

'I'm not in the mood—' Alicia started.

'Who cares?' Megan interrupted. 'He'll be back on Friday. Get over it. Now, movie, fast food, or bowling?'

'Miniature golf,' Alicia said.

Megan and Bess looked at each other, shrugged and Bess said, 'Sure. Miniature golf it is.'

No one knew whose turn it was to drive, so Megan declared it hers and no one argued with her. Arguing with Megan often got tiresome. It was while they were driving to Codderville, the location of the nearest miniature golf course, that Alicia decided to check her messages.

We were sitting at a round table in a conference room on the second floor of the main police station, simply called Reasoner Street, as it resides on a street called Reasoner – clever, these Houstonians – waiting for the lieutenant in charge of homicide, Buddy Nixon, to show up. There were the three of us – Willis, Luna, and me – plus the Hatfields and McCoys, aka Mayfair and DeWitt from Austin, and the Houston detectives in charge of the case, Larry Mann and Dave Marshall, known in the squad as 'Marshallman.' Larry looked like Paul Newman in his later years – in his sixties, trim build, blue eyes, gray hair and a wicked grin. Dave was thirty years younger, small in stature, and totally unremarkable.

We'd talked a little bit – all small talk – and were quietly awaiting the lieutenant's arrival when my cell phone made an urgent sound.

Worried about my kids for all sorts of reasons, I picked it up to see a text from my mother-in-law. Who in the world taught her to text? I'll have their heads! The text said, 'Sending you pic. Bro Joe. Get Luna to ID.' And sure enough a picture came on my screen of two men, one young, one old.

I showed the picture to Luna. 'Vera wants you to ID this guy.'

'Which one?' she asked.

'The younger one, I think. It's her preacher. She suspects him of having murdered her roommate.'

'Like I have time for this?'

We were still looking when the lieutenant walked in, crossing behind Luna and me.

He stopped short and grabbed the phone out of Luna's hand. 'Where did you get this?' he said, his tone gruff.

'My mother-in-law just sent it,' I said. 'It's her preacher. She wants an ID on him.'

'Oh, I can ID him all right!' the lieutenant said. 'He's the prick who killed my brother-in-law.'

SUNDAY
VERA'S STORY

I opened the letter addressed to Rachael. It was postmarked from some town I've never heard of in Florida. Inside was a note: 'Rachael, here's that picture of your uncle Thomas. That's your me-maw he's standing with. If you did find him, honey, stay away! He's very dangerous! Call the police immediately! Love you, Mom.'

I looked at the picture. Two people standing in front of a barn, looking at the camera, a young man with his arm over the shoulders of an older woman. She was scowling; he was smiling fit to beat the band. The older woman was wearing a housedress from the fifties, maybe, her hair in pin curls, wearing shoes and socks, with a sweater pulled over her shoulders. The young man was wearing blue jeans with cuffs, motorcycle boots and a motorcycle jacket over a white T-shirt. He had a hairstyle I remembered from my youth, called a DA – the top slicked back with Brill Cream – and, I'm sure, even though the picture didn't show it, the back was combed into a duck tail. Hence the term DA: duck's ass. The picture was in black and white. He was a good-looking young man, I thought.

Did Rachael run into this man, her uncle Thomas, here at the convention? Is that what happened to her? Her mother said he was dangerous: did he kill Rachael? I sat down on my designated bed. This was getting real. I think maybe I was just playing at this, pretending to be E.J. in my head. Thinking in my heart of hearts that it was just as likely that Rachael had run off with some man or something. But maybe she didn't. Maybe she really was in trouble, or worse, already dead. Uncle Thomas was a dangerous man. Her mother said so. What she didn't say was why.

Well, the picture certainly wasn't of Brother Joe. He was barely older than the young man in the photo. I still didn't like him, but maybe he wasn't a mass murderer like I'd hoped he was.

I finished packing, put the picture of Uncle Thomas in my sweater pocket and headed out the door, taking the elevator to the lobby. I'd just finished checking out when I saw Gerald walking my way. I smiled and walked up to him. He was grinning back at me.

'I got us two connecting rooms at a small – they call it boutique – but very nice hotel in Georgetown,' he said, still smiling.

'Well, I don't know that we need to stay, Gerald. Whoever did away with poor Rachael, it wasn't Brother Joe. Looks like it was her uncle,' I said, pulling the picture out of my pocket.

It wasn't until the picture was in my hand and I was looking at it, then at Gerald, that I realized that the good-looking boy had turned into a good-looking old man. Gerald grabbed the picture out of my hand.

'Brother Joe?' I said, standing up. 'How did he' – I said, pointing at Brother Joe, 'kill your brother-in-law?'

'Not him!' the lieutenant said. 'Him!' And he pointed to the older man. 'I'd recognize that scumbag anywhere! Old man now or not!'

I took the phone back from him and handed it to Willis. 'Who is that?' I asked him.

Willis shook his head. 'I don't know.' Then he stood up and looked at me. 'Ah, you don't think that could be Gerald, do you?'

'Oh my God!' I said. I turned to the lieutenant. 'What did this guy do?'

'He's a real winner,' he said, sitting down at the head of the table. Willis and I took our seats next to each other, holding hands. 'His name is Thomas Gregory, a white supremist who was hording guns back in 'seventy-two, I think. An ATF agent came on his land to deliver a warrant to search the property for illegal firearms, and Gregory shot him dead. The FBI got him and he was arrested. A year later he was standing trial at the federal courthouse here in Houston. On the day the trial was to end and the verdict come out, I guess he didn't like his chances. So he killed one of his guards, severally wounded the other and made it out a window. He was never seen again. My little sister's husband was the wounded guard. He ended up in a coma and, after six months, she had to make the decision to pull the plug.' The lieutenant's hands were balled into fists, the knuckles getting whiter and whiter, his face getting redder and redder. 'Gale, my little sister, was a widow and single mother of two toddlers when she was only twenty-five. So, yeah, I know who this guy is and I want to know where that picture was taken and how to get him.'

Willis and I looked at each other. 'Oh, shit,' he said, and grabbed my phone, still out on the table, and called his mother back. It went to voicemail. 'Mom! Call me! Now! It's urgent,' he said and hung up. He looked so terrified I almost burst into tears. I had no idea what to do now. We were in Houston – she was in Washington, D.C.

I turned to the lieutenant and said, 'She's at the Hyatt in D.C. at a convention. This man is there with her. It's a church choir thing. Can you call the D.C. police? Her name is Vera Pugh, from Codderville, Texas. She's five foot one, gray hair, thin—'

I turned to Willis. He shook his head. 'I don't know if she has any birthmarks or anything,' he said.

Luna was on the phone before the lieutenant had even pulled his out of his pocket. 'We'll find her,' she said to Willis and me. 'Don't worry, we'll find her!'

'OMG!' Alicia shouted from the back seat. 'Listen to this!' She held up her phone and pushed the speaker button. 'Hi, Alicia, it's Mr Jones. I'm in Houston at Mr Big's house. He's Russian, I think. Anyway, they've got this lady here against her will and I think it's that guy's wife, the one who fell off the Driscoll? Anyway, they're torturing her! The house is in River Oaks, but I don't know what street—' And then there was a dead line.

'Shit!' Megan said.

'Oh my God!' Bess said. 'Call Mom! Quick!'

'You call her!' Alicia said. 'I don't know how I can call her and play this back at the same time.'

'Well,' Bess said, 'what you do is—'

'Jesus, Bess!' Megan shouted. 'Just call Mom, for God's sake!'

'You don't have to get all uppity about it!' Bess said, pulling out her phone. She hit the button for her mom's cell and waited. Three rings and she picked up.

'Can't talk now,' Mom said.

'Don't hang up!' Bess shouted. 'We have big news from Mr Jones!'

Alicia grabbed Bess's phone. 'Mom, listen! I just got a call from Mr Jones—'

'Oh my God! How did he get your number?' Mom demanded.

'Later, Mom! He called me. Listen!' And she played Mr Jones's message.

'Let me put this on speaker and then play it again. OK, go.'

After she'd played the message for a fourth time, Alicia asked her mom, 'Now what?'

'Just sit tight. We'll get back to you,' and she hung up.

'What did she say?' Bess asked.

'She said to sit tight,' Alicia said.

'What does that mean?' from Megan.

'Go home?' Alicia suggested.

'Hell, no,' Megan said, hitting the accelerator. 'She can call us just as easily at the miniature golf course as she can at home.'

'You think I should call Mr Jones back?' Alicia asked.

'You have his number?' Bess said, turning around in her seat to gape at her sister.

Looking hang-dogged, Alicia said, 'I should have told Mom that, huh?'

'Only if you want Mr Jones arrested!' Megan said. 'Me? I don't care. But he did save your life, Alicia.'

'True,' Alicia said. 'I'll call him when we get to Codderville.'

'I want it on record that I think you should tell Mom that guy's phone number,' Bess said.

All in agreement, they headed to Codderville.

Mr Jones made his way back to the door of the lab. 'Mrs Unger?' he said quietly.

'Yes?' she answered.

'You OK?' he asked.

'No,' she said.

'I mean, did he hurt you bad?' Mr Jones thought she might be thinking he meant about the whole situation, rather than just the slap on the face.

'The slap?' she said. 'No. I've had worse from his precious Misha before that.'

'Look, I'm going to try to get out of the house today at some point. I haven't heard back from Alicia, my friend, and I called her yesterday. I guess she hasn't checked her messages—' His phone vibrated in his pocket. He pulled it out and saw Alicia's name on the screen. He smiled big. 'Hey! Speak of the devil! Here she is now!' He punched the phone on and said, 'Hi, Alicia!'

'Oh my God, Mr Jones! Are you OK?'

'Yeah, physically, but Mrs Unger's being tortured. They pulled off one of her fingernails!' Mr Jones said.

'Oh, yuck!' Alicia said. He could hear her repeating what he'd said to others.

'You with your family?' he asked.

'Just my sisters. My parents went to Houston with our neighbor, Mrs Luna. She's the pol—'

'Yeah, the police lady. I sorta met her,' Mr Jones said.

'They're looking for you,' she said.

'Well, I'm no friend of the cops, but I think they need to come here with a warrant. Mrs Unger is in the basement in a locked room. There are three other people in the house – wait, what day is it?'

'Sunday,' Alicia said.

'Right. No maids or gardeners on Sunday. So upstairs is Mr Brown, I don't know his real name, but Mr Big's real name is— Mrs Unger, what's Mr Big's real name?'

'Vladimir Andronikov. And the address here is 410 Dalton Lane.'

Mr Jones repeated that information, getting the correct spelling of Vlad's last name from Mrs Unger.

'And the last guy is Misha, aka Mr Green. He's bigger than me and a lot meaner. He's Mr Androno— Whatever, Mr Big's henchman. So tell them to take him down first.'

'What about you, Mr Jones?' Alicia asked, her voice sounding worried.

'Don't worry about me, sweet girl. I'll find a way out of here. Mr Jones always lands on his feet.' He hung up the phone and turned to the locked door. 'You hear all that, ma'am?' he asked.

'Yes, I did, Mr Jones. By the way, what's your real name?'

'Aw, ma'am, I'm not gonna tell you that. I could get in a lot of trouble. But somebody's coming to help you, OK? You hang in there.'

He'd heard Mr Green throw the deadbolt on the door at the head of the stairs, so he knew there would be no way to get out, and even so, they were probably in the kitchen and if they caught him they would more than likely kill him. And he was afraid it wouldn't be fast. He was afraid he'd give out Alicia's name, and start the whole nightmare all over again for her and her family.

But over in the corner, opposite the door to the laundry room, was a window. Big enough, he hoped, to get his shoulders through. Exit Mr Jones, he thought. Ernie Stanton was heading home.

FOURTEEN

SUNDAY

My phone rang again while we were still discussing what to do about what. It was Alicia. I said, 'Hey,' and she said, 'Mom, you still with all the cops?'

'Yes,' I said.

'Then put me on speaker.'

I did and told her she had the room. 'OK. Listen, y'all. I just talked to Mr Jones again. Mr Big's name is Vladimir Andronikov and he lives at 410 Dalton Street in River Oaks—'

'I know him!' Lt Nixon said. 'Really bad guy.'

'Mrs Unger is in the basement in a locked room. There are three men upstairs: Mr Big, his henchman Misha, aka Mr Green, and Mr Brown. We don't know Mr Brown's real name.'

'Nobody else?' Lt Nixon asked.

'No,' my daughter said.

'What about Mr Jones?'

'I think you'll find only three men on the premises,' she said.

'So your Mr Jones is on the lamb, huh?' Lt Nixon asked.

'I'm sorry, I really wouldn't know anything about that. Mom, take me off speaker, please.'

I did and she said, 'Wow, is that guy rude or what?'

'Y'all lock all the doors and windows—'

'We're not at home, Mom. We're playing miniature golf.'

All I could do was shake my head. 'Just be careful, OK?' I said and hung up.

Lt Nixon was talking. 'Luna and me will work on the D.C. problem. Meanwhile, Marshallman, y'all take DeWitt and Mayfair with you to the River Oaks address. You might want to have SWAT back-up. This Andronikov is a seriously deranged socio-path. Now go.'

The four departed quickly, and I turned to my husband and whispered, 'What do we do?'

'Weren't you listening?' he scolded.

I don't like to be scolded. I didn't like it when I was three, and I certainly don't like it now. But his mother was possibly in the clutches of another dangerous sociopath, so I'd let it go for now. 'I was still on the phone with Alicia,' I said.

'Oh, right. Sorry. We're with the lieutenant and Luna. Working on the D.C. problem, i.e., my mother.'

'Who did you talk to in D.C.?' Lt Nixon asked Luna.

'I have a friend in the FBI. Agent Lorraine Jones. I figured this would be FBI jurisdiction.'

'Yeah, ATF agent dead, federal court guards dead. Pretty much FBI worthy. What did she say?'

'She's gonna call me back.'

'Give me her fuckin' number,' the lieutenant said.

While he called Special Agent Jones, I dialed Vera's number again. It went to voicemail.

SUNDAY
VERA'S STORY

'Let go of me!' I screamed. Unfortunately there were so many people in the lobby, all checking out, and making so much noise, that my words got lost in the mayhem.

Gerald didn't let go, but dragged me toward the front doors of the hotel. I tried stomping on his foot, but it didn't slow him down. First time in forty years I've regretted giving up high heels.

We were on the street, and he was still dragging me and I was still screaming. Surely somebody would notice a little old lady being dragged off against her will! Surely?

We were half a block from the hotel when we heard sirens. Black SUVs stormed the hotel. I waved my free arm at the people exiting the vehicles, but nobody seemed to notice.

'Hey!' someone said.

Gerald had stopped, but hadn't let up his hold on me. 'Get out of the way!' Gerald shouted.

I turned away from the black SUVs to see a black kid, a teenager, in baggy pants and a baggy sleeveless shirt, underwear showing, a hat pulled sideways on his head, and neon-yellow running shoes, standing in Gerald's way.

'He's a killer!' I yelled at the kid.

'Oh, yeah?' The kid said. 'Me too.' He pulled a very large gun from behind his back. I think it was a Glock. 'Let go of the old lady and give me your wallet,' the kid said.

Gerald didn't just let go of me, he shoved me away. I can only assume from what happened next that he had a gun hidden on him somewhere. He shot the kid, who shot at him, but somehow the kid missed and got me instead.

Mayfair and DeWitt were in the backseat of Marshallman's car. The two HPD detectives had to open the back doors for the two APD detectives. They'd come at the mansion from the back, no sirens, parked on a side street, and went to the house on foot. A SWAT team was on the perimeter, locked and loaded. Mann, the older detective, held the warrant, hastily signed by a judge, in his left hand. He hit the doorbell with his right.

Inside they could hear the first several notes of 'Lara's Theme' from *Dr Zhivago*. The door was opened by a large man, in his forties, possibly, with thick wavy brown hair, a face with overly large features, and hands the size of baseball gloves.

'We have a warrant to search these premises,' Larry Mann said.

The big guy slammed the door shut and Larry motioned for the SWAT team. They came up fast and used a ramrod to break the door in. Once the door was down, the big guy pointed a large Glock at them and began to shoot, so SWAT team members shot back. The big guy, who Mayfair decided had to be Misha, aka Mr Green, lay dead on the floor. Behind him stood a short, well-built man with his hands up.

'Mr Brown, I presume?' Detective Mann said.

'Yes, sir. I'll go quietly. Just get me out of this house. These people are crazy.'

'Where's Andronikov?' Mann asked.

'Who?' Mr Brown said, his brow furrowed.

'Mr Big,' DeWitt supplied.

'Oh. Downstairs. In the basement with Mrs Unger, I think.'

'But you're not sure?' Mann clarified.

'No, sir, I'm not positive, no.'

'Where's the door to the basement?' Mayfair asked.

Mr Brown pointed toward the back of the house with his head, his arms still raised. 'In the kitchen. That way.'

Mann nodded to two patrolmen they'd brought along. 'Take him downtown,' he said.

'Thank you,' Mr Brown said as they cuffed him. 'Thank you so much.'

Marshall and Mann sent two of the SWAT members to the kitchen in search of the door to the basement, two more upstairs, and the last two to check out the rest of the first floor.

'Got it!' one of the team members called from the back. All four detectives hurried toward the sound of her voice. She and her partner were both standing at the head of the basement steps, the door of which opened into a fabulous kitchen. Mayfair couldn't help noticing that. She'd always wanted a kitchen like this.

Following the SWAT team members down the stairs into the basement, they saw the door Alicia had described with the hasp and lock, only the lock was missing and the hasp was open. Mayfair nodded at the team member who'd called to them, who turned the handle and opened the door.

Everyone had their guns out and pointing inside the room, where Vladimir Andronikov stood behind Elizabeth Unger, a knife at her throat and a gun in his hand, pointed toward them.

'Drop it, Vlad,' Mann said. 'You know you're not getting out of this. We have you on so much shit you won't be seeing daylight in your lifetime.'

'Then maybe I commit what they call suicide by cop, yes?' Mr Big said. 'I slit her throat and then you kill me, yes? Sounds good to me.'

Although Mr Big was shorter than Mrs Unger and his head and body were hidden from view, one of his legs was exposed.

'Or we could do this,' Larry Mann said and shot Mr Big in the knee. Mr Big fell back, but the knife had been close enough to Mrs Unger's skin that it nicked her going down. Mr Big was screaming and the SWAT team members were on him, relieving him of his weapons.

Mayfair ran to Mrs Unger, who'd fallen back against a table and was holding her neck. Blood was seeping through her fingers.

Mayfair grabbed a box of Kleenex off another table, balled a bunch up in her fist, removed Mrs Unger's hand and placed the wad of tissue against her neck.

'It's not serious,' Mrs Unger said. 'I don't think it's much more than a scratch.'

In a relaxed manner, Larry Mann turned to the others, SWAT members included, and said, 'You saw him start to shoot me, right?'

Everyone nodded. Including Mrs Unger, who said, 'You can finish the job now, if you like. I won't breathe a word of it.' Then she passed out.

SUNDAY
VERA'S STORY

Well, I guess all that shooting finally got the attention of those people in the black SUVs with the sirens. Somebody tackled Gerald, or Uncle Tom, or whoever the hell he was. He fell hard on the sidewalk and, God forgive me, I kinda hoped he broke a hip. Somebody else was there taking care of the boy who saved me, and there was somebody hovering over me too, only none of these people were medics.

'Has anyone called for an ambulance?' I asked the person hovering over me, who was a pretty young woman with very short hair – which I feel most policewomen should have. I mean, all these young women on TV who are FBI or sheriff's deputies or police or whatever, with their long hair. How easy would that be for a perp (they call the bad guys 'perps,' you know) to grab that long hair and choke her to death, or at least get hold of her. That's all I'm saying.

'Yes, ma'am,' my pretty young woman with the very short hair said. 'They're on their way.'

'How's the boy? He saved me, you know,' I told her. My arm was beginning to throb, and I took my hand away to look at it. It appeared a large chunk of my arm was missing. Good thing I grew up on a farm or I woulda been puking on the streets of the nation's capital.

'He's OK,' she said. 'It was a through-and-through, almost identical to yours.'

'They were standing right in front of each other!' I said in disgust. 'Both of 'em piss poor shots, I reckon.'

'And thank God for that,' she said with a smile. 'By the way,' she stuck out her hand, 'I'm Special Agent Sanchez, FBI.'

'Sanchez – you Mexican?' I asked.

'Yes, ma'am. From Corpus Christi, Texas,' she said.

I shook her hand and grinned at her through my pain. 'A fellow Texan. Hallelujah!'

She grinned back. 'Sometimes I feel the same way, living here. Ma'am, I need to get your name, and where you're from in Texas, if you don't mind.'

'Vera Pugh, Codderville, Texas. That's halfway between Brenham and La Grange.'

Then they heard more sirens, as two ambulances came to stop near them.

'Two?' Vera asked.

'One for you and your hero, young Tyrone, there, and the other for our prisoner.'

'Where's my roommate? Did he kill her? Maybe he's got her hidden somewhere and she'll die if we don't find her quick.'

'We're still investigating, ma'am,' Special Agent Sanchez said.

One of the EMTs got me on a gurney but I still had a few thousand questions for my special agent. 'Who called y'all? How'd you get here so fast? Find my roommate: Rachael Gregory Donley—' I was trying to get all this out in a hurry, but I was shoved into the back of the ambulance, with Tyrone beside me and no special agent in sight.

'I hear your name's Tyrone,' I said.

'Yes, ma'am,' he said.

'Well, I'm Vera Pugh. I wanna thank you, Tyrone, for saving my life.'

'Ma'am, I seen you there with that old man messin' with you and I said to myself, "Tyrone, what if that was your grams? What would you want someone to do?" So I did it.'

'That's all well and good, Tyrone,' I said, 'but you know you shouldn't steal. And I think you'd look a lot better if you bought clothes that fit.'

FIFTEEN

SUNDAY

While Willis called the girls to tell them about Vera, I called my new friend Lacy Kent, told her what happened, and asked if she'd keep an eye on the girls. 'They're all sixteen, and I trust them to not sneak guys over or anything, but I'd just feel better if there was someone there for back-up.'

'No problem,' Lacy said.

'My mother-in-law is usually our back-up – stays in the house and drives the kids crazy. Or my next-door neighbor, Elena Luna, but she's out of town too—'

'E.J., it's OK!' Lacy assured me. 'I promise I won't take my son with me when I go check on them, either.'

'Oh?'

'He's got a mad crush on Megan. Not that he thinks I know this or anything!'

I laughed with her and said, 'Well, if you did know, you could warn him, but that's what he gets for not telling you.'

'Warn him?'

'Megan's as sweet as they come, but . . . let's just say she's a handful.'

'Aren't we all?'

'I know I try,' I said and we hung up. I took Willis's phone from him. 'Who am I talking to?' I asked.

'All of us,' Bess said. 'We're on speaker.'

'Hi, Mom!' Megan.

'Hi, Mom!' Alicia.

'OK, I just talked to Mrs Kent—'

'Dex's mother?' Megan interrupted. 'He's really cute!'

'And she's going to come by occasionally and check on y'all, make sure everything is OK, so try not to trash the house, all right?' I said, ignoring Megan's need for a romantic entanglement.

'Is she going to bring Dex with her?' Megan asked.

'There should be plenty of food in the refrigerator and freezer. I'm not sure how long we're going to be gone—'

'It's OK, Mom,' Bess said. 'We can take care of ourselves.'

'Bess, you know where the emergency Visa card is, right?' I asked her.

'Yes, ma'am—'

'What emergency Visa card?' Megan demanded. 'We've had a Visa card hidden around here that I didn't know about? Jeez, Bess, thanks for sharing—'

'It has a low balance. I'm not saying how low, and Bess doesn't know. And an emergency only includes two pizza deliveries of a *reasonable* amount of pizza. No parties!'

'Damn,' I heard Megan say in the background.

'Don't worry, Mom,' Alicia said. 'Bess and I will keep Megs in line.'

'Yeah, y'all and what army?' Megan shot back.

'Stop!' I said. 'Don't bother Mrs Luna if she gets home before we do—'

'We know what *she'll* be doing!' Megan said and giggled, the other girls followed suit.

'Maybe you're not old enough to stay on your own—'

'Mom!' Three loud voices as one.

'Just be good,' I said and we said our goodbyes.

I turned to my husband. 'When does the plane leave?'

'We've got three hours before we need to be at the airport. Luna's going to take us to the mall to buy what we'll need in D.C. If we're there for longer than two days, we'll buy more,' he said.

I looked at my husband and could tell he was freaking out. 'Honey, you want to stay here and I'll get you some things? You could make me a list—'

He shook his head. 'No. There's nothing I could do here. I'd just be in the way and do nothing but worry. At least at the mall I'll have something to take my mind off this.'

'The special agent who called said it was a through-and-through, doesn't looked like much damage—'

'Jesus, E.J.!' he said, gritting his teeth and hissing at me. 'She's nearly eighty years old! God only knows what this will do to her! She could have a stroke, or go into a depression, become suicidal—'

'Willis, stop,' I said, putting my arms around him. 'You're going to drive yourself nuts. We can't do anything until we get to D.C. So, come on, let's go to the mall.'

He sighed and stood up. 'Where's Luna?' he asked the world in general.

She appeared and we headed out of the main cop shop down to the mean streets of Houston, blood and fashion on our minds.

ALMOST ONE WEEK LATER

It was Saturday night and we were having a barbecue in honor of Eddie Luna. By the time we'd gotten home from Washington, D.C., Elena and Eddie were keeping house like an old married couple; although they'd been married for twenty-four years, only four of those had been together. I found it amazing that the two of them had kept the fire going all these years. I could only hope that Willis and I will have sustained such a bond over that great a time.

Elena and I had already made all the side dishes and the men, which is the way of suburbia, were dealing with the meat, tonight starring chicken and sausage. Elena and I sat on our deck, watching and giving an occasional opinion.

'Have you heard anything about the Unger thing?' I asked her.

She nodded. 'Yeah. Mayfair called me, told me the whole story. Seems James and Elizabeth Unger, both with PhDs in biology, met when they both worked for a large pharmaceutical company. They got married and left the company to start their own. After three years they discovered what they thought was the cure to childhood leukemia, and they wanted desperately to market it, but they couldn't go the conventional route because they'd already had a bankruptcy and their credit was in the toilet. Somebody told them about Andronikov, who had money to invest. He was more than a little interested, so he backed them. Over a million dollars' worth.'

'Jeez, just to get a pill produced?' I asked.

'Produced and to market. Seems like it's an expensive endeavor. But before market, there are the tests.' She stopped to take a swig of her Shiner Bach.

'And?' I encouraged.

'Well, there's the rub. They found out during the testing phase that it might cure leukemia, but it also caused brain tumors in rats.'

'Jeez,' I said, sipping my white wine. I'm off beer because of my new and improved body. 'But Andronikov had put all this money in—'

'And wanted more money out. Selling the drug as a cure for childhood leukemia would have made him a fortune. He told them to go ahead and manufacture the drug. James said no way. He wasn't going to be responsible for giving children brain tumors. Duh.'

'Yeah, duh. But Andronikov—'

'Cajoled and then threatened, then kidnapped Elizabeth. To give them both credit, when Andronikov called James and told him he had Elizabeth, when she was able to speak to him briefly—'

'Proof of life?'

'Right. She told him to take the flash drive with all their data on it and run. The formula for the drug, their research, and the tests. And he did.'

'And that's where we came in,' I finished up. 'I've told Willis a thousand times that baby-shit yellow truck of his was going to get him in trouble. I'm sure the color is the reason James Unger put the satchel in our truck!'

'I don't know,' Luna said. 'With Smith and Jones following him, I don't think he had much time to think. Anyway, the flash drive is history. Elizabeth destroyed it so no one else as greedy as Andronikov can get their hands on it.'

'Any word on Mr Jones?' I asked.

Luna shook her head. 'I doubt if we'll get him. And I'm not sure I want to. Let's face it, he's sort of the good guy in this thing.'

'Yeah, he is,' I agreed. 'And if what he said about Mr Unger going off the roof being an accident is true—'

Luna shook her head. 'Death during the commission of a felony,' she said. 'But I'm not going to go looking for him.'

I heard another car pull up and Willis went through the gate to the driveway and came back holding a cloth bag loaded with edible goodies, followed by Vera. Her arm was in a sling, but somehow she'd managed to get that heavy-looking bag from her house to her car. She's a little spitfire, that woman.

I got up and hugged her. She hates that. Which is why I do it, of course. 'Hey,' I said. 'How are you feeling?'

'I'm fine. Hello, Elena. You gonna introduce me to this nice-looking young man?'

And so she did, while I set out Vera's offerings on the picnic table with the sides Luna and I had already made. Looking over the bounty, I figured if I had *just* a little bit of everything, I'd be OK. Maybe a little more of that strawberry pie – I mean, it was fruit, right? How bad could it be for me?

Vera joined Elena and I on the deck, and I pulled up another chair. Vera sat down, her face a frown. 'They finally found Rachael Donley's body,' she said. 'He put her in a dumpster at a building site that had been shut down. It took the trash people a little longer to empty it because they couldn't get into the site.' I touched her hand. 'He strangled her. Old man like that. Rachael was young and fit, I just don't see how he managed it. According to my FBI friend, Roni Sanchez, Gerald – I mean, Thomas – had no idea who she was until the convention. She'd told him before that she knew him from somewhere, but could never place him. On the bus on our way to D.C. she must have figured it out. And she asked him to meet her in the mezzanine the following night, told him she knew who he was and begged him to turn himself in – or else she would. Instead, he choked her to death and hid her body in a closet on the mezzanine, then came back in the middle of the night and moved her, using the staff elevator.' Vera shook her head. 'Vicious, just vicious. And to think, all that time I thought he was helping me to find her. Mind you, I never did trust that man.'

I decided to ignore that remark. 'So how are your friends at church dealing with all this about Gerald?' I asked.

'Well, at first they were all aghast, but then something even worse – well, maybe not worse, but equally messy – came out.'

'What?' Luna and I both demanded.

'I was right about Brother Joe. He's a piss poor preacher for a good reason,' she said, at which point she stopped for dramatic effect. Vera does like to enhance her stories just a bit.

'And that would be . . .' I prompted.

'He's not one!' She grinned big. 'He's undercover DEA! Would you believe Angela Barrow and her husband Howard are great big meth dealers? It's true! They run a whole ring or something—'

'Why wasn't I informed of this?' Luna demanded.

Vera shrugged. 'Maybe because it was on a need to know basis, and you, my dear, didn't need to know?'

Luna stiffened, then relaxed. I've noticed she'd been a lot easier to get along with since Eddie's been home. 'Probably. Hell, there's lots of things I don't need to know.'

'Y'all got your little problem all settled, the one that took you to Houston?' Vera asked.

Luna told her all about that. Finally, the meat was done to the satisfaction of our men, so we called the kids and all gathered at the picnic table.

Somewhere during all the food shoveling into faces, Graham said, 'Grandma, did Dad tell you about Alicia and me?'

'Well, I think you're both too young to be thinking the kinds of things y'all are thinking, that's all I'm saying,' Vera said.

'Vera, how old were you when you got married?' I asked with a grin.

'Seventeen, but that's not the point—'

Graham's hands were in the air in a surrender pose. 'Whoa, now! No one's said anything about marriage!'

The look on Alicia's face was enough to make me want to cry. Graham saw it, and recovered nicely. 'I mean right now! We both have to finish school.'

She nodded and went back to her consumption of mass quantities of food.

Graham sighed. 'So, did he ask you about me moving in with you?'

'Of course. And the answer is yes. Wish you could move in now. I have a hard time with just one arm—'

'Mama!' Willis said. 'Why didn't you say so? Medicare has a day nurse thing, don't they? If not, we'll get you one.'

'I don't need a nurse—'

'Nurse's aide,' I said.

'I'll think about it,' she said. 'Or I could stay here for a few days. I have a bag in my car.'

Just when I start to like the woman . . .

NOV 1 8 2013

DAUPHIN COUNTY LIBRARY SYSTEM
HARRISBURG, PENNSYLVANIA